BLOODBATH

Two bodies lay in front of me. They were female, their clothes removed and replaced with a sheet of congealed blood and a blanket of flies. Their arms and legs were pulled apart, sprawling akimbo in death. Neither of them had peaceful expressions on their faces. No, they were both frozen in screams, eyes shut with rigor mortis, mouths drawn wide with the rictus of death. One was average height for a grown woman.

The other was much smaller.

A man without eyelids was propped up against the wall. Bloodstained rope twisted around his body, binding him in a kneeling position, holding him there. He was dead, his throat torn open. The wound yawned apart to reveal the ivory gleam of his spine. He had been forced to watch what had happened in this room before he was killed. Every horrible second, helpless to stop it. Helpless to do anything but watch.

I turned away, chest tight, hot fire burning in my guts. Someone was going to die for this . . .

Books by James R. Tuck

BLOOD AND BULLETS

BLOOD AND SILVER

Novellas

THAT THING AT THE ZOO

SPIDER'S LULLABY

Published by Kensington Publishing Corporation

BLOOD
AND
SILVER

JAMES R. TUCK

KENSINGTON PUBLISHING CORP.
http://www.kensingtonbooks.com

KENSINGTON BOOKS are published by

Kensington Publishing Corp.
119 West 40th Street
New York, NY 10018

Copyright © 2012 by James R. Tuck

All Kensington Titles, Imprints, and Distributed Lines are
available at special quantity discounts for bulk purchases
for sales promotions, premiums, fund-raising, and educa-
tional or institutional use.

Special book excerpts or customized printings can also
be created to fit specific needs. For details, write or
phone the office of the Kensington special sales manager:
Kensington Publishing Corp., 119 West 40th Street, New
York, NY 10018, attn: Special Sales Department, Phone:
1-800-221-2647.

Kensington and the K logo Reg. U.S. Pat & TM Off.

ISBN-13: 978-0-7582-7148-8
ISBN-10: 0-7582-7148-4

First Mass Market Printing: August 2012

10 9 8 7 6 5 4 3 2 1

Printed in the United States of America

Dedicated to The Missus.
She is still the reason the world turns for me.

ACKNOWLEDGMENTS

The list is long and filled with wonderful folks. I mean really, it is absurd how lucky I am to have the people in my life who deserve a spot on this list. In no particular order here goes.

God. 'Nuff said.

The Missus. Thank you, just thank you so much for all that you do, ever. This small thank you is a paltry attempt to cover even a drop of my gratitude for the blessing you are to me.

The Daughter, the Son, and the Nephew. Y'all kick ass and make me proud.

My editor John. I appreciate all your work on my books. Absolutely a pleasure to work with and thank you for seeing the worth in my words.

Craig, Vida, Lou, and everyone else over at Kensington. Lots of ass-kicking going on by you guys.

Gene Mollica the baddest ass cover artist in the world.

Amanda, Ben, Charlie, Gerry, Matt Shafer, Matt Quinn, Kati, Anthony, Patrick, Alex, Adrienne, and Conor, the best damn critique group on the planet.

Annabel Joseph and the ladies at MPERWA for help with that special scene between Deacon and Tiff.

Kevin and Melissa for holding down the Family Tradition Tattoo fort for me.

Derek and Carol at Dragoncon. Hells to the yeah for DC!

My fellow Word Whores. Ladies, I love being a part of the gang.

I have the wonderful blessing of making some great author friends, many of whom I was a fan of before we became friends. There are a ton but a few extra special ones include: Faith Hunter, J. F. Lewis, Linda Robertson, Jeanne C. Stein, Jenna Maclaine, Annabel Joseph, Adrienne Wilder, Alex Hughes, Jessica Page Morrell, Tom Piccirilli, Chuck Wendig, Carole Nelson Douglas, Jonathan Maberry, Larry Correia, Nancy Holder, Debbie Viguie, Jackson Pearce, Janice Hardy, Shiloh Walker, Matt R. Jones, Joshilyn Jackson, and Delilah S. Dawson.

Thank you to every bookseller who loves the series and makes sure it is ordered, stocked, and hand sold. I would buy you a Ferrari if I could!

And book bloggers. For real, I owe you guys. Just let me know if you need any bodies buried.

And you dear reader, the last but not the least. You *are* the reason I do what I do. Thank you.

1

Good days don't last. Not for me they don't. Not for the last five years. Since the deaths of my family, good days are like pet rattlesnakes. I may not know when they will bite, but I damn sure ought to know that they will. Suddenly and sharply. With great venom and without mercy.

But I was having a good day. Scratch that, I was having a *great* day. My friend Tiff had dragged me downtown to a little carnival that had set up in a parking lot. It took some persuasion on her part; after all, I am a big badass occult bounty hunter. We had ridden rides and filled our bellies with greasy carnival food, laughing in the sunshine and making fools of ourselves. We were surrounded by normal humans, families enjoying themselves. There were no monsters. No bloodshed.

So far the only thing that had threatened my life was a rickety Tilt-A-Whirl and some sketchy-looking hot dogs.

And I'd had a good time. Leaving the carnival, I was happy to simply walk down the street, the warm sun on my back, and a good-looking woman at my side.

I was at peace with God, nature, and my fellow man.

And I should have known some asshole was going to come along and screw it up.

"Are you working tonight?"

My eyes cut over to the small brunette walking beside me. Well, I say brunette, her hair was dyed black and had bubblegum pink cut through it in streaks. Tiff matched me stride for stride, even though at 5'2" she was more than a foot shorter than me. The quick pace flipped her short skirt back and forth, flashing a nice length of leg from hem to calf-high boots.

"Nothing's on the books, but you know that doesn't mean anything." I stepped close to her as we walked. "Don't you have to work the club tonight?"

"Nope, I got Kat to cover so that I'm free." She moved close and her arm slid around my waist. Fingernails painted to match her hair lightly scratched through my T-shirt. A pleasant shiver chased up my spine. Her arm rested above the snub-nosed .44 revolver she knew was at the small of my back. I had a lightweight button-up shirt over it and the big .45 semiautomatic that hung under my arm.

"Maybe we could do Indian food tonight then."

Her free hand rubbed her stomach. "I don't know how you can think of food right now. I am completely stuffed."

"I always think about food when I'm not working." I was comfortable walking beside Tiff. Spring was in the air. Warm but not oppressive, like the South gets in the middle months of the year.

Things had been quiet for a bit, which is why there was time to do things like go to the carnival. Normally I am eyebrow deep in monsters. Work had been pretty tame since last year when I had gone up against Appollonia, an insane hell-bitch of a vampire who had gotten hold of the Spear of Destiny. Of course, that job had nearly killed me, but I was still standing at the end of it.

I had survived and managed to kill off a good part of the vampire population in the Southeast. All in all, not a bad day at the office.

That was also the time I had first gotten to know Tiff. The break in action had given me a chance to get to know her better and we had grown pretty close.

We were not dating. I wasn't ready for that. She understood. Hell, she had to. She knew about my family, about what had happened to them. How I had lost them five years ago at the hands of a Nephilim serial killer named Slaine. I hunted him down and found that monsters *are* real. I found that every nightmare you ever had, every story you ever heard that made you lie awake at night and sweat even though you were cold with fear, every damned thing in the dark that made your heart skip a beat . . . it's all real. My thirst for revenge was so great I hunted Slaine anyway, monsters be damned. I chased him even after learning what a Nephilim is.

Nephilim are the offspring of Angels and humans. While tracking Slaine, I came across an Angel. Yes, an honest-to-God Angel of the Lord. Slaine's people were raping her, trying to impregnate her and make more Nephilim, filming it to sell as Angel porn. I killed those sons of bitches and set her free.

After that, I found the bastard who killed my family. Being just human, I was outmatched. He killed me.

Dead.

When I died, the Angel showed up to return the rescue. She infused me with her blood, or whatever Angels have that passes for blood. It brought me back . . . Made me more than human.

I am faster, stronger, and tougher than normal. I heal fast, not like a superhero, but a lot faster than humans. Although it all still hurts like a bitch until I do. I can see almost perfectly in the dark, and I can sense supernatural crap. I killed that evil son of a bitch, and I have been killing every evil son of a bitch I can find ever since.

Oh yeah, I'm Deacon Chalk, Occult Bounty Hunter.

I hunt monsters for a living.

To this day, the deaths of my family sit like stones where my heart was. Sometimes the pain of their memory is crippling. It breaks my bones and grinds my soul. It crushes me. All I want to do is go be where they are. I can't buy that ticket myself, that's a mortal sin according to the Pope. Kill yourself and go straight to hell. Do not pass Go. Do not collect two hundred dollars. So I move on and I keep hunting, waiting for the day I run up on something monster enough to take me out, to send me on my way to be with them. To give me the peace that was ripped away from me with their deaths.

The loss of my family is why I strap up and hunt. I carry the pain and rage of their loss *every day.* It's always there. Always waiting to crawl from the shadows. Always looking to explode and shatter into shards that cut and tear. I miss them every day.

Every.

Fucking.

Day.

And there hadn't been anyone since my wife died.

Until Tiff.

She came along last year in the middle of that shit-storm with Appollonia and the crazy bitch's plan to enslave humanity. Once that was settled, Tiff stayed and made a place in my messed-up life. Somehow, she found a way to make her intentions clear and yet not put any pressure on the situation at all. She knew about my family and what had happened to them. Not the full story, because I still can't talk about it. It's too painful, too sharp. Even without knowing, Tiff still understood. And that was enough for now.

So understand that I was happy when we walked toward the parking lot to leave. All was good and right in this shitty old world, better than it had been in years.

Until we turned the corner and came across a man beating a dog.

The man was large. Dark chocolate skin bulged, thick with muscle. Not quite as big as I am, but a big son of a bitch nonetheless. Fat dreads hung around his head like dirty snakes. They shook as his arm rose and fell and rose again. One hand snarled around a heavy chain connected to a wide leather collar around the dog's neck. The rest of the chain flailed from his other hand, thudding against the dog's sides and haunches.

The dog was curled into a ball, trying to be as small as possible, hiding from the chain as much as it could. Pitiful whimpers mewled with each blow. Blood-slicked shaggy fur picked up dirt and debris from the gravel lot they were in, sticking in layers of brown and gray grit. It was so covered in blood and dirt I couldn't tell what kind of dog it was.

The man stopped beating the dog but was still holding the chain. I could hear his breathing from across the lot, bellowing in and out, short from exertion.

Tiff drew to a stop beside me as I went still. She took a small step away, giving me room to move. Her arm was still behind me and I could feel her hand on the grip of the .44 at my lower back. She had her own in her bag, a CZ-75 9mm, but mine was closer to her hand. She was following the training I had been giving her over the past few months.

Good girl.

The keys to my car were already in my hand since we were close to the parking lot. I handed them off to her. Tilting my head, I spoke from the side of my mouth without taking my eyes off the scene in front of me. "Get the car. Pull it back here and stay in it. Keep the motor running and be ready to go."

I caught her nod from the corner of my eye as she took the keys and moved away. I looked around the lot before I moved. It was at the end of a building on the corner of two streets. The back of the building was a brick wall. Some artist had painted a mural of a girl with a butterfly on her outstretched palm. It was pretty well done. The street side of the lot had a chain-link fence clogged with kudzu that was trying to take over, using the fence as a trellis. Kudzu will grow anywhere. It's like a disease here in the South. Give it a crack in the asphalt to plant itself and it will latch on, getting bigger as each day passes, growing and spreading in little increments like vegetable Ebola. A row of cars lined the fence, leaning on their wheels.

I looked back. No one was coming down the sidewalk. There were a lot of people at the carnival, but they were all far enough away that they looked tiny and indistinct. The coast was fairly clear as long as this stayed quiet.

I took a step, walking toward the man. I rolled my shoulders to loosen them, and flexed my hands open and closed to warm them up. Adrenaline coursed through my arteries, making my heart beat harder. Not faster, the rate stayed the same, but each beat thudded inside my ribcage like a bat to a bell. Each beat slammed an echo inside me and anger rose, pushing more blood through my veins.

People who abuse animals are cowards, especially ones who hurt dogs. Dogs are God's way of showing He still loves us. They only exist to be devoted to us. So when some jackass has to abuse a dog to make himself feel better, it really, really pisses me off.

I am not someone you want pissed off at you.

My whistle cut across the lot, making the guy jerk his head up. Deep amber eyes flashed out under a thick brow.

The scowl he gave wrinkled a wide nose and curled his lips into a snarl. His voice rumbled from a deep chest. "Go away, redneck. This is none of your concern."

"When I go away, I will be taking that animal with me, asshole." I stopped just a few feet from him, finger pointed toward his face. "Walk away now and save me the trouble of kicking the shit out of you before I do."

The man dropped the chain on top of the dog with a run of clinks and a thud. The dog didn't move or run away, just lay shaking as the chain slithered off its huddled form. Turning to face me fully, the man flexed his fingers against each other. The knuckles popped loudly. A shudder ran through him. His chest and shoulder muscles compressed under his black T-shirt, tensing for a fight. He raised his face up to look at me.

The bones underneath his skin *shifted.*

It was subtle, but I saw it. The bones thickened and slipped just ever so slightly, squaring up his skull and widening his mandible. A warm power slid over my skin, rubbing like velvet against the grain. The hairs on my arms stood up. The spring breeze pushed from behind him. The moist smell of cat made my nose wrinkle.

Damn. A lycanthrope in broad daylight.

This changed everything.

My eyes cast around for a weapon to even the odds. Weres are fast as hell and stronger than a motherfucker. I had guns, I always have guns. I even had silver bullets in them, but we were in the middle of downtown on a spring day. There were people around, families just around the corner from where we stood. Hell, we were only three blocks from the local police precinct. Gunshots would bring lawmen a-runnin'. That wouldn't be good. Cops don't have silver bullets. Some of them know about the things I fight, but most are completely in the dark. I try to keep it that way.

The lot was flat and mostly empty, nothing but gravel under my boots. No weapons I could see. I squared my shoulders and started walking toward him again.

"*What* did you just say to me?" His voice was deeper, the edge of a growl rumbling out into the air.

"I said . . ." and with that I closed the space between us, looping my right hand from behind and driving it into the side of his head. My fist slammed into his temple where the skull is its thinnest. It drove his head to the side and pushed him down into a crouch. Fingers closing on a handful of dreads, I jerked his face into my knee, smashing his cheek. Pain made him roar. The volume of it shook me, vibrating through my bones. Velvet power exploded from him, rushing along my body, stinging my skin.

Faster than I could put my foot down, he threw his body back, shaking me off and flinging me backward through the air. My stomach lurched as I sailed above the gravel. One second was all I had to see golden fur erupt from dark skin and his face pull into the shape of a snarling beast. *Lion* sprang to my mind. Then I was crashing into a row of trash cans, spilling garbage everywhere, thinking about nothing but pain.

Something hard rammed into my back just above my kidneys with a grinding crush. Air whooshed from my lungs as my diaphragm spasmed and jerked. I was blind, vision dark from lack of oxygen. The pile of garbage I was in didn't help as it spilled over me. Something wet and sticky smeared across my arm. Dust and debris flew in my face. Scrambling, I got my feet under me. Heaving lungfuls of air, I shook my head to clear my sight.

A pile of old cinderblocks lay on the ground, scattered from where I had slammed into them. As my eyes cleared, I saw the man who had thrown me was now a full-fledged man-beast. Half man, half lion, he stood like a special effect in a big-budget movie. Sand-colored fur covered him and he had grown in size, more muscular than before, bigger than me. Thick black talons flexed in and out at the end of his fingertips. His body shook. Dreads colored like dirty honey bounced around his leonine face. They had grown out into a thick mat of a mane.

Back turned to me, he had the dog's chain again. His arm lifted, making the dog dangle. Pawing at the air, it struggled to breathe through the choking collar. Blood dripped from its fur, spattering the ground at his feet in a crazy pattern of swirls. High-pitched yelps of pain were choked by the collar and still cut over the low growl that was thrumming from the Were-lion.

Violence coiled inside me like a spring, tension tight, waiting to be unleashed. Anger coursed through my body. My old friend rage washed away the pain in my back with a tide of adrenaline. Eyes squinted, my vision narrowed to a laser-fine focus; only the Were-lion was in my sight. The skin on my fingers scraped as they closed on two of the cinderblocks next to me. They weighed nothing in my anger.

One in each hand, I charged, closing the space between us in the blink of an eye. Fury tore from my throat in a scream as I slammed the two cinderblocks together against his skull.

They shattered into shards of concrete and dust from the impact, falling apart in my hands.

The dog fell from the lion-man's grasp, yelping as it hit the ground and immediately curling into a ball of blood-slicked fur. The lycanthrope dropped to his knees, bonelessly slumping to the side. I was on top of him in a second, fists pounding against the side of his face. Anger drove my fist again and again, trying to batter my way through bone. He was still conscious. He stayed half man and half beast, even though his face was slack and his eyes were closed. If he had passed out, he would have shifted back into a human. I kept beating on him, not giving him a chance to recover. Not even one damn second. One second would be too much. Give him even one second of respite and he would recover, and I would lose the slim advantage I had.

There was a flash of motion to my left. I jerked toward it. Something struck me in the side; then I was tumbling across the ground with a wolf trying to eat my face.

Two-inch-long curved yellow fangs snapped viciously at me. Fetid canine breath left the skin on my cheeks moist, and hot spittle flew as I fought to keep that mouth away from me. Everywhere my hands fell on the wolf to hold it back found muscle vibrating with power. Coarse fur rubbed along my arms, feeling like cotton candy made of steel. I was on my back with the wolf on top of me. My mind registered its size because we were pressed against each other. It weighed a ton as it pressed over me, the wolf was damn near as big as I was.

My hands scrabbled, trying to find a weak spot to exploit. Digging, I found the wolf's trachea under a thick ruff of fur. It felt like a softball in my palm. Squeezing with all the strength I had, I clawed my fingers under it, trying to crush it. My arm was burning with effort when I felt it give and pop in my grip with the wet, hollow sound of dislocating a joint.

With a yelp that strangled out in a gurgle, the wolf pushed off, leaping away. It swung its head from side to side, coarse fur ruffling around its neck. It shook from snout to tail, gagging on its own blood. Black nails had dug long red furrows across my thighs and chest. The denim of my jeans gapped open atop the slashes. Thin, hot streaks cut across where the skin was broken, blood soaking out to the edges of the cut jeans.

It hurt like a bitch.

I didn't try to get up. In a fight, you are at your most vulnerable when trying to stand up. Instead, my hand closed on the gun under my left arm and pulled it out. The grip filled my hand with a comfort. My heartbeat slowed and my nerves stopped jangling. I always feel better with my gun in hand. It slid out of the holster like a nickel-plated messenger of death, glinting in the afternoon sun. Colt .45 model 1911, made by John Moses Browning and standard issue for our troops for near a hundred years. The 1911 is as reliable and intuitive as a semiautomatic hand-gun can be. This one was covered with swirls of engraving. The ivory grips were carved into the face of a skull. It was one of a matched set that I had taken off a Yakuza assassin a few months back. The other was at home. One big-bore semiautomatic and a backup gun should have been enough for a day out to a street fair.

Should have been.

The safety was thumbed off the second I pulled it free of the holster. I had it pointed at the group of men who now stood surrounding me. They had been closing around me in a half circle. They stopped midstep when the gun flashed out. It's hard to feel anything but helpless when you are flat on your back, but having a big-ass gun helps. The 1911 holds seven rounds of silver-jacketed death. Eight if you carry one in the chamber.

I always carry one in the chamber.

"Everybody stay right where you are." I swung the gun back and forth from one to the other in a smooth arc, red laser sight bouncing from chest to chest. "Next person to take even one step toward me eats a bullet."

The five men were all different but dressed like the Were-lion was—black military BDU pants, boots, and a black shirt. Each had small touches of individuality, but they still looked like they were wearing some sort of paramilitary uniform.

And they were all lycanthropes. I could feel their power pressing against my skin in a mishmash of sensation. Flashes of fur short and thick, fur coarse and greasy, rubbery skin wet and rough, thick pyramids of horn, and the oil-slick feel of snakeskin. The impressions slithered and crawled over me until they took hold of my mind. Pressure built in my skull as I drew in my power to sense the supernatural, closing it like a fist. I tamped the impressions down in my mind. Pulling my power close inside made the sensations fade. It's a bitch to concentrate when all of that is going on and I was a little occupied.

The lycanthropes around me were all different sizes and shape; the only thing similar about them was the clothes they wore. The one on the left crouched, ready to spring. Yellow eyes gleamed in the sunlight, and they had the same feline cast as the Were-lion's. He wasn't nearly as large as the lion—smaller, sleeker, but similar in build and feel.

Next to him stood a long, thin man with black eyes set in a wide face. His dusky skin was hairless and slick. Even holding his position, he swayed gently back and forth. A bloodless, forked tongue flickered over thin lips. I knew from the feel of him I was looking at some kind of snake. I would bet money he was venomous.

His neighbor was short and stocky, standing on squatty, bowed legs. His skull had shifted, elongating his face into a reptilian snout. Matching black eyes blinked slowly at me, and hard, pebbled skin formed across his brows and cheeks.

A small, greasy man with a wide chest was helping the Were-lion to his feet. Small, sharp teeth flashed in a wide grin, too many teeth for just human, and dark brown hair shot coarse from his head.

The fifth one was a giant of a man. He would have

towered over me, and I am not short. Hell, normally I am the biggest man in any given situation, but this one stood an easy seven feet tall. His head was shaved like mine and gleamed in the springtime sunshine. Everywhere his skin showed it was fish-belly pale. Thick and rubbery, it covered massive limbs. Arms like slabs of beef hung loose by his side. Webbing stretched between his knuckles, skin solid to the first full joint of each finger.

The greasy Were hopped from one foot to the other, tugging on the Were-lion's arm. His voice was a raspy bark. "Leonidas, he is down on the ground, showing his belly." A finger shot in my direction. The arm and hand it was on covered in a thick layer of wiry brown hair. "We can take him."

The Were-lion shook him off with a growl and stepped in, closing the circle around me. Blood matted dreadlocked hair, and his face was twisted with anger. The wound from the cinderblocks was closed up already. Damn lycanthropes. They heal like magick.

"He is right, human. Put the gun away, you are outmatched." A taloned finger flicked a dread from across his eyes. "Put it away. Take your beating like a human and we will let you live."

I didn't move from the dirt and gravel. Sharp rocks dug into my back and shoulders. Liquid heat was building in the muscles of my arms from holding my gun up while lying on my back, but they weren't trembling.

Yet.

"I don't know. I see seven assholes and I have eight silver bullets. I'd say I was matched pretty damn good."

The tension in the group cranked up to eleven. They all began to cast eyes at Leonidas, the Were-lion. I had gotten their attention by saying the magic words: *silver* and *bullets*.

Silver is good against most supernatural threats. It slows monsters down, equalizes the equation. To lycanthropes, silver is poison. They can heal most damage done to them, except for silver. Not only does a silver bullet cause the same trauma to them that a regular bullet does to a regular human, but it sets up a violent, allergic chain reaction too. If they don't get the bullet out of them, it can lead to anaphylactic shock and death. With regular bullets, you have to completely destroy the brain or the heart to kill a Were. Toss silver on the bullet and you have a fast-acting poison to lycanthropes.

It changes the game. Evens the odds.

"Bullshit." This was from the giant. It sounded like the word was stuck in his gullet. He choked it out, wet and messy. "Nobody uses silver bullets. They're too expensive."

My eyebrow cocked up. "You can be the first one to find out."

I could feel the tremble starting in my shoulders. The gun didn't shake yet, but it was getting heavy. Really damn heavy. I was going to have to do something to change the dynamic we were in. A standoff was not in my favor. My arm would quickly fatigue until my aim would be worthless, even at this close range. If I moved and took my gun off them, they would jump on that moment of weakness and distraction like quicksilver. I had no idea how to change the situation without opening fire, so I continued to buy time.

"The name is Deacon Chalk. Surely you didn't roll your furry asses into town and not check out the local players."

Leonidas waved his hand dismissively. "You are not our prey. We don't care who you are."

"Turn around, leave the dog with me, and clear the hell out of my town." The tremble that had been twittering in my shoulders now ran down my arm, spasming my triceps muscle. Fire poured into every fiber of my arm. The muzzle of the gun moved side to side. Tightening my grip steadied it. But only a little.

"Be warned, asshole." My own voice was a snarling growl now. "I will shoot before I lose control of my gun. Make your choice right now. Walk and live. Stay and die."

There was a moment where time froze, clear and sharp and fragile. None of us moved. None of us breathed. We just stayed locked in a bubble of potential violence and bloodshed. Tension crackled the air, ozone hot.

Then, the pressure changed.

All of them leaned slightly forward, drawing into themselves, getting ready to leap in tandem, murder in their eyes. My finger tightened on the trigger, arm tensing to absorb the shock of recoil that would happen the split second the hammer fell.

Death held his breath, waiting for blood to be spilled. I would not be able to take them all out before they tore into me. But some of them were dead meat, they just didn't know it.

A midnight black hot rod roared into the lot, grinding gravel under its wheels as the brakes locked down.

Its monster grill loomed like a killer whale over a family of seals. Dust flew forward, swirling over the hood and front tires. The engine snarled with pure American horsepower. The 1966 Comet Cyclone is the epitome of what a hot rod is supposed to be. It stood with attitude. Badass black with chain-link steering wheel and a growling engine that put the lion to shame.

She is a beauty and she is all mine.

The heavy door swung open. A small brunette with bubblegum streaks stepped out. A shotgun racked in her hands, its distinctive sound *click-clacking* loud over the engine's growl. She brought the barrel down, sweeping it back and forth over the lycanthropes that were regrouping. They had been driven back by the car's entrance.

"Which one of these assholes do you want me to shoot first?" Tiff's eyes flashed, black and pink hair swirling out.

The cavalry had arrived.

God bless her.

I scrambled to my feet, using the distraction of the car to my advantage. The lycanthropes looked from me to Tiff. The bowlegged one made a swift, shuffling move toward her. She pointed the shotgun at the middle of his chest.

"Take one more step!" The words pushed from behind clenched teeth.

My .45 was still pointing at the Weres. Moving and adrenaline had washed away the burn in my muscles. "I'd listen to the lady. That gun has double-aught silver shot in it. She can't miss your ass from there."

Those black eyes turned toward me. Slowly, he took a step back. I shook my gun, waving them back. "Keep moving. All of you move your asses back."

Leonidas motioned with his hands, now covered in golden fur and ending in inch-long black talons. Everyone took a few steps back. Moving over to the dog, I crouched down. Reaching out my left hand, I gently touched blood-slicked fur. A whine escaped its lips. It was still alive. It looked like hell warmed over, but it was still alive.

Softly I examined it. Sorry, her, softly I examined *her*. She was small, maybe sixty pounds, but when healthy she looked like she would fill out to a nice ninety to one hundred. She was long-limbed, and her fur, where it wasn't covered in gore, was thick and soft. The color was a deep russet that made the blood hard to spot where it was drying. The thick collar had rubbed and worn away the fur around her neck, leaving the skin under it raw and chafed. I pushed my power out to her, letting it run down my arm and roll over her. The feedback I got was the feel of skin and the smell of a city park in the moonlight.

Just as I thought, another shape-shifter.

As gently as I could, I slid my arm under her, trying to find a purchase on her limp form that would allow me to pick her up. It was harder than you would think. It would have been cake if I'd had two hands to use, but I still had my gun out in my right hand and pointed at the bad guys.

Finally, I got her into the crook of my arm. Her head lolled limply against my skin, leaving smears of blood, brown and crimson. Lifting her confirmed she didn't weigh anything. Carefully, I backed over to the Comet's passenger door. There was a click as Tiff hit the button to unlock it, causing the heavy steel door to yawn wide and swallow us.

The toe of my boot slid behind the front seat and hooked the lever, which folded the back down. It was awkward to lean in and lay her on the backseat. I piled the chain up into loose bundles in the floorboards. Standing up, I raised the .45 to cover the Weres again.

I pushed the front seat back upright. Standing with one foot in the car and one foot on the ground, I drew the .44 snub-nosed revolver from the holster at my lower back. Now I had both hands full of gun pointed at the bad guys. Nodding to Tiff made her slip in behind the wheel and close her door. I felt the car bump a bit as she put it in gear, foot on the brake.

Seven angry lycanthropes glared at me in the spring-time sun. Leonidas pointed a clawed hand at me. "This isn't over. I will have what is mine."

I gave him my best smile, the pit bull grin. "The only thing yours around here is a silver bullet." I waved the guns from one to the other of them for effect. "Get out of my town. If I see you again, I will shoot you in the face."

I dropped into the seat and Tiff put the pedal to the metal. The Comet's door slammed shut as she lurched forward, scattering Weres like bowling pins and covering them with dust.

I had been right. An asshole had come along and ruined my perfectly good day.

I hate being right.

2

Kat covered the stage with clean bar towels for me to lay our rescue on. They were freshly bleached and gleaming white, so the blood and dirt from the dog's fur screamed out against them. They were stark black marks even in the low light of the club. She grabbed the first-aid kit behind the bar and hauled it over, dropping it heavy on the wooden surface.

Kat is very efficient. That's why she manages Polecats, the club I own. Before she came into my life, it made enough money to fund my war. With her at the helm, it made a killing.

I found Kat while on a hunt. Her little sister had been savagely killed by vampires. Kat had tried to go after them herself, looking for the bloodsucker responsible by playing groupie in the vampire scene. She had been willing to let them bite her, drink from her, and have her to try and find the vampire responsible for killing her sister. They discovered what she was up to and enslaved her, turning her into a bloodwhore. They handed her over to a sadistic bastard named Darius, and he put her through a level of sexual torture that most people would not survive.

For months.

I found her, rescued her, and helped her get revenge on them all. Since then, she's had a deep-seated, violent hatred for anything vampire. She's like a sister to me and is dedicated completely to what I do.

She bumped me out of the way and set the duffel bag we use as a first aid kit on the stage next to the dog. Inside that bag was everything you might need to deal with any injury short of major surgery.

Occult bounty hunting is a rough job.

Pulling her straight, thick blond hair back in a ponytail, she secured it with a hair tie from her wrist. Unzipping the bag, she reached in and slipped on a pair of latex gloves. They were bright pink and smelled like powdered rubbber.

I looked down at where I had carried the lycanthrope into the club. My arms were so filthy with dried blood, dirt, and fur that you could barely see the tattoos covering them. Standing up, I stripped off the black button-up shirt, leaving me in a black A-shirt, or a wife beater as they are called. The button-up was to cover my guns; the wife beater was to keep my shoulder holster from chafing. Father Mulcahy tossed me a wet towel and I began to clean off my arms.

It was odd to clean off blood and none of it be mine.

Nodding, he moved over by Tiff. His left leg dragged just a bit, giving him a short limp. Father Mulcahy is the Catholic priest who tends bar at Polecats. Mass on Sundays and tending bar the rest of the week. He has been with me since I first started hunting monsters after my family was killed those years back. Only he knew the details of my family's deaths and what happened afterward. Only he had any inkling of what it did to me. I needed someone that I could rely on when everything went tits up.

Father Mulcahy was as reliable as cancer.

The dog lay limp like she had since we rescued her, but the convulsive shaking she had done in the car had slowed to a tremble. Whimpers and whines came from her muzzle as Kat probed her for wounds. Kat has a lot of experience being a medic. She's usually the one who patches me up. No, I am not a dog, but technically neither was her current patient.

Lycanthropes are humans who can change into animals. It's a supernatural virus. It is contagious, but not all that easy to catch. Not like in the movies where a scratch will make you furry once a month. You need blood-to-blood contact or blood-to-mucous membrane. It works a lot like AIDS, actually.

Also, the virus mutates with the host DNA, so it is different from lycanthrope to lycanthrope. Some shape-shifters can change form anytime they want; some can only change in the height of the lunar cycle. Some can change into partial animal forms, like a half-human, half-animal combo pack. Some can only change completely into their animal form. Some shape-shifters retain their intellect while shifted, some don't and they remember what their animal half did as a dream. And all these variants had more variants.

The only two constant rules about lycanthropes are as follows: First, they all lose control during the full moon. They go completely, out-of-control, batshit crazy. Transformed and vicious. Different lycanthropes handle it differently. Some lock up, some dope up, and some go north to northern Georgia where a wealthy Were-possum has a fully fenced and portioned off hunting preserve that covers an entire mountain. If the Weres are not a predator, they just stay home, but the dangerous ones have to take precautions.

The second constant is that silver is the great equalizer. Every lycanthrope in the world has a violent allergic reaction to silver to the point that it negates their healing ability and can be deadly.

Other than that, all bets are off.

There are also shape-shifters who have nothing to do with lycanthropy. I know a family of Tengu here in Atlanta. They own a drive-through sushi joint called the Bento Box. Tengu shift into ravens and raven-human warrior forms, but they are not lycanthropes. They are Tengu. There are also skinwalkers, selkies, and animals who turn into men. I am an acquaintance-who-doesn't-kill-each-other with an ancient three-headed dragon who spends his days as a professional hitman. He is apparently a Werekin, whatever that means. Silver worked on some of these, some it didn't. But even if a shape-shifter could shrug off silver, I was still delivering a bullet.

I wasn't one hundred percent sure, but the one Kat was examining felt like a lycanthrope. It's hard to describe, but I felt the night and the moon in her, but not the forest. A Were-dog instead of a Werewolf, she looked tamer than any kind of feral canine. My ability to feel out supernatural crap in others filters through my natural senses, but it is very impressionistic and I have to do a lot of interpretation. It's a guessing game that I win only sometimes.

Kat sat back on her heels, kneeling on the stage next to her patient. "There are some definite broken ribs, but I can't be certain of much else. There are a lot of cuts and contusions." Her gloved hand was filthy as it waved over the Were-dog's abdomen. "But I am really worried about this area, though. It is swollen, solid, and hot to the touch. It's probably an internal injury, but I can't tell without an X-ray or an ultrasound."

"Well, we can't just swing her over to the local vet."

"We could take her to Larson. He's been treating lycanthropes for a few months now and is equipped to handle something like this."

Larson is a former wannabe vampire hunter who had been used as bait in a plot to kill me by the same hell-bitch vampire from when I met Tiff. In the final standoff he had been seriously injured by one of her minions. That had been months ago, and since then he had become our local mad scientist and go-to guy for research on the supernatural. He lives and works in a lab that I fund through the club.

It was the least I could do, the man was hurt helping me save the world.

I nodded. "Let's load her back in the Comet and get her over there then." I knelt down and started using the towels to wrap the dog.

Some small noise I couldn't identify made the muscles on the back of my neck tense. I stopped working for a second, waiting to hear it again. A tingle started on the back of my scalp, getting stronger as the seconds ticked away.

The entrance doors swung open. Light streamed into the dim club silhouetting three people as they walked in. They were indistinct in the bright light. A deep voice rumbled. "You are not taking her anywhere. We are here to collect her."

My gun was out just seconds before Kat's and Father Mulcahy's.

The doors closed, shutting the light off with a snap. With the streaming light cut off, the three people could now be seen. One was a short, stocky man with a wide chest and a wide jaw to match. Scars covered his neck and arms where his skintight T-shirt did not hide them. Deep-set eyes glared bright gray from under a heavy brow full of scar tissue. They rolled and jittered in his thick skull, making him look crazed. I had seen the same look in the eyes of punch-drunk boxers and soldiers with post-traumatic stress disorder.

The middle one of the group was a woman. Tall and lithe, she stalked into the club like she owned it. Her skin was golden brown, like expensive caramel, and her hair was a mass of thick ringlet waves that were pulled back and pinned to show her face. High cheekbones cut between sultry lips and deadly eyes the color of mahogany. She was striking and aristocratic, noble and elegant. She looked like you would find her face stamped on a coin in a foreign country.

The third member of the party was dressed impeccably in a three-piece suit with a smart charcoal stripe. His skin was darker than the woman's, a dark cocoa to her caramel, and his hair sprouted in tiny dreads the color of blond rolled in dirt. I had seen his face about an hour ago.

It was the same face as the Were-lion that had beaten the dog.

They stopped just inside the club. The man in the suit had his arms outstretched, hands empty of weapons; the other two stayed just behind him. The woman stood straight, hand gently resting on his outstretched arm to the right, whereas the other man leaned his chest against the left one, straining to keep from moving forward. All our guns stayed on them, ruby dots dancing on center mass.

Mentally I cursed at us for leaving the door unlocked in the hurry to see to the injured lycanthrope. I had relied on someone else to get the lock since my arms were full of dog. I would have to stop that. I opened my power up. The same nose-wrinkling smell of cat came to me as earlier, double strong since I was inside and there were two cats in front of me. I would bet dollars to donuts they were both lions. They felt like a mated pair.

The other man gave off the feel of violence. Blood and cement, the taste of fur and metal. Power rolled off the three of them in three distinct flavors: regal and aloof power, calm and peaceful power, and barely contained power that wanted to shed blood.

The lion in front lowered his head just slightly, not deferring, just placating. His arms stayed out to his side, hands held loose, looking as human as I am.

Which isn't all that human, to be honest.

His voice was deep, a slight purr in his inflections that soothed the ears. "She is one of mine. I thank you for rescuing her, but we are equipped to care for her now. Let us have her so we can tend to her."

I moved the laser dot up his chest until it flared across the planes of his face. Golden amber eyes blinked in the glare. The dot stopped in the center of his forehead. "I don't think so. She is under my protection now; I'll see to her medical care." I stood up and took a step forward. The red dot stayed on his forehead. "Just who the hell are you people?"

"We are her friends. Her family. We just want to take her to a safe place and nurse her to health."

"Some asshole named Leonidas is the one who did this to her." I studied his face. "He looked a lot like you, so you have to understand why I am having a hard time trusting you."

"That is my brother. We are nothing alike and have nothing to do with each other."

The scarred one growled low and raspy. The rumble in his chest tightened his jaw into a bulge. The lion turned his hand and touched him on his arm. I think it was meant to be a calming gesture.

It didn't work.

"You're not one of us. You can't protect her like we can." The scarred man's jaw was thick and heavy while he talked.

I laughed—a head-back, full-throated guffaw. "You weren't there when we saved her from the piece of shit who was trying to beat her to death. So take your protection and care, turn it sideways, and shove it up your ass. And while I'm at it, get the fuck out of my club. I need to get her to medical attention."

I felt the air move before I saw the stocky one come at me. In a blink, he was around the other man's arm and charging toward me. He was a blur of superhuman speed as he plowed into me, knocking me off my feet. The Colt .45 spun out of my hand and away. Powerful hands clamped on my wrist and throat as we rolled across the floor. I managed to swing my elbow into his face, pain flashing across my arm as his teeth broke skin, but I landed a solid blow to his mouth. I knew because I felt it jolt all the way up to my shoulder. Hot blood spurted, arcing over my forearm to hit me in the face.

We came to a stop in the middle of the floor with him crouching in front of me and me sprawled on my side. Red dripped from his lower jaw. It could have been his blood or mine. I knew I had broken some of his teeth, but I could also feel blood pulsing out of my forearm and running hot down to my wrist. I got to my feet in a scramble, crouching low like he was. Dirty napkins and beer bottles littered the floor between us, and the carpet was soaked with dozens of leftover drinks. We had knocked over a trash can in our tumble.

Kat's voice called from behind me. "I have no shot!"

I was between her and the lycanthrope that still crouched in front of me. Muscles bunched across his chest and shoulders, white fur sprouting through the scar tissue on his neck and arms. His face was more canine. Jaw wider, lips pulled into a joker grin. Pit bull flashed in my mind. Fucking great. I couldn't get into a fight with a Were-Labradoodle? No, of course I couldn't. Who was I kidding?

He wasn't fully shifting, but he was edging toward it,

probably from the adrenaline. He crouched, muscles bunching as he panted. He had attacked me but wasn't trying to kill me. It made me want to keep from killing him back.

I try to not kill shape-shifters. They are human most of the time, and I try to only kill 100% monsters. This one wanted to fight for the lycanthrope we had rescued. He was trying to hurt me, but not kill me.

Not yet anyway. I was willing to play the game only as hard as he did.

But the only way he was leaving with the Were-dog today was over my dead body. Things would change when he figured that out.

Two silvered knives were tucked into my boots, but there was no way I would get to them before he would be on me. My eyes darted for some kind of weapon, sweeping the floor. My fingers closed around the long-necks of two beer bottles. I stood, smashing the two bottles together with a brittle crash. The sound of the old-fashioned Southern Switchblade opening. It's a sound that makes blood run cold when you are in a late-night honkytonk with a woman you just met.

Nothing cuts nastier than a broken bottle, not even lycanthrope claws.

My power unfurled from inside me and I felt the animal beneath his skin. It snapped at him, snarling and clawing to get out. Blind with rage. It wanted to hurt me because I was in front of it. Hell, it wanted to hurt anyone. His will hung like a fraying rope around the neck of his beast, barely restraining, ready to snap.

I held the bottles in a fighting stance, one out toward him, one back and ready to strike. "Easy, Fido. I don't want to hurt you, but I will."

"I am not fucking Fido." He growled, voice thick and wet. One big, meaty fist paw thumped his chest. "My

name is Cash. Let us have Sophia and *I* won't hurt *you.*"
Muscles shifted under his skin in a roll of power that
scraped along my skin. Short white fur sprouted up his
arms and neck. His jaw pulled even wider, pushed apart
by thick teeth. The canines were blunted from chewing on
bone. His forehead slanted and stretched, becoming a flat
ridge of skull as his eyes spread apart over his muzzle. "At
least not much."

"You are not getting her. She is under my protection
now."

"She is my mate." His eyes cut over to the lion and lioness. They said nothing to stop him. "Mine to protect."

"Piss off." Anger surged in my words. "Until she wakes
up and is coherent, *nobody* is taking her."

"Give her to us!" Spittle flew as he roared.

"Kiss my ass one more time."

I settled into myself, loose and relaxed, ready to react
the second he moved. His wide head shook side to side.
I watched closely as his eyes snapped up at me and he
tensed, muscles standing like cables along his arms. The
air sang with potential violence.

He threw himself at me. Spittle flung in thick strings
from his jaws as they snapped toward my throat. I shoved
the bottle out in front of me. My shoulder jolted as it
punched into his neck, tearing and ripping the loose skin.
I twisted the jagged edge into thick folds. Glass splintered
with the shrill sound of thin crystalline edges grinding together. Blood splashed warm over my hand as I pushed up
and away. Shoving him up, stretching him back. The other
bottle flicked out crossways, slashing across his stomach.
The skin opened up with the green, ripe smell of intestine.

He thudded to the floor in a slosh of blood and the spill
from the trash can. My big boot swung out, moving to
kick his face. Scrambling away, he was a white blur. I lost
him for a split second. My eyes had to track the blood

he left in a trail to follow his movement as he leaped over the bar.

Over the bar Tiff was behind.

Cash was in full dog-man mode as he grabbed her. One paw slapped across her face, pushing her head to the side to expose her throat. Wicked canines dripped just inches above her jugular. His other arm wrapped around her waist, trapping her against him.

Noise exploded around me as everyone started yelling. Kat and Father Mulcahy, the two lions. My heart hitched in my chest and all the sound in the room faded to a buzz. Someone yelled "Stop!" before my head filled with static. My mind reset itself to murder as I watched the rabid Were-pit bull hold Tiff.

Tiff stood still, eyes wide behind the paw that held her. She swallowed her fear, throat muscles working as Cash lowered his muzzle even closer to her skin. He took a long sniff through a nose gone black and canine. His voice was thick and gnarled, coming from a throat more dog than human. I could barely understand the words he spoke. Homicide pulsed inside my mind.

"She smells like a raw steak. Delicious and bloody." His eyes cut up to me. Daring me.

Father Mulcahy yelled at him. "Don't do this, son. Let her go. This is a mistake."

Cash growled. "The mistake is trying to keep Sophia from us."

The priest's gun was still trained on the lions. "You are not going to listen to reason are you, young man?" He shook his head sadly. "You are trying to kill yourself."

"Myself?" The laugh was a bark. "Not myself." His cheek rubbed on Tiff's. "But if you don't give us Sophia, I will kill this—"

The silver bullet took off the top of his head.

A spatter of gore painted the wall behind him. Chunks,

thick and red, ran down the bottles of liquor like homemade marinara sauce.

I was over the bar before his body slumped toward the
floor. My hand closed on Tiff's arm, steadying her as the
body released her to fall down. My eyes searched her over,
looking for any sign she might be hurt. "Are you okay?"

She nodded. Her pink and black hair was spackled
with blood that wasn't hers. Her voice tremored. "I am.
I'm fine. I'm okay." She took a deep breath. Pulling it in,
holding it hostage, then letting it go. I watched as she
pulled herself back together. She looked up at me; there
was a little too much white around her pupils, giving her
a wild look, but the tremble had disappeared. She took
another breath and closed her eyes. When she opened
them again she was almost normal.

One side of her mouth quirked up. "Thank you."

"Anytime." I looked down at her. "You all right?"

Small hands pushed me away. "Go back to work. I'll
be okay."

The snub-nosed .44 smoked slightly in my hand. I
turned to the two lions who were still in place, still covered by the priest and Kat. The man had tears streaming
down his cheeks and a look of horror on his face. The
woman was unmoved, face impassive as a stone. Her
coloring had deepened into a more burnished copper
tone, and I could feel her anger from across the room.

"Let me be clear." I added the gun in my hand to the
ones pointing at them. "You are *not* taking Sophia and
you *are* getting the fuck out of my club."

As I stepped around the bar the man's mouth moved
to speak. I waved the gun at him like a librarian's finger.
"No, no, and no," I said. His mouth closed into a tight
line. "I don't care what you have to say and I don't want
to hear it." Leaning in toward him, my voice dropped to
a growl worthy of an animal. "*You* brought this down.

You let him push too far." My finger pointed at Cash's body. It had fallen and was propped on the bar. Blood puddled on the waterproof surface in a thick, chunky soup spilled from the bowl of his skull. "This is what happens to anyone who threatens one of my people. If you ever forget it, you'll be the next one to fall." I stepped back. "Now get the hell out."

The Were-lion stared at me. Pride clashed with prudence on his face, making his dark features twist sourly. I stared at him. I don't know what my face looked like. My old friend rage was bubbling under the surface of my skin. He gathered himself and turned toward the door. The woman with him did not move. She stood and seethed. His arm flashed out, pushing her toward the door as she glared at us. They were almost there when I whistled. The shrill sound cut through the air, getting his attention. He turned toward me. My finger stretched out, pointing at the body on the bar.

"Leave with what you came with. We don't take out other people's trash here."

3

The Comet growled at me, motor low and angry, crackling through the exhaust pipes. I wasn't driving her like I usually did. Normally, I am from the "drive it like you stole it" school of driving. Pedal to the metal, balls out, ninety to nothing kind of driving. The Comet is a hot rod. She eats asphalt like a fat kid at a cake buffet. It's what she was made to do. Right now, though, she was an ambulance.

Sophia was stretched across the backseat, blankets wadded around her frail form to keep her as still as possible. Air pulled through her muzzle in ragged fits, hitching and jerking as the breath drew in. As her lungs filled you could see knuckle-shaped lumps of broken ribs jutting up through her skin. The breath would leave her in a long wheeze, pushing thinly through her throat. The end of it always snagged, drawing short and spurting out wet and choked. It took longer than it should to draw another one in.

I was worried about her condition but didn't want to make it worse by driving recklessly.

I had changed my shirt and jeans while Kat had bundled her up. My other ones had been filthy from the dirt and blood, as well as torn by Werewolf claws. I had also added the other Colt .45. Both of them hung openly against my new T-shirt, which read, "GOT SILVER BULLETS?"

Kat sat next to me. She had insisted on coming. Tiff stayed behind to shower away blood splatter, and Father Mulcahy would mop up and get ready for the evening opening of the club. I didn't mind since Kat was the one who knew how to get to Larson's. She was alternating between looking out the window and turning to keep an eye on Sophia. Her thick blond ponytail swayed as she turned to and fro.

She wasn't talking other than giving directions and making comforting noises to Sophia, so I reached over and turned the music up a touch. A cocksure guitar riff soared up over the rumble of the motor calling out the sweet sound of Chicago's South Side. Muddy Waters sang about how he was a "Hoochie-Coochie Man" and he was gonna work his mojo and his black cat bone. That one-in-a-million voice coaxing some sweet young thing into believing all the claims he made. I settled into the rhythm of driving and let him sing and play me away into a memory.

It was my first year of hunting monsters. I was new and raw, still figuring out how to do it right. A little girl was missing, gone without a trace from the woods not far from her school. Taken from a field trip with a group of people between one eyeblink and another. No one knew how she had disappeared so quickly.

Search parties were formed. They brought in blood-hounds. Dogs trained to fearlessly trail a scent. Never giving up until they found its source. Relentless and unswerving no matter how dangerous their prey.

They had all huddled together, shaking and pissing themselves, refusing to move or search.

Her father had contacted me. He had been given my name by one of the investigators on the scene. I had already developed a reputation for handling weird crimes and cases. He had begged me, eyes burning like raw red wounds in his face, to find his daughter if I could. His hand shook as he gave me a picture of her, taken the day she disappeared to document her first field trip while in school.

Kaylee Ann Dobbs had been missing for eight hours. She was a cute little girl, about six years old with a mop of unruly ash-blond hair, brown eyes that sparkled even in the picture, and a dash of light freckles across her delicate little nose. She was smiling in the picture, holding a brown paper bag lunch and wearing a pink paisley sundress. He fell to his knees in front of me. *Please bring her back, no matter what you have to do. I'll give you anything.*

My family had been taken less than nine months earlier.

My daughter had a dash of freckles across her nose too.

I took the damn case.

After a lot of work and more than a little luck, I picked up a trail the bloodhounds couldn't have followed. At the site of the disappearance there was an energy that my ability to sense the supernatural picked up on. It made my stomach draw into a dull gnaw of hunger. Itchiness crawled over my skin and when I scratched, it was hot to the touch.

Following the energy, I tracked it to a house on the edge of the forest. It sat in one of the 'hoods that hang on the outskirts of the city. It was a squatty little crack house in a run-down ghetto. Despair rode the air currents, tainting the atmosphere. Sad vinyl siding sagged on the outside over stubby azalea bushes with flowers curled brown from crackhead piss. The windows were covered with plywood like it was waiting for a hurricane that would never come.

The houses around it were just as depressing. Ramshackle government housing; all the same drab gray siding and rickety states of disrepair. Yards that were more dirt than grass, and cars that didn't run sitting beside SUVs with gleaming rims. One neighboring house had burned to the ground. Nothing left but a cracked foundation and the charred stumps that used to be the bones of a home.

Sad figures shuffled in and out of the crack house as I watched. They used to be people, before the crack burned them out, turning them into husks of humanity. They would look up at a camera that was mounted above the steel door, then someone inside would buzz them through.

It was a bad scene. Lots of civilians. Lots of witnesses. A nasty part of town that I stuck out in like a sore thumb and I was alone, without backup. Every bit of logic said to come back later, better prepared.

Kaylee Ann Dobbs had been missing for eleven hours.

I stepped out of the Comet and the air slapped me with a buzz of something not natural. Back then I hadn't yet learned how to pull in my power. I couldn't tamp it down or put it away. It was like an open nerve, raw and swollen and sore to the touch. Like the hole in your tooth that you just can't keep your tongue out of. It hurts and makes you shiver, the pain tremoring, leaving that funny feeling deep below your belly button, but you just can't leave it alone. Impressions assaulted me from

the house. The same impressions I'd found in the woods
but on steroids.

Or crack.

The feel of something fever hot and aching with dull
hunger. My skin began to itch and my stomach growled
at me.

Reaching inside, my hand closed on my Mossberg
500 shotgun. It had an eight-round tube, loaded with
steel-core Mini-missile slugs for the first four rounds
and silver-plated buckshot in the back half. Six extra
shells of silver shot were strapped to the stock, standing
out green against the black. The front of the barrel was
capped by a breaching shroud, a jagged tube of steel, designed to grip doors to hold the barrel steady as a lock
was blown away. A Desert Eagle .357 rode under my left
arm, snug in its shoulder holster, pushed tight against my
arm by the Kevlar vest I had strapped to me. Yes, I was
hunting something supernatural, but crack houses and
gun-toting drug dealers go hand in hand like . . . well,
like crack houses and gun-toting drug dealers. I wasn't
taking chances on getting shot by some low-life piece of
scum. A compact Glock .40 caliber snugged into the
small of my back as a backup gun.

Before I closed the car door, I grabbed a rag out of the
floorboard that I used to check the oil in the Comet.
Maintenance is better than repair, my dad used to say
before he left this shitty world. I stuffed the oily rag into
my back pocket and wiped my hand off on my jeans so
I wouldn't compromise my grip on the shotgun.

Locked and loaded, I crossed the street. Moving
quickly, my eyes scanned the broken asphalt for anything that might trip me. The tread of my boot ground
against tiny shards of glass that glittered underfoot—
busted bottles and shattered crack pipes. The fever-hot

hunger my power sensed thickened with each step, gelling around me, coagulating into something to wade through. I had one boot on the bottom step when a woman came around the corner of the house, dragging a stick-thin child behind her.

We stopped, staring at each other. Her hair jutted out around a bobble head on a scrawny neck. Scabs covered her cheeks and arms. Some were thick as oatmeal. Some were picked away and dug into by dirty, broken finger-nails so that the flesh showed bright pink. The sores were stark against ashy, bitter chocolate skin. Yellow, phlegmy eyes rolled at me inside sockets that sunk into the bones of her skull.

The girl she had by the arm was as thin as her mother, but from being undernourished, not corroded away by drugs. She looked to be about twice Kaylee's age. Black hair was pulled tight in cornrows and capped off with a rainbow of tiny plastic clips. She was barefoot despite the broken glass that littered the ground. Big brown eyes watched me carefully.

The woman couldn't stand still. Her shoulders and neck kept moving back and forth and side to side. She looked like a cobra somebody had jumped up on methampheta-mines. Her lips were crusted with something white and flaky that cracked when she talked. I could hardly under-stand her through the mouthful of stubs she had. Crack had eaten most of her teeth into stumps that hung black to her pink gums.

"What you doin' here wid dat big-ass gun, whiteboy?"

My left hand pulled out the picture Kaylee's father had given me. I held it toward her. "Looking for this little girl. You seen her?"

She closed one rheumy eye as she leaned forward and

looked at the picture. "Why you think she'd be in this neighborhood?"

"I just do. Have you seen her?"

Her head swiveled. She squinted, one bulging eye looking up the steps to the house. "You think she's in dat house?"

I nodded.

"Muddafucka!" She turned and shook the little girl at the end of her arm. The girl flopped around but didn't make any noise. "You hear dat? McMahon done got himself a little white girl, he ain't gonna want you! Now what am I gunna do? I gots to get my fix."

I stepped closer to her. The nerve under my eye started twitching, throbbing hard enough to make my eyelid flutter. The skin on my hands felt swollen, my palms itched with the desire to clench into fists. "Start by letting her go and knocking that shit off."

She turned on me, her voice rising. "You tellin' me how to raise my own child? Who da' hell you think you is?" She was making too much noise. She was going to draw attention to us in any second.

My fingers shot out, closing on the greasy skin at the back of her neck. I yanked her close. She smelled bad. Like she hadn't washed in a week or maybe she'd had a shit sandwich for breakfast. "Who is McMahon?"

"He da' crackman! Dis his house you at."

"What does he want with a little girl?"

Both her hands clasped on my arm. I stared at her broken fingernails. There was blood dried on the ones where she had been scratching and picking at herself. Something gross was caked under her middle finger, some unidentifiable chunk hanging against the splintered nail. She wasn't fighting, just holding on and staring at me sullenly. At least she had let her daughter go.

The girl stood there, watching us. The crackhead's eyes narrowed as she studied me.

"What kinda cop are you?"

I jerked her close, making her look in my eyes. "Do I look like a fucking cop?" I shook her like she had shaken the little girl earlier. Corroded stumps of teeth clacked together. "Answer the question."

"He likes dat. He give a big fat rock if you bring a girl for him. Ever'body know dat!"

My blood ran cold. The anger that had heated my skin dropped like a stone, congealing in my stomach and curdling. I had to shove her away to keep from breaking her neck. "Get out of my sight." Words stuck to my clenched teeth. "Leave the girl. Run away."

She stared at me sullenly. "What you give me for her?" She hopped from foot to foot, arms bouncing at her side like chicken wings. "I gotta get sump'thin."

I raised the shotgun and pointed it at her head. "I'll give you your worthless, miserable life. Now get the hell away from me."

I watched her over the top of the shotgun barrel. I watched her draw in a breath. I watched her rotten mouth open. A flake tumbled away from her chapped lips, leaving a pink square uncovered.

"WHITEBOY WID A GUN! WHITE BOY WID A—"

The back of my hand flew off the gun, whipping around and smacking her on the cheekbone. There was no resistance as she dropped to the ground like a sack of bricks. The girl watched her fall and then turned big intelligent eyes up toward me.

I knelt down beside her. "I'm not going to hurt you."

"I know." Wide brown eyes blinked at me. "You said you were here to save that girl."

"I am."

She thought about it for a moment. Her tiny forehead

furrowed as she pondered. "Could you save me, too, mister?"

My heart twisted, drawing my chest tight. "What's your name, sweetie?" My throat was tight as I asked.

"Mary."

I pointed at the Comet. "You see that car over there, across the street?" She nodded earnestly, her eyes following my finger. I pulled out the keys, separated out the door key, and handed them to her. "Go wait in the car. Lock the doors and lay down in the backseat. Stay there no matter what happens outside the car or how much noise you hear and I will come back for you when I am done."

"Are you really going to come back?" That little face held a lifetime of disappointment. Broken promises filled her eyes.

I smiled at her. "I have to. You have the keys to my car." I softly put my hand on the top of her head. "Go on now, Mary. I'll be done soon." She watched me for a second. She looked down at the keys in her hand and then back up to me. Turning, she took one step toward the car, then spun and threw her thin arms around my neck in a hug. She squeezed with all she had, let go, and then ran to the car. I watched her, wiping hot wetness from my eyes. The car door closed behind her and I heard the click of the lock. With a deep breath I stood, stepped over the crackhead mother, and walked up the steps.

Pulling out the oily rag, I smeared it over the camera lens, turning it into a greasy blind eye. For extra measure, I tossed the rag over the camera. It draped and hung, covering me from sight. My fingers swiped down my denim-clad thigh to wipe away the oil again and then closed on the slide of the shotgun.

The door was steel. It opened to the inside and was secured with a giant dead bolt. I shoved the breeching shroud just above the lock, leaning into it. Steel met steel in a soft clang. The barrel was aimed down toward the lock, stock pressed securely into my shoulder.

One deep breath in. Hold. Release.

Pull the trigger.

The end of the shotgun exploded, shooting fire out through the tiny gaps between door and shroud. I rocked back through my knees. Taking the kick of the gun. Absorbing it. Pushing back toward the door. The world closed down around the blast, my ears gone silent behind the roar.

The lead-covered steel ball blasted through the lock. Shoving metal apart. Ripping a tunnel through. I pivoted left, jacked the slide, squeezed the trigger, and blasted another round through. Pivot right. Jack the slide. Pull the trigger. Absorb the shock.

The lock was gone. Smashed to smithereens. A fist-sized hole glared out at me.

Spinning to the side of the door, my fingers pulled extra rounds off the stock and shoved them into the breach. With the gun fully loaded again, I turned to the door, leaned back, and planted a size thirteen boot beside the doorknob. The steel door flew in, smashing against a crackhead holding a pistol. The skinny man yelled out in pain and grabbed his arm that held a gun. I shouldered in, twisted, and slammed the stock of my gun across the side of his head, right across the temple. He bowled over into the wall, dropping the pistol, and crumpling into a heap. My fingers flicked on the light mounted to the tactical rail. A halogen beam cut through dim shadows as I started walking down the unlit hallway.

The hall was narrow and short. Walls closed in toward me, made dingy by a sickly sweet haze of crack-pipe smoke that hung in the air. I tried to breathe shallow and keep as much of that poison out of my lungs as possible.

That shit is corrosive, which is why crackheads have train wrecks for smiles. The crack smoke erodes enamel and dissolves the tooth. A lot of crackheads suck the pipe the same way, time after time putting it in the same place as they smoke. Those crackheads will have a perfect hole eaten through their smile like it was etched in acid.

Trash carpeted the floor. Paper, bottles, rotten food, discarded clothing. It all lay on the floor in piles and heaps, kicked to the side, shoved against the baseboards. I stepped carefully, sweeping the light back and forth. Inside the house, the hot itch was almost unbearable, so choking that the back of my throat was dry and scratchy. My stomach gurgled, roiling around on itself.

My hearing was clearing up, sounds coming back to me. Yelling. Screaming. I kept moving, clearing the first room by the door quickly. It was empty except for filthy broken-down couches occupied by filthy broken-down people. Most of them stared at me, openmouthed. Two were so far gone they didn't wake up, dead asleep or just dead, wasted away again in Crack-a-ritaville. One stared at me while still holding a small butane lighter to the glass tube stuck between desiccated lips, held by corroded teeth.

They were no threat; I moved on.

Noise came from the end of the hall, where it turned to the rest of the house. Moving quickly, I closed the gap. Two gangbangers rounded the corner. Pants sagging, shirts three sizes too big, with bandannas noosed around their heads and arms full of jailhouse ink, they raised cheap pistols at me. Spinning on my foot, my back slammed into the wall as I pushed out of their line of fire.

Time shrank, wrapping us in a bubble. The one in front jerked his finger on the trigger, spitting death into the space I was just in. He held the cheap semiautomatic sideways, playing a video game in his head. The slide convulsed back, hot shell casings flying to plink him in the face. My shoulders flexed, bouncing me off the wall. Three giant strides put me right up in his face. The shotgun swung up over my head.Pushing off the ground,the top of my boot tightened across my instep. I rose up and drove the butt of the gun into the top of his skull. The shock jolted to my shoulders as I bashed him to the floor. His knees went out as he dropped, both legs going into a split. He slumped to the ground, face thudding into the litter-strewn hallway. I let the momentum spin me around as I landed. The shotgun swung down, pointing at the second gangbanger's face.

Acne scars stood out on sallow cheekbones as his cardboard brown complexion washed white in the halogen gleam of the tactical light mounted on the shotgun. Sweat popped out below his bandanna, glimmering in trails down the sides of his baby face. White showed all around dark brown irises, pupils shrinking to pinpricks in the harsh glare of the light on the shotgun. Sweet Jesus, Mary, and Joseph, he looked to be about fifteen years old.

"Sssshhhhhhhhhhhhh," I hissed at him. I kept my voice low. "Drop the gun." His fingers opened, sleek Berretta 9mm tumbling to the floor, lost in the litter. It was a nice gun.

His Adam's apple bobbed up and down as he swallowed. "It's cool esse, it's cool." His voice was brittle with fear.

"Who else is on your crew?"

"Nobody, Holmes. Just me and Jaime." I believed him. The stink of fear rolled off him like cheap cologne.

"Where's McMahon?" He shook his head, lips pulled tight, refusing to speak. I pushed the barrel of the shotgun to his face. Blood welled up around the teeth of the breeching shroud as it bit his cheek. "Do you think I'm playing with you? Where. Is. He?"

He jerked a thumb behind him. "Back there. Please don't shoot me, man. My grandma's sick. I needed the money." Tears streamed out of his eyes.

He was a kid. He should have been in high school, playing baseball or rugby or something. A tiny spot inside my chest loosened up for him as I looked into that baby face and those fear-filled brown eyes.

And then I remembered.

This "kid" was a drug dealer. He sold poison to people, watching them become animals a twenty rock at a time. I remembered the crackhead in front of the house, bringing her daughter to trade for drugs. This "kid" would have been the one answering the door, taking the girl to this McMahon, handing over the nugget of crack cocaine. This "kid" knew about little Kaylee Anne Dobbs, missing now for almost twelve hours.

That tiny spot in my chest hardened to concrete.

My boot lashed out, steel toe cracking across his shinbone. I felt it give under my foot with a wet snap. The kid dropped to the ground. A high-pitched scream ripped out of his throat on the way to the floor. He rolled over, still screaming. His hand came up with the Beretta. He had found it in the trash on the floor. He pointed it at me. From two feet away he wouldn't miss. I whipped the shotgun barrel down, across the bones of his forearm. The steel tube might as well have been a baseball bat and I might as well have been Babe Ruth. His arm snapped over just below his wrist. Ivory bone popped through the skin in a well of dark blood as the Beretta went flying. The kid made a moist choking sound as he stared at his arm.

Then he passed out cold.

I stepped over him, moving back through the house. The hallway turned at a ninety-degree angle. I rounded the corner, gun ready, and stepped into a new layer of supernatural weirdness.

My stomach jerked into a knot and the air took on the consistency of a blanket that had been drenched in boiling water. Everything was hot, so smotheringly hot I could barely breathe.

Down the hallway were two openings between me and the back wall. On my left was a steel gate, like prison bars. It had a big lock on it. I swept the light inside the bars. There were shelves lining each wall stacked with bins. In the center of the room was a long, cheap table. At the table sat naked women stuffing little white rocks of crack into small ziplock bags. They were naked so they couldn't steal crack from the drug dealers, so high they moved like automatons. Robotically, they swung their arms from piles of crack to piles of plastic bags. So far gone that none of them looked over at the big scary man with the shotgun and the halogen spotlight. I turned away, moving on.

A few steps down the hall was a wide-open archway. Warm yellow light spilled out, cutting a space open on the floor of the hallway. The carpet of trash abruptly stopped just short of the opening, leaving a clean hardwood floor under the spilled light. I pressed my back against the wall and listened. There was a clinking noise, low and chiming. Not repetitive, but similar each time it sounded. My mind couldn't pick out a pattern to it or place where I had heard it before. The supernatural taint to the air was oppressive. I took a deep breath to center myself. The inhale brought me up short.

I smelled pot roast.

The scent of cooked meat tore through the air, so out of place in the environment I was in that it was jarring. The smell clashed in my mind, reminding me of Sunday dinners at home with my family after Mass.

I shoved that memory away. I couldn't get caught in it, especially back then. They still sneak up on me even today. Memories like that, they blindside you. Memories like that could drive me to my knees. Memories like that could drive me insane. Memories like that could get me killed, and there were two little girls waiting on me to save them: Kaylee Anne Dobbs and Mary with the big brown eyes who was waiting in the Comet. They needed me. I couldn't fall apart because of a memory. So I ripped it out of my mind and crammed it deep down, pushing it away violently.

The smell still jangled on my nerves. So out of place. My skin was tight, every muscle primed. Adrenaline simmered in my veins as I swung around the archway to face whatever was in that glowing, yellow room.

I found a man sitting at a table eating supper.

The man was huge. His silverware looked dainty in hands the size of catcher's mitts. He was well-groomed, red hair and full beard neatly kept. The clothes he wore were very suburban. A light blue polo shirt strained over shoulders the size of bowling balls, and I could see khaki pants covering his legs under the small table where he sat. The hems of the pants sat on loafers the size of shoeboxes that stretched out between the table legs.

He didn't look up, even with the shotgun's light shining on him. He just continued eating the last of the meal on the plate in front of him. The knife in one hand cut meat with a clinking scrape. The fork in the other stabbed the meat along with potatoes and carrots, and scooped them up to his mouth.

"What the hell are you doing? Are you McMahon?"

Ignoring me, he tucked away his last bite, chewing and savoring it. With a sigh, he wiped his mouth with a wad of fabric and looked up. His eyes were beady and black, set in a wide face. There was still a bit of potato stuck in his beard.

"I am McMahon. Who the hell are you?" His voice had an Irish lilt to it.

"Where is Kaylee Dobbs?"

"Oh, you are here about the girl." His hands came down on the table and he looked like he was going to stand up. I swiveled the shotgun and squeezed the trigger. Thunder roared out of the barrel as the last breecher slug smashed into the refrigerator beside him. Racking the slide kicked the spent shell out to fly over my shoulder and dance on the linoleum floor. Another shell slipped into its place like a familiar lover.

"Stay where you are or the next one will blow your skull apart." I took a step closer to him. "Where is Kaylee? Answer the question or I won't wait for you to move."

"You are not a cop." He said it as a statement.

Most people, even men his size, get nervous when a gun is pointed at them, especially a shotgun. Most people shit their pants. He was sitting calmly in the fifties-style kitchen and talking to me as if I were an acquaintance.

My shoulders grew tight. This was a dangerous man. There was something more than his size that made the hair stick up on my arms. My finger tightened, taking the slack out of the trigger, one twitch away from shooting him in the face.

"What I am is the man who is about one second from blasting a cap in your ass if you don't tell me where Kaylee is."

He sighed. "Do you know how easy it is to get a little girl to come with you? The classics still work, even in this age of heightened awareness." His smile was wide, making the tiny piece of potato tumble from his beard and onto his shirt. "'Little girl, do you want some candy?'"

He chuckled and shook his head. "For instance, sweet little Kaylee just wanted to help me find my lost puppy."

My stomach churned in disgust. I turned, squeezing the trigger again. The shotgun bucked and roared, blasting into the stove. The oven door fell off and heat washed into the room. I racked the slide and pointed the barrel back to his head, fighting to keep from squeezing the trigger.

My voice was a snarl. "No more warning shots. Tell me where she is!"

"Sweet, delicious Kaylee is gone. I just finished her off, as a matter of fact." His hand twitched, knocking the wad of fabric he had used to wipe his mouth off the table. It tumbled slowly to the floor, billowing out.

It was a tiny sundress made of pink paisley fabric.

Revulsion slammed into the back of my throat, bile churning in my mouth. I roared out, squeezing the trigger. The shotgun bucked, spitting a load of silver shot across the room.

The pellets smashed into the small table, absorbed by the thick wood.

Faster than sight, the big man had snatched the table, putting it in front of him as a shield. Before I could rack the slide, he raised it up and threw it across the room at me. I ducked to get out of its path, twisting away. The heavy wood struck across my shoulder. Numbness flashed down my arm like lightning. The shotgun tore out of my hands, spinning through the air and clattering inside the open oven. It rattled around and stopped, hung up on the wire oven racks.

I was knocked to the ground. My face slammed into the slick linoleum and there was a hot gush as my eyebrow split open from the impact. White sparks flew across my vision. I threw my weight to the side, scrambling. I wound up with my back against the dishwasher.

My right hand yanked the Desert Eagle from its holster and my left hand wiped blood from my eye. I swept the room with the gun, the tactical laser burning trails through the air.

The man was standing in the center of the room.

Massive shoulders hunched over, veins standing like cables on his arms. The polo shirt ripped at the seams as he screamed to the sky. His muscles were swelling, twitching, and jerking as they grew. I watched his arms and legs twist. Joints distended as his legs became thicker. The supernatural in the air was like soup. Heat washed over me, my skin felt like it was on fire. The desire to plunge in salty, icy water consumed me.

The man roared as his ribs broke with a snap and a jerk, chest expanding into a barrel. The bones in his neck grew and his skull re-formed itself. His face pulled into a snout, big and square. Head thrown back, I could see his teeth grow. All four incisors split gums, shooting out into four-inch-long enameled daggers. A thick tongue lashed out to lick the blood off them. His nose colored black as it changed shape, becoming a square at the end of his snout.

Power rushed over me in a tide. My stomach tore itself apart in hunger. I wanted meat, red and raw and briny. I wanted to lick salty blood off the ice. I wanted to rend flesh, to tear blubber from bone in strips to swallow it whole.

The man convulsed as his body swelled. His skin thickened over muscles that had reknit themselves to three and four times their size. His clothes were shredded, hanging in rags. His square skull brushed the ceiling. Hands and feet had elongated into paws, razor-sharp black talons jutting from the end of each former finger. A deep guttural grunt tore out of him as one last convulsion ran from the bottom of his feet to the top of his head. In its wake, white fur sprouted from his skin, lengthening and growing into a thick pelt.

Inside the kitchen, inside a crack house in the 'hood, stood a fucking polar bear.

Holy shit.

4

I scrambled to my feet as the bear turned to look at me. A roar tore through the air, washing hot and moist over me. My finger squeezed. The gun in my hand kicked back, its roar shorter and sharper, but just as loud as the bear's. Four .357 Magnum bullets in four blinks of the eye. They slapped center mass into white fur.

And disappeared.

The bear jerked his head down, looking at where the bullets had vanished. His skull convulsed, shrinking back with a shift of bone until it was a mix of bear and man. The voice that came out of that mouth was completely inhuman. It sounded like a garbage disposal trying to form words in English.

"Silver? You shot me with silver?" That mutated face looked at me. "What the hell are you doing with silver bullets?"

My finger squeezed the trigger in response.

The next two bullets disappeared into that expanse of white fur.

"QUIT SHOOTING ME!" he screamed. "IT BURNS!"
Sure enough, I could see black spots forming where I

had shot him. Tiny wisps of smoke curled out between strands of white fur.

I pulled the trigger on the last four bullets.

The air shook as the bear screamed out. Between my pulling the trigger and the bullets reaching him, he turned, grabbed the refrigerator, and yanked it in front of him. It was so fast I didn't see it happen. One second he was standing in my line of fire, the next he had the refrigerator in front of him. The bullets splatted against the insulated side of the fridge, tearing holes and leaving marks, but not penetrating through to hit him.

The slide of my pistol locked back, open and empty.

Dammit!

Thumb sweeping the release button made the clip drop out of the bottom of the gun. It fell and clattered on the floor. My left hand had a fresh clip and was already moving to the opening. It slid home and clicked into place. I flicked the slide release and it jerked forward, stripping a round off the clip and seating it in the chamber.

The bear threw the refrigerator at me.

Time shrank around me again as I watched hundreds of pounds of metal fly toward me. The door swung open as it flipped toward me in the air, food tumbling out. Mustard, ketchup, carton of eggs, head of lettuce; my mind took stock of these on one track. On the other was the thought: *That damn fridge is going to crush me.*

Without thinking, I threw my feet out and dove under the flying hunk of metal and insulation. My shoulder slammed into the floor as I rolled. The door to the fridge whirlwinded over my face so close it brushed my goatee. I kept tumbling to a stop as the refrigerator smashed into the wall behind where I had been standing. Sheetrock exploded into dust, raining down over the kitchen appliance. I was on my stomach. Pain throbbed across my shoulder and my breath was gone.

Get up!

I pulled my knees under me when something slammed across my back like the fist of God and drove me back to the floor. Another blow hit me across the kidneys, this one with a tug and a ripping sound. The Kevlar vest jerked around my body, edge of the collar rubbing a cloth burn across my throat that blossomed lava hot immediately.

I rolled away. The bear was standing over me, pieces of my Kevlar vest hanging off black talons. Kevlar is just a cloth. The weave and layering is what makes it stop bullets, but it isn't worth a damn against bladed attacks. That included bear claws.

I swung the Desert Eagle up, pulling the trigger, absorbing the shock through my shoulder, letting the recoil carry the gun up in an arc. Silver bullets stitched a haphazard line up the bear's body from knee to neck. The skin convulsed around the entry points, white fur rolling back to expose black holes.

There was no blood. There should have been blood.

The bear's skin was too thick for the .357 bullets to penetrate. The rounds were lodging in the layer of blubber that protects polar bears from arctic chill. The .357 is a hot-loaded .38 caliber bullet—more powder, more kick, more penetrating force. It's a substantial bullet, good for almost anything, but it was still about the size of a large pea. They just weren't enough to do any real damage to something as big as a bear.

The slide locked again as the bear pawed the air in anger. Before I could grab another clip, the polar bear began to fall. On top of me. Two tons of killing machine fell like a redwood toward me. My heels dug in and I pushed off the floor, clambering to my feet as it crashed down on all four paws where I had been laying.

My foot landed on the mustard bottle that had flown

out of the fridge earlier. I jerked myself to a stop so I could keep my feet. That massive square head, the size of my chest, swung around. Black lips pulled back on jaws full of murderous teeth. Faster than sight, they clamped down on my right arm. Both sets of incisors punched through my bicep in a shower of blood as the jaws closed just above my elbow.

Agony exploded in my arm, spasming from fingertip to shoulder, then running down my lat and across the small of my back. Pain splashed across my chest, and my heart closed like a fist. It held shut, skipping beats, locked in the throb of sheer agony. With a sharp shock it thudded back to life. My mind went blind for a second and the world disappeared.

My bones vibrated as the bear growled in victory. The vibration carried more pain in its path as it jolted through my skeleton. Acid boiled in my stomach, growing hot and queasy. Left hand reaching back, it closed on the Glock tucked in my waistband. I drew it out and pressed it against that bog white skull. My finger jerked the trigger.

Nothing happened.

Semiautomatics jam at the worst possible times.

Anger chased pain, clearing my head. I drew back and whacked the pistol across that black snout. Beady, brown, bear eyes closed and he snorted around my arm. The bear's head shook, yanking pain through my arm and chest again. I began to pound the useless gun into its head. Over and over. Bringing it up, slamming it down. My strength leaked away with each hit. The skin split across the snout. Blood ran freely, staining the white fur crimson. Thin nasal bone crumpled under the butt of the gun.

The bear tossed its head back, lifting me off my feet. Killer jaws opened at the top of its swing, flinging me away. My stomach flipped as I sailed over, landing on the stovetop. I banged to a stop, hanging off the counter and stove.

I couldn't see. I was blinded by pain. My arm was a throbbing, sticky mess, the fingers completely useless. I shook my head to clear it. My sight came back in a tunnel of dark gray. The polar bear was gathering itself, readying to charge.

My guns were gone, both of them knocked out of my hands. I was lying in a pile of broken ceramic shards with cookie crumbles scattered in the pieces. My useless arm was under me, hand on an overturned knife block.

My left hand snatched a handle from the block, drawing out a thirteen-inch butcher knife like Excalibur from the stone. The bear charged. It thundered up, jaws snapping toward my face.

My hand flashed out holding the knife. I slashed down with all the strength I had.

And stabbed it in the mouth.

The blade slid through the bear's tongue with no resistance, the pink tip of it flew past my ear to smack the wall behind me. A thin arc of blood from it whipped hot across my cheek. The blade punched through the bottom of the jaw, between the bones. Blood and saliva washed over my hand as I shoved it to the hilt and let go.

The bear jerked back, paws swinging toward its face. Swatting, trying to grab without fingers. Blood streamed down the blade where it jutted out of the bottom of the jaw. The gore blared out, day-glow bright against the white fur of the bear's chest. It kept trying to close its mouth, ramming the handle against the roof of its palate. This drove the knife even deeper, which made the bear try harder in a cycle of pain and frustration.

The Were-bear fell over, rolling on the floor. Its throat convulsed to try and dislodge the knife. Blood smeared across the linoleum in weird abstract patterns.

I sat up and slid off the counter. Heat from the open oven baked against my leg. I looked down to find the shotgun still lodged in the oven rack. My left hand closed on it. The skin of my palm burned, the barrel hot from being inside the oven.

I didn't care.

I managed to rack the slide, juggling the shotgun with one hand as the bear finally shook the knife free. It skittered across the floor, slinging blood droplets in its trail. The bear looked up at me. Natural polar bears don't have expressions besides calm indifference and kill. This polar bear had murder in its eyes and blood on its fur. It roared as I pointed the shotgun in its face. I squeezed the trigger as it turned away. The silver-shot blast tore across its snout, ripping away the bottom jaw, leaving it to hang askew on one thin, bloody tendon. The stump of its tongue splatted on the ceiling, sticking there like some gigantic, gory, obscene spitwad.

The bear fell into a puddle of its own blood. Seizure convulsed it, jerking the bear's body into knots. It began to shrink, its body re-formed, writhing back into the form of a man. Pushing off the stove, I walked unsteadily to the bloody, naked man twitching on the linoleum. As the last dregs of bear washed away from McMahon, he sprawled out, arms and legs akimbo, muscles still bunched into charley horses.

I racked the shotgun again as I stepped over him. The lower half of his face was a red ruin. Gnarled hands batted at my legs weakly. His eyes rolled around, looking wildly from side to side as he made *ghuk*, *ghuk* noises from what was left of his throat. Silver poisoning ran black from the edges of the wound. I swung the shotgun over his face, putting the barrel against his eye socket.

"This is for Kaylee Ann Dobbs."

I pulled the trigger.

* * *

Exhausted, battered, and injured, I fell into the Comet's seat. The armload of guns I had carried from the house clattered into the passenger side, some of them spilling into the floorboard. Weary from blood loss, I felt like a piece of beef jerky. Pulled tight and dried out. The bicep on my right arm was tourniqueted with my T-shirt. It wasn't pretty, but it should keep me alive until I got to medical attention. I had torn the shirt and tied the knot with my teeth. Each heartbeat throbbed through the arm, sending a cutting pain all the way down to my fingertips. I couldn't see out of my left eye. It had swollen shut, and the skin was sore and mushy to the touch. The eyelid had sealed shut with clotted blood from the split on my eyebrow. I would take care of it when I got back to the club. My head was fuzzy, full of ache and cotton. That would be the combo pack of abuse and blood loss. My left hand fished in my pocket, looking for the keys. They weren't there.

Dammit.

"You okay, mister?"

I jumped, one open eye jerking to the rearview mirror. I was too spent to react more than that. In the small rectangle of glass I saw little Mary sitting in the backseat. Her eyes were wide as she stared at me.

I relaxed, tension washing away. "Yeah, kid. Why do you ask?"

She slid forward, putting her thin arms on the back of the front seat. "You don't look so good."

"You should see the other guy." I laughed at my own joke. Laughing made my stomach spasm and turned into a wet, hacking cough. I caught it in my hand. When I looked there were tiny droplets of blood on my palm. I wiped them away on my pants. Mary didn't seem to think it was funny. "Do you still have my keys, sweetie?"

Her arm came forward over the seat. My keys dangled from the end of her thin brown fingers. I reached over to get them with my left hand and that sent a jolt of pain across my arm that made my head spin. When it passed, I leaned up and tried to put the key in the ignition with my left hand. I dropped them to the floorboard with a curse.

"Let me help." Mary scrambled over the seat and ducked down to snatch up the keys. Unmindful of the guns, she scooped up the keys. They jangled as she shoved the right key into the ignition and turned it. The Comet roared to life, happy to see me. I nodded a thank you to Mary. She pushed guns in the floor and pulled the seat belt around her thin frame. I shifted the car to Drive. Before I could go, Mary spoke up, "Where's the little white girl, mister?"

The thought of Kaylee punched me in the gut. I was going to have to tell her father what had happened to her. I didn't want to tell her father what had happened to her. I would. That's part of the job. The shitty part, but still a part I had to do. I looked over. "She didn't make it, kid. I was too late to save her."

Mary sat for a second. Absorbing. One tiny tear trickled down her cheek. "I'm sorry." She said it simply, not realizing how much it really meant.

I stepped on the gas, pulling away from the hell of that neighborhood and the hell of that house.

"Where are you taking me, mister?" No fear in her voice, just trust mixed with curiosity. Anywhere I was taking her had to be better than where she was.

"Call me Deacon. I'm taking you to see a friend of mine named Father Mulcahy. He will find you a new home. A good home."

"Mister Deacon, did you kill McMahon?"

I kept looking forward as I drove.

"Dead as hell, kid. You never have to worry about him again."

She settled into her seat belt, relaxing.

"Good." Her hands clasped together in her lap, she leaned back into the seat and closed her eyes. There was a smile on her face.

"That's it there."

Kat's voice pulled me out of my reverie. I spun the wheel and turned into the driveway for a low cinderblock building. There was a handicap access ramp from the front door, and all the windows were painted black.

My fingers reached up to rub the wide, flat scars on my right bicep. The skin was slick and hard to the touch even more than four years later. That was the first time I had run up against a lycanthrope.

My mind flashed to the Were-dog in the backseat, the lions, and the gang of other lycanthropes I had run into today. I had learned a helluva lot since that first time, and it looked like I was going to wind up using every bit of it before all of this was over.

Yippee-ki-yay.

5

Larson looked completely different than the last time I saw him. His ginger hair and beard had grown until it hung around almost delicate features. He had lost enough weight to give him the hollow-eyed look of a Russian Orthodox icon. His skin was pale from being inside too much. Cheekbones that could have opened envelopes sat above his tangled beard.

And he was in a wheelchair.

Larson had been mixed up in the fight with Appollonia last year. She had set him up without his knowledge to be bait for me in a trap of her devising. It failed. Things got really weird and she apparently changed her plans. Then she tried to use his family as hostages to force me to do what she wanted.

What she had wanted me to do was her.

I said it got really weird.

It all came down to a big fight that left Larson without the use of his legs. I realized, now that he was in front of me, I had not seen him since he had been in the hospital.

Come to think of it, that was pretty shitty of me.

What can I say? I had been busy.

He wheeled back from the doorway to let me and Kat

inside. I was carrying Sophia wrapped in one of the blankets from the backseat. I stepped in. Kat shut the door behind me, locking it.

"Larson." I did the guy nod.

"Deacon." He nodded back. Arms corded with wiry muscle, he spun his chair around. He began rolling down a hallway. "Let's go see to the patient. Follow me to the lab," he called over his shoulder. I motioned Kat to go ahead of me.

The hall was short and dim, completely bare of any decoration. It ended in a ramp that led down into a mad scientist-style laboratory. The room had tile floors and white walls. A desk stood in one corner surrounded by bookshelves that had no books on them. The books were piled on and around the desk instead, haphazardly slid and stacked. The rest of the room had countertops lining each wall. On these were a lot of equipment I did not recognize, but it all looked medical or scientific of some type. The lab smelled like a cross between a laundry mat and an herb shop. A flat table stood in the center of the room with telescoping lights arranged above it. Larson pulled a sheet of thick white butcher paper over it and motioned me to lay the Were on it.

It was a relief to set her down again. My back was burning from being thrown into the cinderblocks, and my arm throbbed and ached with every heartbeat where Cash had opened it up with his teeth. I slid Sophia off my arms and onto the table as gently as I could. She didn't whimper like she had when I picked her up from the backseat of the Comet, but I felt her tense, holding her breath tight.

Once I got out of the way, Larson went to work. Tenderly, he moved the blanket and began examining her. Her eyes opened for the first time, one liquid brown, the other a crystal white-blue. She looked at him warily; then her brown eye rolled around to me, fixing me with a stare. A dog's eyes can look remarkably human. A Were-dog's eyes are eerily human. Even the difference in their color didn't ruin the effect.

"Tell me what happened to her."

I held the Were's gaze as I answered. "I don't know any details or anything that happened to her before I found her. But she has been choked and beaten with a heavy chain by a big sonuvabitch of a Were-lion. He looked like he was trying to kill her."

"That sounds brutal."

"It was."

"I assume she's a shape-shifter of some kind. If not, she would never have survived that kind of beating."

I nodded. "She feels like a lycanthrope. Some form of dog Were, even though I don't recognize the breed." Larson knew about my ability to sense the supernatural.

"Her name is Sophia." Kat leaned over the back of Larson's chair, her blond hair and left breast brushing across his cheek. He didn't pull away. Neither did she. Her hand lightly touched Sophia's stomach, fingers fluttering like a butterfly against the skin. "This area is swollen and fevered. It's different from her other wounds."

Larson leaned forward as Kat pulled back. I arched an eyebrow at her when she looked up. A blush popped into her cheeks, but she didn't turn away. Larson's voice was soft and comforting. "Sophia, I am going to push in on your abdomen, let me know if it hurts in any way."

Before his hands could touch her, she turned and snapped, lips pulled back, sharp teeth biting the air. Her body curled around into a ball, covering her belly. The snarl stayed on her mouth. A low growl rumbled, vibrating off the table she was on.

Larson leaned back, his hand up and moving with him

away from the teeth. A low "hmmmmmmmmmm" came from him as he sat looking at Sophia with a tilted head. Kat had to quickstep out of the way as he wheeled backward, spun, and rolled to a counter across the room. He slid open a drawer, rummaging around it and throwing stuff on the counter. His voice was a low mutter to himself that I couldn't make out. Something told me that if I could, I still wouldn't understand it. He gave an "Aha!" and held up an empty syringe. He left the drawer open as he wheeled back over to the table. Sophia eyed him warily but wasn't growling and her teeth were behind her lips.

Larson looked her in the eyes, voice still calm. "Is it okay if I take a small blood sample? I will be as gentle as possible. There is no harm that can come from this to you."

There was a drawn-out pause as she looked at him. He kept his eyes down and his hands open where she could see them. Finally, her tail thumped the table twice. Slowly, her paw stretched out toward him. With a murmured thank you, he slipped the slender needle into her skin. A quick hand motion had thin red liquid streaming into the syringe. He withdrew the needle and rolled over to another counter where he began doing things while muttering to himself again.

Sophia licked where the needle had gone in, then lay her head down and closed her eyes. I wanted to reach out and pet her, to comfort her. In my mind, I knew there was a human inside and she was not truly a dog, but I wanted to pet her.

Ah, to hell with it.

I reached out and put my hand on her head, fingers curling through the ruff of fur behind her ear. She leaned into my palm, rubbing her cheek and jaw against it. It was a little strange. Very gently I stroked her face and head. Her fur was dirty, but soft. Long and thick, it felt like spun cotton. She made that small purring sound that dogs make when you scratch them behind the ears. Her brown eye opened again and I could see the intelligence inside. Quickly, her tongue licked out across my hand. I kept petting her until Larson rolled over.

"Sophia, do you know that you are pregnant?"

Pregnant?

Two thumps on the table from her thick tail said, yes, she did know.

Larson's arm went around Kat's waist and squeezed. He looked up at her. "Will you go in the kitchen and bring back some food? High protein, I think there is some tuna in the pantry and I know there are some protein bars." He kissed the back of her hand. "And bring some water."

Kat nodded and moved off through another door. Larson looked up at me. His blue eyes were red-rimmed, bloodshot, and deep sunk in bruise-colored hollows. He looked like he had been burning the candle at both ends. With a blowtorch.

"The pregnancy may explain the slow healing she is experiencing." He looked down sadly at Sophia. "We'll get some food in her for fuel and hopefully speed up her metabolism."

"Okay." I went back to petting her head while we waited. She didn't seem to mind and it wasn't weird once I got used to it.

It wasn't long before Kat returned with a plate heaping with meat. I smelled the tinny fish smell of tuna along with a bloody meat smell. A large piece of what looked like liver covered one side of the plate too. She showed it to Larson and he nodded that it was fine. Looking back at me, he jerked his head to the side, indicating I should follow him to the other side of the room.

I patted Sophia and moved. Kat slid into my place and began spoon-feeding the tuna into the Were's muzzle.

Out the door on the other side of the lab was another short hallway. I followed Larson through. He stopped in the middle and spun his chair around. The footrest banged into the wall, stopping the chair from turning with a jerk.

Larson's voice was a snarl as he yanked on the wheels of the chair. "Fucking piece of shit chair!" The footrest gouged a chunk out of the drywall as it broke free. It was the newest one of many in the narrow hallway. Looking around, I noticed that there were a lot of black skid marks on the doorframes at the beginning and end of the hallway too.

Straightened out, he sat for a second, head down. He took a deep breath, held it, and let it go in a long stream of exhale. He looked up at me. "Sorry about that."

I waved it away. "It's cool."

His hand hit the armrest of the chair. "I'm still not used to this damn chair."

"It has to suck in a major way."

"More than you can imagine."

I shrugged. There was nothing left to say. He was in the wheelchair. Nothing could be done and there was no use in going on about it. He nodded and the moment passed. I knelt down so Larson and I were eye level. I kept my voice low, assuming he had wanted to move away for privacy. "All right, what's the real situation?"

"She should have healed her injuries by now. Lycanthrope metabolism works at a hugely accelerated rate repairing damage almost as soon as it occurs."

I knew this. I'd had to inflict damage on lycanthropes in my line of work before. I had actually done it just a few hours ago. "You think the pregnancy is taking her ability to heal?"

He looked into the other room. Kat was sitting on the table, cradling the Were's head in her lap and hand-feeding her. He turned back to me. "I think it's the most likely scenario. If we can't get her healing to kick in . . ." his voice trailed off with a shrug.

"What could happen?"

Larson sighed. "Anything. Nothing good. I won't bother you with the medical stuff, but suffice to say, her blood is extremely abnormal, even for a lycanthrope. Its alkalines are all off the charts, and the proteins are extremely low. The fevered skin over the fetus is worrisome. It could be an injury from the beating or it could be something unknown. Either way, it probably means trouble." He rubbed thin fingers across his eyes. "Lycanthropy is hard on pregnancy in any case. The high metabolism of the mother mixed with the high metabolism of the fetus usually results in early miscarriage. Weres have a tough time carrying a pregnancy to term in the best of situations. Add injury to a need to change and the probability goes to hell. She could kick-start her healing if she shifted, but I bet she won't because that might terminate the pregnancy in her condition."

"Will she recover from her injuries without shifting form?"

He looked past me to the other room where Sophia and Kat were. "If we can speed up her metabolism . . . maybe. I doubt it, though."

"So she has to change form to kick-start the healing process?"

"That is the main trigger for lycanthropes. The change might make her abort, though."

Damned if you do, damned if you don't. My mind wondered if the Were-lion who had beaten her knew she was with child. Or pup. Whichever. I looked at Larson. "So it's wait and see, then."

He stopped looking me in the eye, turning away and looking down at his hands in his lap. "There is one thing we can try."

Not looking at me is bad. I had a feeling I was not going to like his suggestion. He did, too, that's why he was suddenly obsessed with looking at his own thumbnail. I waited for him to speak.

"Remember last year when you had the Spear of Destiny and you used your power to heal Longinus and Charlotte?"

My mind tripped back almost six months. After killing Appollonia and taking the Spear of Destiny from her, my ability to sense magick was boosted. Holding the Spear allowed me to reach in and heal Longinus, the immortal owner of the Spear. I had been able to do the same for Charlotte, a Were-spider who had been Appollonia's familiar. She had been forced to serve that hell-bitch until I set her free. They had both been wounded, Longinus mortally so, and I had been able to call out their supernatural abilities to heal them.

I looked down at Larson's legs strapped into the chair he sat in. He had been there, bleeding from the wound that took his legs, while I healed them. Because he was only human there was nothing to call out of him. Nothing paranormal inside him to bring healing. So he got the hospital and the wheelchair. It would have made me feel guilty if I had a conscience about that sort of thing. I don't. War is war and he signed up. His situation might suck, but it did no good to wring my hands over it. Push it aside, keep moving.

I seem to do that a lot.

"I don't have the Spear, it went back to Longinus."

His hand clamped on to my arm. It was full of wiry strength he did not have last year. "I don't think you need it. From what I've heard, your power has changed and grown." I nodded that it had. "I think you still have the ability to manipulate the supernatural like you did that night."

I didn't say anything.

His eyes went back to the lab. I turned to look. Kat had finished feeding Sophia and now sat on the table with the Were-dog's head in her lap. Larson pointed past me. "It's worth a try, I think. For her and her baby."

Dammit.

I am used to my ability. I use it, but I don't like it. It smacks too close to magick, and magick always, always ends badly. A lot of people claim white magick is different from black magick. Bullshit. Magick is magick, and it always goes dark. The only solace I held was that mine came from a transfusion of Angel's blood. How black could it be if it came from an Angel?

Don't answer that.

Since I used it holding the Spear, I *had* felt a difference. Since then it had been stronger, easier, and the impressions were more detailed and intimate. I could feel the supernatural with a depth and texture I had not before. Now I had to make conscious efforts to *not* use my ability. It was always there, ready to spark at the first hint of anything paranormal. It felt like more a part of me, almost as natural as the ability to hear or smell.

I had also felt it pull me like that night long ago with the Spear. Tugging me to change the supernatural I had run up against since.

I had been ignoring it.

Now Larson was asking me to push it even further. To do even more with it. It didn't sit well with me. I almost said no. The word sat behind my teeth, bitter as chalk.

Then I looked at Sophia.

She lay limp on the table. I watched her breathe, dragging air into her lungs. The effort of each breath made her tremble with pain, the shiver running across from her tail to her muzzle. The whine she'd had earlier was back, low and sad, cut by the effort of simply drawing in air.

Dammit.

I stood up.

"Okay, let's do it." I started walking back into the lab, Larson rolling behind me.

Going back into the lab, we found the plate licked clean and Kat pouring water from a bottle in her hand for Sophia to lap at. More water was getting on Kat's jeans than in the Were-dog's mouth and a big wet spot had formed, making the denim dark.

Larson motioned me to the table and reached to help Kat down. He leaned in close to Sophia, his voice back to low, soothing tones. "We are going to try something to help you. It may not work, but it should not hurt. We have to try to get you healed for the baby's sake."

Sophia watched him warily for a moment, then lolled her head back toward me. I stroked her head again. Her tail thumped the table twice more.

"Okay. Just keep your hand on her, close your eyes, and reach out with your power until you can sense her."

My eyes shut to darkness and I reached down inside myself where my ability sits. I had a sense of Sophia's lycanthropy. It felt like night air in the city. The clean taste of moonlight that came with all lycanthropes. Just the surface impression I get automatically, but Larson wanted more. He wanted me to reach inside and make her lycanthropy sit up and do tricks.

Dammit.

Pulling breath into my lungs, I settled down into the

center of myself. My ability sat like a hard cluster inside me. I let it go and let it unfurl. It soared up through me in thin streamers and went down my arm. I felt the tendrils flow out of my fingers and into Sophia. The tendrils probed for a second, feeling around, taking stock.

With a click, they locked into place and I could feel her like I can feel myself. My nose filled with the warm smell of dog, pleasant like roasted peanuts. The world tilted for a second as I adjusted to the metaphysical mind theater. Sensations swirled and whirled inside me. Should I be on two legs or four? The feeling passed quickly and I came back to myself. I shook my head and looked around with my mind's eye.

Her human side was pushed deep, curled up and hurting. I felt the uncivilized pulse that was her lycanthropy rushing and swirling around. I found tiny knots of life, three of them, wild and fierce inside her. In my head they shone like brilliant candle flames in the dark.

Sophia was carrying triplets. Strange.

Outside, a voice spoke, muttering in a guttural, broken tone. A crackle of force zapped into the connection between me and the lycanthrope. Everything around that crackle pulled taut, stretching tight. Sophia whined, feeling the sting like I did. My taste buds burned with acid. I swallowed it back down. My nostrils clotted with the scent of soured milk. The force invaded, pushing whip cracks of pain along its path.

My gun was out and pressed against Larson's head.

I cracked my eye open to look down at him. "What the *hell* do you think you are doing?"

Larson's eyes were big. His mouth hung open, caught mid-syllable. The spell he had been chanting was cut off and hung dying in the air between us. Slowly, his jaw closed and he swallowed, bobbing his Adam's apple.

Sweat ran in a trickle from under his hair, rolling around the slide of the Colt where it pressed against his temple.

He swallowed with a gulping sound. "Trying to help."

"Don't." I pushed the barrel harder against his skull. "Not with magick. Not ever."

His mouth closed and he nodded slowly. His head moved only a scant half inch up and down. Kat stepped forward, her hand soft on my arm, voice soft in my ear.

"Deacon, please . . ."

I whipped the Colt back into the holster under my arm. The leather dug into my shoulder as I shoved the gun home. I looked him in his red-rimmed eyes. "Don't start fucking with magick. It never ends well. Next time you pull that shit, I *will* pull the trigger. No 'ifs,' no 'ands,' and no 'buts' about it."

"I believe you." He was smart enough not to say anything else.

I didn't know Larson had been messing around with magick.

Sorcery.

Hoodoo.

Witchcraft.

Whatever name you used, it was still bad news. There is no getting in and getting out unscathed with magick. It leaves a residue on your soul that begins to taint your every action. And it's as addictive as crack cocaine on steroids. Too far down that road and you lose your way. Once you lose your way with magick, you can't find it back. I would have to keep a better eye on him.

The taint of broken magick coated my tongue like a sickness, triggering my memory.

My head filled with symbols. Symbols written on the walls of my home in blood. My family's blood. They burned through my memory, seared into my soul. My ears filled with the cries of my children over the phone as I tried to get to them. The dreadful knowledge I never would make it bringing a cold, clammy sweat to my skin. My eyes burned, tears threatening. Hands clenched. Teeth grinding.

STOP!

I took a deep breath. Held it. Exhaled. Calm down. Calm down. Easy, easy. It's okay. Be cool.

My family had been slaughtered in a magick ritual. I listened to their cries and screams on the phone as I tried to get to them. They had been killed to make magick.

I can't talk about it anymore, it is still too painful.

Pushing it out of my mind, I closed my eyes and turned my attention back to Sophia. I concentrated, pushing my power back out, looking for the tie between us.

The connection between us locked back into place. It had the same feeling as a spinal adjustment, my power and her beast sliding together with a hollow, wet pop. Her lycanthropy came rushing back to fill the theater of my mind. Her beast was wounded but strong. I coaxed it gently to myself, pulling it out. It sniffed me and the temptation was there to pull it into myself and ease my aches and pains.

I couldn't do that. The only thing I can do is sense the supernatural and manipulate it. Sometimes better than others. But I couldn't steal it or use it myself. I couldn't, but she didn't know that, and her animal side wanted to help me. I guess Were-dogs are like real dogs. They just want to help. It could feel that I was hurt and it wanted to metaphysically comfort me. It made new anger flare inside me at the douchebag Were-lion who had hurt her.

I pointed the dog in my head to her own wounds, encouraging her to heal herself. Inside my skin I felt her beast lick the wounds. The tongue was thick and wet, not very gentle at all, almost like getting slapped with a raw steak. What I felt was an echo of what was happening inside her. Behind the licks followed a warmth that spread healing. Golden fibers of light painted over every injury, flashing brightly as they healed.

My real eyes cracked open and I watched as skin began to move under russet fur. Two ribs that were jutting from her side slid wetly into place with a jerk and pop. Her breathing evened out and lost the thread of wheeze it had.

I stepped back, moving my hand from her. My fingers were outstretched, pulling through the connection between us as it stretched. The connection stayed, but it lessened. It thinned and the sensations through it became muffled. Like watching a movie through a swimming pool.

A small curl of nausea rolled through me. I could feel the drain of using my power like this. I can sense supernatural stuff with no problem, but when I try to manipulate it, things start to go haywire. This wasn't too bad, just an annoyance. I would guess that her lycanthropy being so compliant and helpful was taking some of the burden out of what I was doing. I closed my hand into a fist and pulled in my power. The connection severed with a snap of metaphysical energy that made my hand tingle all the way to my wrist.

Sophia gathered herself and stood on the table, her muzzle even with my face. She was still filthy, but she no longer looked frail or pathetic. Even though she was still small and still thin, she wasn't weak. She was like the blade of a knife. She would take your life to protect the babies inside her.

A small spring carried her off the table to the floor in front of me. She landed with only the slightest click-click of nails on tile. I looked down at her one blue eye and one brown, having a hard time focusing on her gaze because of the discrepancy. Her head butted my hand; then she turned and sat by my left leg, body leaning just enough to touch me.

Apparently I had just inherited a watch Were-dog.

6

The Comet ripped into the parking lot of Polecats, chain-link steering wheel slipping through my hands. Cars filled the lot, sitting like empty shells of dead insects all put in a row by a child with OCD. Neon flashed across the entire front of the club, throwing pastel light around the lot like it was free. On top of the building blue neon whipped out the name of the club, and a pink cartoon girl with a cat tail climbed a pole and slid down it over and over again. Yes, I went for the classy. I drove on through the lines of cars, heading to the underground parking for employees.

My fingers pushed the button to lower the volume on the MP3 player mounted in the stereo. The Texas boogie blues of ZZ Top looking good and looking for "Tush" faded down to a nice buzz we could talk over. Kat sat in the passenger seat twirling a blond lock of hair through her fingers. Sophia was freshly washed, her head over the back of the seat between us. Her fur smelled like some girly shampoo Larson had in his shower. I turned to Kat and asked the question that had been on my mind since we got back in the car.

"So . . . you and Larson?"

She turned and she had a look on her face. I had never seen that look on her before. Her eyes were distant and her features had gone soft. Kat is serious business. Always. To glance over and see her look like a smitten schoolgirl was strange. She looked damn near wistful.

"Yep, me and Larson."

"Interesting." I pulled into the corralled entrance to the parking lot for employees. Hitting a button mounted in the dash made the metal gate slide up so we could slip inside. I spoke out of the side of my mouth, smirking, "How is that working out?"

Kat's face went from wistful to all business in a flash. "The only thing that doesn't work is his legs."

From the backseat Sophia made a noise that sounded suspiciously like a doggie snicker.

Wheeling around, I backed into the space set aside for the Comet. The employee parking was the loading dock when the club used to be a warehouse. I had sunk a lot of money into building up the concrete walls and adding roll-down steel gates to make the employee parking safe and secure. We got out of the car, Sophia moving like quicksilver to trot by my side. Kat moved even quicker, getting to the door before me, using her key and slipping inside. The door shut before I reached it.

I guess I had made her mad.

Swinging open the door, I let Sophia in and shut it behind. I stuck my key in and turned, which fired the hydraulic cylinder in the center of the steel door. Three-inch bolts shot into the steel and concrete frame. Nothing was getting through that door. Kat was already halfway up the stairs to the club, feet hitting each stair like a prizefighter.

Dammit. I hate running up stairs.

I took the stairs two at a time, pulling myself up using the steel handrail. Music from inside the club got louder with each step. I caught Kat ten steps from the utility door to a short hallway just off the main floor of Polecats. My hand fell on her arm. She stopped and I leaned back on the steel railing, catching my breath. It's hard to run upstairs two at a time. Besides, I am built for power, not speed, so when I run, it takes a lot out of me.

"You gonna make it, old man?"

I took a deep gulp of air. "Kiss my ass. I'm only a few years older than you." I said it with a grin.

"Yeah, but your years are like dog years." She looked down at Sophia, who stood a step or two below us. "No offense."

Sophia shook her head side to side.

"Ha. Ha. Ha." I stood up, breathing back under control. "I was just poking fun back there, not trying to piss you off."

"I'm not pissed off. I like Larson." She crossed her arms. "Actually, I like Larson a lot, but it's new. So I'm still uncomfortable with the way it feels around people."

"That's why you didn't say anything?"

"Didn't say anything to *you*. Father Mulcahy knows. The girls know. Tiff knows."

Everybody but me? "Why didn't you tell me?"

"Well, I didn't want to hear your smartass comments, and you have been a little preoccupied lately. With Tiff."

Ah, here we go. I was wondering when Tiff would come up. Kat hit my arm. Hard.

"Get that look off your face. I'm not going to give you shit about it. Tiff's a good girl, and everybody can see how you two are."

"We're not dating." I knew I said it too quickly, protesting too much. I could feel it.

Kat stepped in; her hand moved up and touched my face. "You act like I don't know you have more baggage than an airport. We all do around here. But I watch you with her and I can see you letting go of some of the pain you've carried since before I met you." Her hand dropped to my shoulder. The other one joined it on my other shoulder. Her eyes were glittering even in the low light. "Since she's been around I've even seen you smile and laugh once in a while."

She pulled me into a hug, squeezing tight so I wouldn't see tears spill down her cheeks even though I could feel them puddle hot through my T-shirt. Her face was over my shoulder as I hugged her back. "Not to mention the fact that she's the only one I can trust to watch this place and you boys while I am finding my own reasons to smile and laugh with Larson."

I held my friend Kat. I'd never seen her well up like this. I had seen her cry. She had been crying when I rescued her. She had cried when we killed Darius, the vampire who put her through hell as his personal bloodwhore. I had found her crying sometimes early in the morning, holding a small framed picture of her dead sister.

But I had never seen her cry from happiness.

It was long overdue, so I did the only thing I could. I held her and let her cry and didn't ruin it by trying to talk.

7

Music blasted into the stairwell. The door to the club swung open and a small, stacked brunette stepped out, holding the door open behind her. Kat and I moved apart. She wiped thick trails of tears out of her eyes. I just blinked mine away.

Thick high heels tapped on the concrete. The brunette was agitated. Not because she was only wearing a white micro bikini top and matching white micro shorts. Ronnie, Veronica onstage, was a dancer and was well used to being underdressed for her curves.

Polecats isn't really a "strip club," because the city ordinances allow only nude dancing *or* alcohol sales. We chose alcohol sales, which meant the girls were always dressed—in as little as possible, but dressed nevertheless. Customers still poured in and the place made money hand over fist, which is good since it was the main funding for my war against monsters. Bump and grind to fight things that go bump in the night.

Stepping up, I took over holding the door, motioning Kat, Ronnie, and Sophia inside. We stood in a cramped little hallway meant for only one person. The end of it opened into the club itself, and I could see the cocktail waitresses carrying trays of drinks back and forth. It reminded me of a lurid, moving postcard.

I looked at Ronnie. She was a good girl and had been working the club since I rescued her from a Santeria street gang. I had been too late for her little brother, Gomez, who had given his life to keep her safe. I had pulled her from the fire on his behalf, literally. She still had the slick scars on her palms from then and the vague scent of voodoo smoke that refused to leave her skin.

I looked around the hallway, checking the ceiling and the corners. It took a second, but I spotted them. Above our heads were ghost spiders. They were big, the size of a child's palm, and translucent, their skin almost see-through, kind of like a fogged car window. They were highly venomous and creepy as hell. Why didn't I call an exterminator?

Because of Ronnie.

The spiders were imprinted on her. They followed her everywhere. I didn't know how many there were. When they hatched, there were hundreds, but now I had no idea. You never saw more than a few at any given time. But where you saw Ronnie, you saw spiders. They were deadly, and creepy, and psychically connected to her. If she thought about something they could do, they just did it. She never had to find her keys or the remote anymore because the spiders would do it for her. They used to drop down and take money offered by the customers when she danced. Thankfully, she had been able to stop that, but God help anybody who got too touchy-feely with her.

"What's going on?"

She smoothed her fingers over dark hair that was teased up eighties style. Small white teeth found her bottom lip, leaving crescent-moon scars in her crimson lipstick. "When the club opened, a group of Weres came in. A bunch of them." She saw me tense, and put a small hand on my chest. I could feel the slick, hard scar tissue on her palm through my shirt. "Father Mulcahy has them in the conference room. Tiffany wanted me to tell you that they are not the ones from earlier and that Charlotte was with them."

Okay. If the good Father had them corralled together, then this wasn't an attack.

Not yet anyway.

Kat squeezed past us, making Ronnie step closer to me. I caught her faint sage-smoke scent. "I'll go take the club over. I'll send Tiff your way." She turned and was off into the heart of Polecats.

A roomful of lycanthropes could turn into trouble in a split second. Charlotte being there was a comfort. She had been enslaved by Appollonia last year. Charlotte is a Were-spider. That hell-bitch had spiders as her familiar animal, which meant that she could use them as slaves, controlling them with her vampiric powers. I freed Charlotte from that hell-bitch's control and she had been there at the end, fighting on my side.

Appollonia's death left behind a lot of homeless Were-spiders, so Charlotte helped them relocate and settle into the area. Now she was the mother hen of the southern Were-spider cluster. A cluster composed of many different kinds of spiders, which was unusual, but she made it work.

She was also a friend. She came by with cookies for the girls and gourmet coffee for Father Mulcahy. We spent time together in a camaraderie born of blood shed with each other. Her, Tiff, and I had spent many off nights drinking and talking. Sharing things we couldn't share with normal people.

Hell, the ghost spiders that were bonded to Ronnie were her offspring. It's a long story how it all happened involving an ex-Yakuza assassin with a Japanese demon trapped under his skin.

A long story for another time.

Her being here was a good sign.

That didn't mean I wasn't going to get more weapons and ammunition.

Oh, hell no it didn't.

8

The tension in the conference room spiked to a thousand when I walked in.

It could have been me. My reputation as an occult bounty hunter was well-known in the furry circles. It could have been the big-ass Smith & Wesson .500 Magnum strapped to my right hip.

The Smith & Wesson .500 is the world's most powerful handgun, with bullets damn near the size of my thumb. Designed for hunting big game, it is the only pistol with enough power to bring down a lycanthrope without a head shot.

If you do get a head shot with the .500 Magnum, then you have no head left.

If I hit a lycanthrope anywhere, and it was loaded with silver, then they were done. Her name was Bessie and she hung against my thigh in a western-style holster, complete with big-ass bullets in loops, and a silvered Bowie knife to balance her out on the other hip. I still had the two Colt .45 semiautomatics under each arm, too, and no overshirt to hide them anymore.

I was betting it was the big-ass gun that made everybody nervous, but I would be damned if I would rely on there being another bottle lying around if needed.

It's very aggressive to go into a room with enough firepower to kill everyone there. It makes a statement. Sometimes lycanthropes respond negatively to aggression and have to meet it with an equal show of their own. Alpha-male, dominance, pack mentality, whatever term applies. Sometimes being aggressive around them just sets them off.

I didn't give a damn.

Submissive has never been my thing.

The conference room was actually a conference room inside the strip club, not a room designed for something strip clubby and doing double duty. Big oval table surrounded by chairs and a coffee maker. There was a state-of-the-art, Web-based information display also, but that was Kat's department. I can do what any normal person can with a good search engine, but Kat is a wizard at it.

Father Mulcahy stood at the back of the room, near a broom closet that was cracked open. I knew there was a shotgun loaded with silver shot inside. The priest really likes to use his shotguns, and he could have it out and aimed at the room in a blink. A cigarette dangled from his lips, smoke curling up from it. He took a sip from a Styrofoam cup in his left hand, nodding to me over the rim of it. I have no idea how he can sip coffee and smoke at the same time without either ashing into his coffee cup or soaking his cigarette through, but he does.

He was leaning against the wall, his weight held mostly on his right leg. Last year in the mess with Appollonia he had gotten a vicious wound on his left leg. He could get around fine, but now he favored it when he could and it gave him a small hobble to his walk.

I sat in the only empty chair at the table. I didn't actually sit, I flopped into it casually and threw my boots up onto the table in front of me with a clunk. My hands went across my stomach, not touching each other, ready to draw guns if need be. Taking a deep breath, I shoved my ability down, compressing it inside me so that I wouldn't have to wade through everybody's lycanthropy. It gets too distracting to deal with that many kinds of supernatural feedback if I don't have to.

Six people looked at me with varying expressions on their faces.

Charlotte was immediately to my left. Her spine was perfectly straight; she always sat as if she were posing for a portrait. She had cut her hair since the last time I saw her and it looked good, styled into a semi-sixties Jackie-O. Her business blazer was over a light green blouse that went well with her wide hazel eyes and deep chocolate skin. When she was in spider-lady mode, she creeped me out; but as a human, Charlotte was quite a lovely woman.

I looked to Charlotte. "I am assuming everyone you brought knows who I am." It was a statement, not a question, but she still nodded her head. "Okay, how about we go around the table with introductions, name and animal, so we can all be even. Then you can tell me what y'all want."

Charlotte nodded again and turned to the bulky man to her left. He was a thick man. Shoulders rounded like boulders and arms heavy as logs on the table in front of him. He wore a crumpled white shirt. A thin black tie had been pulled loose and left hanging askew at his neck. The shirt didn't fit, adding to the look of bulk on him. A thick layer of coarse black hair covered his arms, tufting out below the rolled-up sleeves. The contrast between the hair and the shirt somehow made his skin look paler than it actually was. His features had been pasted on his face, thick and heavy like an unfinished sculpture.

A wave of her hand and he grabbed a cane I had not seen leaning against his thigh. With a deep breath, he stood, using the cane to support him on one side.

Before he could speak, the door to the room opened. Tiff breezed in followed by Sophia, who was still a russet-colored dog. Tiff had changed for the opening of the club. As assistant manager, she didn't dance, but she liked to dress as if she did. Tonight she had gone cowgirl. Scandalous red cowboy boots cupped shapely bare calves that stretched into shapely bare thighs that disappeared beneath a fringed miniskirt. More fringe than skirt, truthfully. Not that I was complaining.

Her top was a short-cropped, fringed western cowgirl vest that had a single button in the center and covered just about as much as a Wonderbra. She had curled her hair into a pink and black swirl that flared out from under a matching Stetson hat. She looked like a fifties pinup of a cowgirl, all sassy and sexy and sweet.

Every eye in the room followed her in except Charlotte's, the priest's, and the Were with the silver hair.

Yes, even mine.

She loved that outfit because it allowed her to wear the Colt. The Colt used to belong to my friend Western Jim, a monster hunter from Texas. He was a cantankerous old bastard. Mean as a rattlesnake and twice as likely to bite, but I liked him. I had used the Colt to kill him last summer after he had been turned into a vampire under the thrall of Appollonia. I had taken it with me when I left and it was all I had of his.

The gun wasn't anything special except that it was old as dirt and had killed a ton of ghoulies. It was a Colt Peacemaker, single-action revolver in .45 caliber. Tiff loved it and was a pretty good shot with it. Like most things with Tiff, she wore it as part of a costume but never treated it with disrespect. She understood that it meant something to me because it had belonged to my friend, so she took care of it. She cleaned it after each practice session, and I think even though he was a crotchety SOB, Western Jim would have been pleased with her love and care for his old gun.

She leaned against the wall to the right, midway down the table, and hooked her thumbs in her gun belt. It pulled down on the belt and skirt, revealing the smooth bottom swell of her stomach and the valleys beside her hipbones . . . which was distracting as hell, but I knew she'd be able to draw the Colt in a split second. Standing where she was made a four-sided box with me, her, Charlotte, and the priest. The room was covered if it all went tits up. Her training with me was working well. Sophia sat beside her leg.

The bulky man blinked twice. He shook his head and swallowed deeply, making his Adam's apple jerk up and down. His head turned to me, but it took a second for his eyes to follow. His voice was deep when he spoke, coming from far inside that wide barrel of a chest.

"I have met you before. My name is George and I am a silverback."

Silverback? Last year I had a run-in with a Were-gorilla who was the familiar of a vampire named Gregorios who I made dead. I didn't kill the Were, just shot him. In the knee. With a silver bullet. I pointed at his cane. "Is that from last year?"

"It is."

"Sorry about that."

Thick hands came up and waved in the air. "No, no. To be free of that vampire bastard I would gladly lose my whole leg."

I nodded, not knowing what else to say. That was two people I had seen today whose legs I had injured. I was even more responsible for George's limp than I was for

Larson's wheelchair. I didn't feel bad about either. Things happen in my line of work. It could have been worse for George. I could have shot him in the face.

I turned to the girl beside him. She was a young woman, maybe twenty years old, and very average. Average height, average weight, straight brown hair. The only thing out of the ordinary about her was the size of her glasses. They were huge on her face. Round lenses thick as coke bottles filled the horn rims. They magnified her brown eyes, giving her a cute, almost cartoon look. Like an anime girl from a Japanese cartoon. Without them, she had to be blind as a bat.

She stood as George sat. Thin fingers fluttered around her glasses, leaving smudges behind. Her voice was a thin squeak of nervousness. "My name is Lucy and I share skin with a rhinoceros named Masego."

"I don't know what 'share skin with' means."

If she had been born with an Adam's apple, it would have bobbed up and down as she swallowed. "My family was cursed by an African shaman for poaching rhino horns many generations ago. As punishment for my great, great, great uncle's crime, the oldest offspring of each generation shares a body and a life force with a kindred rhinoceros totem. The one I am tied to is named Masego."

Curious. "So you are not really a lycanthrope?"

"No." Her head shake bobbed hair around thin shoulders. It made her look really young. "I am a shape-shifter, but not because of lycanthropy. Masego and I are totally separate. We get along, but we are not one and the same."

I nodded and indicated she should sit. I would keep her story in mind. Just because she was here did not mean her animal would want to be. A push of my booted foot spun my chair slightly to look at the other side of the table. It was just as interesting.

Across from the girl with the coke-bottle glasses sat a man taller than me. Smooth muscles played under a designer T-shirt so tight it could have been painted on. He had worked hard for his physique, but those muscles had not come from work. They were gym muscles. It didn't mean he wasn't strong, but his body had the polished look of a male model.

Shiny aviator glasses hid his eyes, reflecting back the room. His chiseled jaw was scraped smooth. Even though he looked to be only around twenty-five, his hair was steel gray and cut in a stylish hundred-dollar haircut. You know, the kind that looks like your hair hasn't been cut at all. That's why I shave my head with a straight razor. It costs me nothing but time in the shower every other day.

He was also the only lycanthrope in the room wearing a gun.

I couldn't see it, but I have worn a pistol in the back of my waistband for years now. I know it makes you sit differently. He was too forward in his chair to be comfortable. Leaning up just slightly so that he could reach back to his gun if need be.

I had never run across a shape-shifter who carried a gun. They all relied on tooth and claw. I would be keeping my eye on him. Tilting his head down, he stared coolly back at me over his sunglasses. The irises of his eyes were a pale red like watered-down wine, glowing almost pink below thick steel-gray eyebrows. No wonder he wore the sunglasses.

"I am the Templar Rex of the Red Clay Warren. My name is Boothe, with an E." The words came out languid, relaxed, with just a hint of southern drawl.

"What's your animal?"

His chest thrust out. "Rabbit."

That explained the pink eyes. I liked the fact that he didn't try to make his animal sound more impressive by calling it a lagomorph or something equally retarded. He said the word *rabbit* as if it were something to be proud of.

I liked that.

"What are you carrying?"

His face broke into a slow grin. "I knew you were going to pick up on that." He reached behind himself and slowly drew out a square, black, semiautomatic pistol. His fingers splayed out, away from the trigger as he held it up. "Springfield XD. Forty caliber." It was a good gun. Easy to carry and reliable.

I nodded. He put the gun back behind him. Father Mulcahy took his arm out of the broom closet, and Tiff's hand slid back to her belt and away from the handle of the Colt.

The man beside him moved to draw my attention from Boothe. He was almost preening to get me to look at him. He was also a pretty boy. Thin and lithe, built like a runner or a swimmer. Athletic, but not bulked up like Boothe. His clothing was strange. Everyone else was dressed like normal humans, but he looked like he had been called from the Renaissance Fair to this meeting. His shirt was a light green linen and done in a poet style. I would not be surprised if when he stood up he was wearing tights of some sort. Shaggy, fawn-colored hair kicked wildly around his head, framing two of the largest eyes I had ever seen on a man. I had to admit, his eyes were beautiful. I felt the pull of them from across the table. They were like pools of everything good and noble in the world, seasoned with a current of wildness.

What? I am secure enough to say he had the prettiest eyes I have ever seen on a man.

"And who the hell are you?"

Chest puffed up in an attempt to make himself look bigger, his voice was a nice tenor that he tried to deepen when he spoke.

"I am the Lord of the Forest."

I laughed, I couldn't help it. Tiff swallowed a giggle, the priest coughed, and the Lord of the Forest looked annoyed. "You are being serious?" I asked.

Fire flashed in those big eyes. Hot energy roiled across the table at me, touching my power even down where I had hidden it. I smelled the dark loam of the woods and felt the crisp touch of air shielded from the sun by a canopy of great oaks. The bones in his face moved under his skin, and his hair slid apart as antlers began to grow from his head. The table shook as he slammed hands hardening into hooves down on it. The antlers grew faster, becoming thick tines that were pointed like daggers.

"Do not mock me!" he screamed, chest working like a bellow. His lycanthropy boiled across the space between us, rushing over me like a wind.

Tiff took one step forward and shoved the barrel of the Colt behind his ear.

Everyone froze. The click of the hammer being pulled back sang across the room like a whip crack.

That's my girl.

9

The Lord of the Forest vibrated as he tried to sit still. Anger seethed off him in drips. Through clenched teeth, he growled. "Human, if you don't remove that gun, I am going to—"

Father Mulcahy cut him off. "Don't do that, son. I had to mop up the last one of your kind who threatened her just this morning." Cigarette smoke curled up, making him squint as he kept talking. "I don't particularly fancy doing it twice in one day."

I stood up. My hand found Bessie's handle and rested on it.

"I get it." I did not yell when I spoke. I did not raise my voice at all. "You are The-Pretentious-Bastard-of-the-Forest-Who-Is-Not-to-Be-Mocked. You're some kind of deer Were." I leaned in, pointing with my left hand, the right one still on Bessie's handle. "You would do well to remember that you came here to me. This is *my* club, my little corner of the fucking universe, and you are not in the forest anymore, Bambi. Threaten me or my people again, and you will never taste another acorn in your life. Understand?"

He nodded. The muscles in his jaw stood out like

cables and his antlers were still slowly growing, but it was something. I gave Tiff the signal to step back. She did but didn't decock the Colt or put it back in its holster. It hung ready in her hand, hammer back and one tiny squeeze away from spitting death.

The Lord of the Forest closed his eyes, took a deep breath, and leaned back in his seat. He sat meditating, antlers still growing slowly from his head. I watched him through narrow eyes before sitting back down myself.

I looked over at the last Were at the table. The old man had not moved during the whole confrontation. The only difference in him since the meeting started was that now he was smiling. Thick, silver-shot hair flowed into a beard that gnarled its way down to a massive chest. Long yellow canines showed through his smile. Black eyes stared out at me under overgrown gray eyebrows. A scar pulled one side of his face up, the skin taut over his cheek and forehead. His hands sat on top of each other like washed-up driftwood. Brown liver spots covered their backs. The knuckles were swollen twice as big as the finger bones with arthritis. He was a grizzled old Were, still dangerous despite his age. Maybe even more so because of it. When you can't rely on strength anymore, you learn cunning and brutality.

"Ragnar." His voice had a guttural lilt to it. Almost a Scottish brogue but more primitive. "Wolf."

"We don't have many Werewolves here in the South."

He shook his head, gray strands shimmying to and fro. "The local pack is small and moves in and out of the area. I live alone and am the only one who lives here permanently."

"That is because we chase all of your kind away." The Lord of the Forest's antlers were in full display, wide racks of bone sprouting out into branches of points. His face had smoothed and pulled while I was looking at the wolf. Those big eyes were now farther apart and toward the side of his face, so that he could look at the wolf without turning his head to the side. He snorted. "We only tolerate you because you are too old and feeble to be a threat."

A rumble vibrated across the room, coming from Ragnar's chest. "Keep talking, whitetail, and you will learn just how feeble I am." Tension cascaded between them like a building thunderstorm. Cool, deep forest clashing against cold, craggy highlands.

"That is *quite* enough." Charlotte did not stand. She did not raise her voice. Merely emphasizing the word *quite* with a sharp edge gave her the attention of everyone in the room. Chocolate brown skin was now covered in a fine gray fur. Her face had elongated to accommodate six extra eyes, which stacked in rows above her two original eyes, all of which now glowed red. Behind her, four legs rose and moved in the air. A chill went down my spine.

Like I said, Charlotte in her Were-spider form creeps me the hell out. She's a brown recluse and her bite is necrotic, meaning her venom kills and then dissolves flesh. I have watched her reduce vampires to puddles of goo with her bite, and I never want to be on the receiving end of it.

Charlotte also changes form unlike any other lycanthrope I have ever watched. She can switch forms from one thought to the next almost instantaneously. Most lycanthropes have a painful rearranging of their body to form their beast, but not her. I wasn't sure if that was just her gig or if it applied to all Were-spiders.

I should make a note to ask.

Charlotte turned to me, alien spider face tilted, weird eyes unblinking. She gave a small shiver and changed again. It was like water washed over her, taking away the spider-lady and leaving Charlotte in its place. Her noble human face smiled at me.

I knew Charlotte was actually a nice lady, a good guy, one of the white hats, on my side and all that.

But she could be one scary bitch.

"The reason we came here together is we need your help, Deacon."

My feet went back up on the table. "I'm listening."

"I know you are familiar with lycanthropes, but I don't think you know much about lycanthrope society."

I shrugged in admittance that what she said was true. "Usually when I run across one of you guys it's not a good situation." Not for the lycanthrope involved, that is.

She took a deep breath. "The world of Weres is divided very similarly to the natural animal kingdom. We have predators and prey. If you are a predator, regardless of the species or your power, then you are left alone except for members of your own species establishing dominance. However, if your animal happens to be a prey animal . . ." Thin hands gestured at the end of thin arms. "Well, then you are at the mercy of any predator who comes along."

"What does 'at the mercy of' mean?" This from Tiff. Father Mulcahy continued to smoke, a nicotine-laced fog streaming from his nostrils.

The Lord of the Forest did not turn when he spoke, but short brown hair swirled from his hairline, down his neck. "A predator can demand anything a prey animal has. Their life. Their money. Their flesh." His big eyes rolled around. "A predator can kill, maim, rape, or steal from a prey with no consequence at all, because that is the natural order of our unnatural state and it has been for centuries."

Boothe leaned forward. "Speak for yourself, asshole. My rabbits are nobody's prey." Even behind the glasses his eyes flashed. Veins popped out on his forearm as he jabbed his finger toward the Were-deer. I liked this Boothe more and more.

The Lord of the Forest opened his mouth to respond.

Charlotte tapped a needle-thin nail on the table, leaving behind a scratch. The snik-snik sound of it hung deadly in the air, shutting the Lord of the Forest up. "Regardless, this is how it has been for centuries, and it has caused much evil among our kind. Not every predator takes advantage and abuses, but too many of them do." She leaned in, liquid hazel eyes blazing. Her voice took on the fervor of a missionary. "Now we have a man who will *change* that. He has the ability to set things right and bring equality to our society. He can make peace between predator and prey."

For some reason I had a cold knot of dread in the pit of my stomach. "Who is this messiah of goodwill?"

"His name is Marcus. He was here earlier with his mate, Shani."

That knot began to unravel and unwind through my body, spreading coldness in its wake. "Were-lion in a suit? With a tall lady and a psychotic bodyguard? That him?"

Charlotte nodded once.

"Get the hell out of here."

10

"Are you serious?" George blinked at me as he asked.

I stood up, pushing my chair back with my legs as I did. "Yes, I am. Get the hell out. I am not helping that douchebag after what happened earlier." Anger seethed inside me. It was his fault that he didn't control his bodyguard and his fault I'd had to kill someone mostly human. Was I holding a grudge? Damn right I was holding a grudge.

The Lord of the Forest threw up his hands. Wide nostrils flared with a wet snort. His eyes rolled around the room. "I told you he would not help." Fingers gone black with a rim of hoof thrust in my direction. "He is the reason Marcus is without protection, and yet he refuses to help. He does nothing but kill our kind. He is nothing but a cold-blooded murderer."

I froze. Muscles tensed along my arm, screaming to draw my gun and prove him right. My right hand rolled into a fist so that I would not draw Bessie. Drawing Bessie would be a very bad thing with the Were-deer making me feel like hunting season.

"Listen up, Bambi." My voice deepened with rage. "If this Marcus is without a bodyguard, it's his own fault.

He should have kept the one he had on a shorter leash instead of letting him run wild." I rose up halfway out of my chair. "I am not a cold-blooded killer. If I was, you would be venison right now."

My hand was on Bessie's grip. I hadn't put it there on purpose. Pulling air deep in my lungs, I held it and then let it out slowly. When my gaze turned back to him, my voice was calmer. "Why don't you go and keep him safe yourself?"

Charlotte touched my arm with her long, thin fingers. "Deacon, look at us. We are the strongest shape-shifters in this area, but how many predators do you see?"

I looked at the group and counted. Two. I saw two predators. One was Charlotte. But even though spiders are predators, they are not hunters. They lie in wait for prey to come along and fall into their trap. They are almost like crafty scavengers instead of stalking hunters.

The other was the old, arthritic wolf. He should have been killed long ago in the natural order of things, taken out by a younger, faster, stronger wolf. Everyone else was a prey animal. They may have been big and strong, able to keep from being victimized, but they were not predators.

I made an assumption that the people trying to kill Marcus were the same lycanthropes I had rescued Sophia from. It was too big of a coincidence to have two new groups of lycanthropes in town headed by a pair of brothers for them not to be connected. I had faced those guys down. They were killers to the bone, every one of them.

"So you want me to help because I am just a cold-blooded killer of Weres?"

"We need your help because we *might* be able to protect Marcus, but you can make him *safe*."

Safe.

In other words, I could kill the people out to get him.

My friend was implying I could be a glorified assassin. It was hard to hear.

I don't kid myself about what I am and what I do. I kill monsters for a living and I don't feel bad about it. It's dirty, violent work. Being wracked with guilt over what I do to keep humans safe serves no purpose. It's stupid and I try very hard not to be stupid.

"I don't take hits. I am not a paid assassin."

Boothe leaned up. "Listen, Marcus's safety be damned. Leonidas and his crew are too dangerous to just let them do whatever they are in town to do. You appointed your-self the Sheriff of Monstertown. If you *don't* do something to stop them, then people will get hurt."

An objection formed in my mouth. It shriveled to nothing as my hand was bumped by something covered in soft, russet fur. I looked down. Sophia sat beside me, head rubbing my hand and blue eye tilted up at me. I thought about how Tiff and I had rescued her. I thought about the asshole who had tried to beat her to death, or at least beat her until she lost her babies. For that . . . well, for that I could kill someone. She sat up on her hindquarters and put her front paws up in the air.

I hate it when a woman begs.

"So you want me to protect this Marcus, even though you chose to stay with me instead of him earlier?" She put her paws down and bumped my hand twice with her head. Yes.

Charlotte spoke, "The ones who mean him harm are the ones you saved her from earlier today. If they try for Marcus, you could have revenge on them."

"What makes you think I want to match up against them again?"

Charlotte just looked at me, one sculpted eyebrow rising.

I put my hands up in surrender. "You're right. I want

to give those bastards what they deserve and get them the hell out of my town."

A cell phone sounded off. Some crap metal song for the ringtone. Boothe pulled it from his pocket and stood, moving to the corner of the room. I ignored him and turned back to Charlotte.

"If I do this, you all have to pitch in and help guard this Marcus. There are too many Weres for just me to handle without heavy explosives."

She smiled. "We are all committed to his mission of peace. We'll be there when you need us."

Boothe slapped his phone shut and stepped back over to the table. "That was Marcus. The Brotherhood is there and they brought the local Werewolf pack for backup. Shani and him are holed up in their room, but he says they could attack at any minute." He turned to me. He pulled off his glasses and gave me a hard pink stare. "So we've got to go. The question is, are you coming with us?"

Dammit. This was going to be more trouble than it was worth. I just knew it. I took a deep breath and let it out slowly, all eyes in the room on me.

"I'm in."

Tiff stepped close to me. Her hand touched my arm. "Am I going with you?"

I looked over her head around the room. All the shape-shifters were moving toward the door. We were going to face off against some stone-cold killers who had supernatural strength and speed. Killers as deadly as they come.

Killers as deadly as me.

I looked back down into Tiff's blue, blue eyes.

She had gone on some hunts with me, training, learning the ropes of the job. But it had all been easy stuff. A drunk goblin raising hell at the Atlanta PRIDE parade, a bugbear at a miniature golf park, and an outbreak of pixies on April Fool's Day. This? This was over her head. Like Mariana Trench level of over her head. "Not this time, darlin'." I said it softly. Still, her eyes turned just a little sad.

"I could wait in the car, ready to go when you get done."

I shook my head. "I know your heart is full of courage, little girl, but we're walking into a situation already gone tits up and I need you to stay here. If you're there I won't be able to concentrate on the bad guys. It sucks, but that's what I need from you right now."

Her lip poked out, full and petulant. Their movement drew my eyes like a magnet draws steel. "It does suck." She moved even closer, reaching up to brush her fingers through my goatee. The light touch made me feel funny inside my chest. Her voice was low and breathy as she spoke two words. "Be. Careful."

I leaned down, bringing my mouth close to her ear. The warm honeysuckle scent of her drifted to me. Soft. Intimate. The sweet smell of her skin as intoxicating as a double shot of whiskey. "Never fear, little girl. I *will* come back to you."

Her hand slid up to the side of my face. Her full lips parted. "I like it when you call me that."

I smiled. "I know."

The world was contained in her slightly parted lips. Everything that men cross oceans for and fight wars to possess. Her hand made the slightest pressure on my cheek and I was swept forward. I began to fall toward those lips and all the promise they held only an inch away. Her eyes closed softly. Mine did, too, as I was pulled in. Close, so close.

The door slammed into the wall with a *BANG!* as George the gorilla burst in. "We're loaded up. Everybody's waiting on you, Deacon."

The moment shattered like a windshield in a car crash.

George looked at us both as we stepped back from each other, his thick face pasted with bewilderment. "Sorry. Did I interrupt something?"

Dammit.

Now I was ready to kill somebody.

The Comet was full of lycanthropes as we raced down the road at top speed. Windows down, the cool night air rushed in, carrying the smells of the South in spring mixed with the scent of motor oil, gasoline, and exhaust fumes of a good old American hot rod.

I love my car. Made in 1966, the Mercury Comet is a fine example of automotive engineering. A 351 Windsor-motor pushes her down the road like a scalded dog. Badass black, with the bare minimum amount of chrome, and a chain-link steering wheel, she looks like a beast. She's loud, fast, and drinks gas like an alcoholic kleptomaniac working at a liquor store sloshes back the inventory, but I love her.

Charlotte pressed up against me as we pulled through a curve, her weight warm against my shoulder. Next to her, Boothe pushed silver bullets into clips. The full clips went into loops on ballistic vests, one for him and one for me. At his feet lay two Bushmaster AR-15's looking black and evil. I had grabbed them on the way out since we had no idea how many lycanthropes we would be up against.

You always want more bullets than enemies, and the

AR-15 holds thirty-three bullets per clip. That's why it has been standard issue for SWAT teams for decades. I still had the two Colt .45's locked, cocked, and ready to rock in their holsters, and Bessie on my hip, but I had no idea what kind of situation we were walking into. The AR-15 should keep me from running out of ammunition.

The backseat held the Lord of the Forest, his giant rack of antlers, and Ragnar. The stag was apparently still upset and kept his antlers out so there wasn't room for anyone else in the back. I think the old wolf rode back there just to annoy him. George the Were-gorilla and Lucy the rhino were following in his tiny Mazda and doing a good job of keeping up with me. We were heading for a crappy little no-tell motel on the outskirts of town. The people who ran the place were the kind who didn't ask any questions. They didn't want the answers they might get from the whores, dealers, and assorted criminals who stayed there. It was a good place to hide out if you wanted off the radar.

I'd spent two days there once recovering from a run-in with a nymphomaniac poltergeist. The ghost had been killing the johns of hookers who frequented the motel, so the hookers hired me to put her down. At the end of it all, I had spent two full days in and out of it from ecto-plasmic poisoning while the working girls nursed me back to consciousness.

Music poured from the speakers, rising over the rumble of the engine. Cinderella cranked out their version of blues-rock. Tom Keifer's whiskey and sin growl ripping out, singing about love gone bad. The guitar hummed along with the motor, making a sweet sound. I hated to turn it down, but we were close and needed to talk. My fingers pushed the buttons on the MP3 player, fading the whiskey-soaked blues down under the roar of the engine.

The Lord of the Forest chimed in from the backseat. "Thank you for turning that shit down. This car is loud enough to wake the dead without that noise."

My middle finger rose up to answer. The Comet is *not* loud enough to wake the dead. Trust me, I would know better than he would. I ignored his sour look in the rearview mirror as I turned slightly toward Boothe.

"So, tell me what you know about this Were-lion who's trying to kill this Marcus cat, no pun intended."

"His name is Leonidas and he is Marcus's twin brother. But where Marcus is striving to bring peace between predator and prey, Leonidas is more than happy to hold the status quo." Charlotte put her hand on the dash as I pulled to a stop at a red light. The rosary swung to and fro from the rearview mirror.

"It is hard to give up a free pass to rape, pillage, and plunder," Ragnar gruffed.

"You would know," the Lord of the Forest snapped.

The growl from the old wolf was real now, matching the engine in rumble. "Shut up." He turned toward the stag man. "Do not ever presume to judge me again. You do not know me. What I have seen nor what I have done." His brogue was deepening along with his voice, anger making him sound more animal.

The light turned green and I put the pedal down. The Comet responded by leaping forward, the G's in the car pushing everybody into their seats. I spoke to the backseat. "Both of you knock it the fuck off. We're almost there. You two children can bicker on your own time."

Boothe slapped a full clip into one of the Bushmasters and racked the bolt with a *klick-klack* that snapped as loud as a gunshot inside the car. He leaned forward and turned to put his back against the door so he could look at me. His words were crisp and clear when he spoke. "Leonidas is the ultimate alpha predator. He's a dick who takes full advantage of the predator-prey dynamic to have anything he wants when he wants it. He's surrounded himself with like-minded thugs of various types, and they call themselves the Brotherhood of Marrow and Bone. They'll be without weapons, but they have trained to fight as a unit under Leonidas's command."

"So they go by BOMAB?"

"Usually by the 'Brotherhood,' but sometimes yes."

"That's a dumbass name."

"It is, but don't underestimate them. They are vicious and without mercy. They work together with paramilitary precision."

The motel sign blared out into the night as we topped a hill. I touched the brake to slow us down so we could make the turn into the parking lot. The Comet responded with a low-throated growl, exhaust crackling and popping through the muffler.

Boothe kept talking. "Marcus has been traveling the country, preaching nonviolence to lycanthrope communities. He will get the predators and the prey to work together, but once he leaves, the Brotherhood sweeps in and undoes everything he accomplished. They do this with terror tactics that would make the Nazi SS blush. Every member of the Brotherhood is a confirmed killer. No need to hesitate."

"Never fear," I assured him, "I wasn't planning on it."

Pulling hard on the steering wheel, I slid the Comet into the parking lot. I whipped the big car to the entrance and put it in Park. The motel was an old-style side-of-the-road rat trap with a décor that hadn't been updated since the seventies. Pink stucco walls and hacienda-styled tile roofs made the buildings, and cracked asphalt, white pebble rock, and sad palm trees in planters made the grounds. The motel stayed in business renting rooms by the hour to crack whores and adulterous couples. I switched off the car, then took the vest and rifle Boothe handed me. George's Mazda pulled in behind me, parking with a chirp of tires.

Stepping out, I slipped on the vest, the full clips pulling down, making it hang heavy on my shoulders. Charlotte slid out behind me, transforming into a spider-lady between one step and the next. Boothe and I pushed the seats forward, letting the two Weres in the back get out. Ragnar took a minute, pulling himself out of the car with a grunt. He stood holding on to the car for a second, slowly stretching up to a full standing position. The Lord of the Forest took a minute because his antlers got tangled in the seat belt.

Once everyone was out, I pointed to George and Lucy. "You two start at this end of the motel, knock on doors and clear any humans out of here. Tell them the place is being raided by the cops and they will hightail it out of here without any fuss." I checked the slide on my rifle to make sure it was loaded. "If you hear a big ruckus, shift into your strongest form and get your asses over to us."

They nodded and headed off in opposite directions. Turning back, I saw Ragnar had pulled on a pair of armored gloves. Long spikes jutted from each knuckle, neon gleaming off their silvered edges. His hair was longer and shaggier; black-ringed amber eyes blazing from under his heavy brow. He smiled at me, baring longer yellow teeth under an animalistic snout. He still looked human, but barely.

A warm rush of power washed over me from behind, carrying with it the scent of loam and land never farmed or tamed by humans. I turned and the Lord of the Forest had stripped off his clothes and stripped off his humanity. His body twisted in on itself, making nooks and crannies of flesh. Limbs stretched with wet pops as he re-formed himself. Brown fur crawled over bare skin. He lay in a heap of quivering flesh beside the car.

After a minute, he pulled a deep breath into his lungs, swelling his chest. Slowly, he rose, pulling his legs underneath himself. Shaking his head swung a rack of antlers grown even more massive through the air. With a snort and a stomp of a hoof, he stood tall and proud. He had transformed into a gigantic, magnificent stag. His head was even with mine at 6'4", antlers spreading wider than my arm span. The horn bough of them as thick as my arm, spikes jutting up like bone daggers. Liquid brown eyes the size of my fists stared out at us. Under his luxurious pelt, muscle stacked with power and agility. In this form he truly deserved the title Lord of the Forest. I nodded at him in appreciation. He snorted in my direction and turned away.

Yep, still an asshole.

Reaching inside, I let my power go. I could use it to find lycanthropes in hiding if we were going to be ambushed. They had to know we were here by now and since I didn't hear any big commotion, I assumed they were laying low, waiting to sucker punch us. It unfurled in a sweep of sensation. The air was charged with lycanthropic energy, like ozone after a lightning strike. It made my skin tingle and my mouth run dry.

There was a wide, arched corridor that stretched through the center of the buildings to a courtyard parking lot. We had to get through that to the backside of the motel where the two Were-lions were holed up.

With a nod I began walking toward the back of the motel. Boothe flanked me to the right, sweeping the area with his AR-15 in militaristic precision. I never served in any military, so our movements were strikingly different.

His steps were silent, booted feet rolling heel to toe,

knees bent, shoulders hunched around the stock of his rifle. I walked like I normally did, chest wide and one foot in front of the other, rifle pointed down but ready.

The Lord of the Forest stalked behind him, hooves click-clacking on the asphalt. Ragnar loped along in the rear on all fours, looking more canine as the minutes passed. I could feel him behind me, his wolf pushing toward the night under his skin. With his animal rising, he moved better than he had when he was more human, loping with a grace and ease his joints denied him as a human. Charlotte traveled along the ceiling, spider legs moving like clockwork to carry her forward.

Cars began driving out of the motel from George's and Lucy's efforts. Good, I wanted as few civilians in the way as possible; plus, without them in the line of fire, we would have more time until someone in this part of town called the police. Even automatic gunfire wouldn't make most residents of this side of town anxious to call the cops. Not unless it was directed at them.

With each step I could feel the power in the air growing. There were some angry Weres just up ahead. Rage clouded the atmosphere like an oncoming thunderstorm. My hand tightened on the grip of the rifle. I raised it up to my cheek.

I stepped around an ice machine that sat in the corridor we walked down. As I cleared it, a door on the other side opened. I caught a blond-haired blur from the corner of my eye a split second before it knocked into me. Spinning with the blow, I used the momentum to drive the barrel of the AR into that mass of blond hair, knocking her to one knee beside the ice machine. My hand tangled in those yellow curls, yanking her to her feet and shoving her against the ice machine. The business end of the rifle pressed into her throat. Big eyes the color of ice crystals sprung wide in recognition. Thick lips made for indecent things broke open into a smile that exposed dainty, almost delicate fangs. Her whiskey-throated southern drawl was molasses thick.

"Well, sugah, I haven't seen you in forever."

12

"Hello, Blair." I pressed harder on the rifle barrel, raising her delectable jawline. "What the hell are you doing here?" The last time I had seen Blair I had left her unconscious in a puddle of her own blood after she had given me a lap dance.

It's a long story.

The short version is, she was a vampire I'd had to let go in that mess last year while tracking down Appollonia. I hate letting vampires go, 'cause they always pop back up. They are all evil, vicious predators. Every one of them. They prey on humans. Drinking blood. Destroying lives.

Finding Blair here may or may not be a coincidence. Normally, Weres and vamps don't work together, but I didn't know much about the situation I was in. It could be one big happy freakfest.

Blair's eyes narrowed as she looked at me. "I am just like any other girl here, sugah. I'm just trying to make a living." Her tongue slid over sinful lips, leaving behind a wet trail. They glistened in the yellow light of the corridor as she pouted. She made an effort to keep her fangs sheathed as her bottom lip poked out, full and moist.

"Sometimes I get a snack, too, but I'm not hurting nobody."

I looked down at her then. She was wearing more than the last time I saw her, but then again, the last time I saw her she had been giving me a lap dance, which doesn't lead to many clothes.

Again, long story.

A paper-thin cutoff T-shirt clung to big fake breasts, accentuating the fact that she was not wearing a bra. Generous hips curved under a denim skirt narrow enough to be a belt. Long, spray-tanned legs led down to stripper heels that had a confederate flag motif to match her shirt.

She was a knockout, all lush curves and feminine sex. Too bad she was dead. Dead and evil. I would bet she had lured many, many victims to this hotel using her looks for bait. They would have thought they had hit the jackpot. Won the lottery of lust, until she turned on them and they learned exactly what their ticket had gotten them. Being a soulless bloodsucker, she would give a john a lot more than a case of herpe-gono-syphil-AIDS.

My finger tightened on the trigger.

"Wait, wait, wait, sugah." Her voice was strained, words spilling out fast. "You don't want to do that."

I did not ease the pressure on the trigger, but my finger stopped moving. "Why the hell not?"

That deadly, saccharine smile came back across her face. "You are not here for me and right now you have bigger problems to deal with."

From behind me I heard Boothe curse and break into a run. Looking over my shoulder, I saw Lucy being dragged by her hair through the asphalt courtyard at the end of the corridor. The Were that had her was gigantic, eight or nine feet tall and swollen with thick, rubbery muscle. Battleship gray skin gleamed in the moonlit parking lot. He had no neck; instead, a wide, triangular head jutted from his shoulders ending in a gaping maw that bristled with row upon row of triangular teeth. Round black eyes sat above and in front of gill slits that ran both sides to his shoulders. Now that I was paying attention I could hear him draw bellowing gasps of air through them. It took my mind a second to put together just what I was looking at.

A fucking great white shark.

I had never seen a Were-shark. He looked like something out of a horror movie. Lycanthropes look like monsters if they can pull off a hybrid form, but the Were-shark just looked *wrong*. It belonged in the depths of the ocean, or the far reaches of outer space. It was alien, mind-bending, and just *off*. It was something you would see in the ninth circle of hell. Not in a no-tell motel courtyard on the outskirts of town.

Boothe's rifle sounded off, rapid pops zinging bullets toward the monstrosity. The shark turned, jerking Lucy up by the hair to his chest, using her as a shield. She screamed as her feet dangled in the air.

Boothe, Ragnar, Charlotte, and the Lord of the Forest all cleared the corridor's exit, stepping into the parking lot. Shadows moved from the edges as other lycanthropes closed in.

The pressure against my rifle barrel disappeared, jerking me forward. I looked to see Blair moving with unnatural speed around the corner.

Her southern drawl floated back to me as she vanished out of sight. "Until next time, sugah."

Slippery bitch. I am *going to kill you one day.*

I turned to join the battle.

13

Chaos reigned in the parking lot at the end of the corridor. The Were-shark still held Lucy by her hair in front of him. George had shifted into a full gorilla and was swinging a limp Werewolf by the hindquarters, using the body as a bludgeon against the four wolves that surrounded him. He roared as he spun. The Werewolf in his hands flew out, slamming into the pack attacking him.

The Lord of the Forest chased a hyena around. His great rack of antlers swished through the air as he swung his head to and fro trying to gore the skittering bastard. The hyena was quick, bounding back and forth, occasionally flipping backward to swipe at the Were-deer with a handful of long black talons. Blood slicked the Lord of the Forest's back and sides.

Ragnar was circling two lycanthropes. A Were-lizard, his skin gone scaly brownish green and head elongated, and the Were-snake from earlier. A hiss escaped the Were-snake, long, forked tongue darting in and out of a thin-lipped mouth. Black, lidless eyes stared unblinking. Two fangs curved out of his mouth nearly a foot long. Pale yellow venom ran off them. Ragnar swung his bladed gloves in a weave of death, holding them off.

Charlotte hung on the side of the building above Boothe, using her spider legs to knock aside the wolves trying to dart in on him.

I tossed my rifle up and looked through the green reticle sight, getting a fix on the wolves dancing around under Charlotte. Between breaths I squeezed the trigger and the gun chattered death in three-round bursts. One of the wolves jerked to a stop with a sharp yelp of pain, blood slinging into the night. Two more bursts caught another one, stitching into him and flipping him over onto his back to lay still.

Charlotte scooped up the last one as it turned tail and tried to run. Long spider legs pulled it into the air and up to her. Ruby lipsticked mouth parted and closed on the wolf's back, over his spine. The wolf convulsed with a human scream. Charlotte dropped him. He fell to the ground, twitching on the asphalt as fur ran from his skin, leaving a dead naked man with a hole dissolved in his back to reveal spine.

Spooky bitch. Boothe's gun chattered out and I watched the bullets rip holes through dorsal fin. Blood spurted and ran down the Were-shark's back. The shark looked like he was screaming, mouth thrown wide, head tossing back and forth, but he made no noise. He was probably mute in that form. Sharks don't have vocal chords. But he did jerk around and drop Lucy, who scrambled away.

Charlotte launched herself out into the air. She spun, full of deadly grace, pulling spider legs in to tuck around her as she arced overhead like a jump shot in a pro basketball game. She hit the Were-shark's back, unfolding around him like a net made of Were-spider. Her legs latched on, hooking in with sticky pads as he tried to sling her off.

I felt a push of air at my back. The piss rank musk of

cat washed over me, coating my throat with a foul taste. I spun. A giant cougar charged. Muscles bunched and moved under a thick tawny pelt. I tried to swing the rifle up to fire, but he was too fast, lycanthrope speed too unpredictable. Bounding up, claws unsheathed, he tried to maul me.

I fell and rolled flat on my back.

The cat sailed over me, hind legs catching against the rifle and wrenching it out of my hands. The sling was still wrapped around my arm, but it was out of my hands. Rolling, I scrambled to my feet as the cougar landed lightly and turned toward me.

My hands filled with Colt .45. The 1911 is the finest handgun ever crafted. The standard sidearm for American service men for three quarters of a century, it is reliable and intuitive. My hands closed on the grips, thumbs flicking safeties off without a thought. Both guns were pointed at the cougar before he could take a full step.

Yellow eyes glared at me. Wide shoulders bunched with tension as the Were-cougar tensed to jump.

"Don't," I said.

His long, thick tail fell down, thudding the ground to act as a balance for his leap.

My fingers twitched against the triggers.

The 1911 has a five-pound trigger pull and a travel distance of one quarter of an inch. It is nothing, a breath, a thought, to fire them.

The guns jerked back into my arms, bullets slapping fur-covered chest mid-leap.

Blood and muscle blossomed under his neck in a gruesome flower of death. The impact changed the direction of his upper body, cartwheeling him around to land at my feet in a limp heap. Fur ran back into skin as the corpse morphed into a human. I stepped over it, reholstering the .45's under my arms. Pulling the strap for the

AR-15 secured it across my back. My hand settled on the pistol at my hip. I drew Bessie from her holster.

The Smith & Wesson .500 Magnum is a huge gun. It's a revolver and dead reliable. Semiautomatics, no matter how well made, will jam eventually. Revolvers don't. Pull the trigger and a bullet comes out. The .500 cartridge is a huge load, designed for killing big game. Most pistols are not powerful enough to hunt with, Bessie was purposed for it.

Sighting down my arm, I pointed the barrel at the great white. Charlotte still hung to its back, fingers morphed into needle-thin claws dug into gill slits. It spun around, trying to dislodge her. Lucy stood in front of them. Thin fingers dug into the skin of her chest, wadding it into two handfuls. Lucy took a deep breath, yanking her hands apart. Her skin pulled like taffy until it shredded. A three-foot horn slid out of the hole.

Lucy screamed into the night as the horn continued to push out of her chest. It was a long wail of pain that carried out until she ran out of breath. Choking on the scream, her skin exploded.

Bits of Lucy flew across the parking lot, sticking wetly to the Weres fighting around her. In her place a black rhinoceros stood, glistening in the sodium lights of the lot. Masego. He blinked and snorted. With a shake and a stomp, he flung thick goo in streams around himself. He was massive. A thick tank of an animal built for nothing but power. Lowering his head, the rhino charged the Were-shark, driving his horn deep into that gleaming white stomach.

I jerked Bessie up, pointing her to the sky. My shot was gone, blocked by Charlotte and now Masego the rhino. A howl turned my attention to Ragnar. The bow-legged Were-lizard had fully transformed into a Komodo dragon. Its jaws latched on the old wolf's leg. Ragnar crumpled to his knees, the Komodo dragon still holding on, jaws moving as he chewed.

The Were-snake that Ragnar had been holding off lunged forward. Stepping close to the fallen old Werewolf, he drew himself up. His head came back, neck flaring like a hood. The thin bottom jaw unhinged, dropping down almost to his breastbone. He leaned back to strike with those vicious fangs. Venom splatted on the Werewolf's upturned face and began to smoke and sizzle, blisters rising immediately as Ragnar screamed again.

Bessie swung down and I centered her on the back of his serpent skull. Squeezing the trigger kicked the gun up, recoil trying to break my arm. Thunder rolled and a ten-inch spout of fire split the night as the bullet flew at the Were-snake like the Judgment of God.

And completely missed.

The Were-snake jerked his head out of the way with that supernatural speed that lycanthropes have, turning toward me with a hiss I could not hear. My ears had closed down with the blast of the gun. The Were slithered toward me. I squeezed the trigger again, aiming for the center of his body.

He slipped the bullet again.

His body twisted as if he no longer had a spine, or at least not a human one. He kept moving forward, his torso twisted, bending bonelessly. Three more bullets flew at him and every one of them missed as he wove and spun with liquid lycanthrope grace.

And then he was on me.

Long, scaly fingers, much longer than human and without joints or bones, clamped on my arm. That oilyslick head drew back, foot-long fangs jutting to strike. I didn't have time to draw another gun or the Bowie knife at my hip, and Bessie was out of bullets.

So I cracked him across the mouth with the empty pistol.

One fang snapped off and spun into the night air. Scales along that cheek split apart, revealing bright pink flesh underneath. Blood and venom began to pour as the Were shrieked—a shrill hiss that made my skin ripple. He pulled away with a jerk, trying to scramble to safety.

Not so fast, you slippery bastard.

A twist of my wrist clamped fingers on his arm. There was no bone, just a tube of scale-covered muscle. Pulling him close, I slammed the pistol against his skull again. Soft snake bone caved in. Gore, black in the sodium lights of the lot, spattered across my arm, burning hatefully with venom.

Empty, the Smith & Wesson .500 is four-and-a-half pounds of stainless steel. I used it as a club, as a hammer, pounding it into the Were-snake's face and head. His struggles became weaker after three blows and stopped with five. I let his arm go and he slid to the ground and lay in a boneless, quivering heap of scales. He stayed a snake-man, so he wasn't dead, but he was damn sure out of the fight.

I holstered Bessie, not having time to reload her. The Komodo dragon still had Ragnar pinned. It lay across his back, weight pressing him down. Those jaws chewed, working on his leg. Ragnar was unmoving underneath the dragon as it tore a hunk of flesh off his leg. A flip of its elongated head tossed it back down its gullet. Jaws working, it swallowed the hunk whole. Bone lay bare, glistening ivory tucked in the bloody mess of the wolf's leg.

The AR-15 swung around into my grip and I fired off a burst aimed at the dragon's wide side. It darted away and only two of the bullets punched into its thick tail. Blood spurted black into an oily trail behind it. I ripped off another two bursts as it zigged and zagged across the lot. Bullets chewed the asphalt but missed the Were as it slithered away into the dark.

My finger hit the button to release the clip on the rifle. It slid out, clattering to the pavement. My left hand had another one and was pushing it into place when I heard Boothe shout my name. His gun came up, spitting bullets in my direction.

I had time to flex my knees so I could leap away from the gunfire when a sledgehammer with claws knocked me ass over teakettle across the ground.

14

Black flooded my vision, rushing in like a tidal wave. Air was driven out of my lungs in a hard, sharp blow. My hearing shattered, a shrill ringing filled my ears as my head bounced off asphalt. My eyelids were thousand-pound weights, pulling me into the darkness, dragging me under to its peaceful depths.

Get up!

My mind screamed at me through the fog, clawing its way back to alertness. I shoved my eyes open, trying to focus on what was happening around me. I shook my head to clear it. Asphalt scraped the skin, raw and on fire, pulling me back up.

A lion-man stood over me, mouth open in a snarl, one clawed hand slicing the air to tear out my throat.

Violently, I twisted my body away. Razor claws raked across my chest, biting into and slashing through the tactical vest I was wearing. It fell apart like wet tissue paper, held on by one shoulder and the waist section. I kicked out, boot heel driving into the Were-lion's stomach. He staggered back.

Hands and knees scrabbling, I moved as fast as I could. Something banged hard on my arm. My fingers found the barrel of the rifle that was still hanging on my arm by the sling. Scrambling, I got my feet under me as fast as I could, clutching the AR-15 upside down by the barrel.

Leonidas roared in my direction. Carrion breath, sickly sweet, swept over me even from seven or eight feet away. The world swam, waves of distortion riding from the edges of my vision to the center. I stumbled back a step. Dizzy, I kept myself from falling by using the rifle as a cane.

The Were-lion sprung, claws unsheathed.

Both fur-covered arms swung toward me trying to scissor down around me. To trap me so that lion mouth of his could close on my jugular or some other soft, fleshy bit. Without thought, I swung the rifle as hard as I could. The polymer stock flashed up and caught the lion just under his jaw. Leonidas jerked to the side from the impact, his forward charge stopped cold.

He stood for a second with his head to the side, eyes squinted shut. His head moved back down to face me. We were only an arm's length apart. He made a noise with his throat, tongue working around in his cheek. Pulling a face, he spat. A white tooth arced to the ground, stuck in a thick, bloody puddle.

"That hurt." Blood trickled down his chin as he growled.

Clawed hands clamped on the rifle, yanking it away with a ripple of muscle. Both hands closed on it and with a jerk of his arms, the rifle snapped in two pieces. He looked up with a feral smile on his face.

Both Colt .45 barrels were pointed at his face.

I pulled the triggers. Thunder rolled out of the barrels and bullets seared toward his head.

I missed.

Leonidas just wasn't where the bullets were. He threw himself backward with shape-shifter speed. It was so fast he seemed to blink out of existence for a second. My eyes tried to follow him, but they kept jerking off track. I emptied both clips in his direction, squeezing the triggers until the slides locked back empty.

With a curse I shoved the one in my left hand back in its holster and pulled out a new clip, which rode under each gun in the shoulder rig I wore. Practice let me drop the clip out of the pistol in my right hand. Leonidas crouched about ten feet away. It was a distance he could cover in a blink.

I shoved the clip toward the bottom of the gun, trying to get it in before Leonidas could attack. My hands trembled. My head swam, doing an Olympic-level breaststroke. Through wavy vision I saw the muscles along the Were-lion's chest and shoulders bunch, getting ready to jump. The clip rattled against the opening it was supposed to slip into, jangling out of place.

Fuck! I was *not* right.

Head injury. The thought was detached, coming from the back of my brain.

The Were-lion drew a huge breath for his victory roar and I fumbled with something I should have been able to do in my sleep. I dropped the clip, frantically reaching to my waist, hoping I could get the Bowie knife out in time. My fingers danced around, clumsily tearing at the small strap that held it in place. I had to get it out before he attacked or I was a dead man. Leonidas tensed. He pushed off the asphalt, body stretching in the air, coming to kill me. To kill me dead.

A rhinoceros slammed into him, driving him through the motel wall.

Masego staggered back from the wall, shaking his head, and fell on his wide, black ass. Blood streamed from holes that had been gouged in his thick black hide. On one shoulder he had a triple row of serrations that looked like a shark bite. Fur was glued on his horn with blood where he had gotten in damage of his own, but he was hurt bad. He fell over on his side and lay, his great big ribcage bellowing in and out.

I took a second to look around and take stock. Ragnar was sitting up now. His gnarled arthritic hands wrapped his shirt around his leg, making a gore-soaked mess. The Lord of the Forest lay still on his side. His head still had that great sweep of antler, but he was a man now. His eyes were glassy, empty of life, tongue hanging from between his teeth. A hyena sat on his body. Heavy jaws pulled gobs of flesh out of a hole where his stomach once was, tossing them in the air and swallowing them whole.

Boothe knelt on the ground, surrounded by a heap of dark furred bodies that were slowly changing to bare skin. One arm cradled against his stomach. It was twisted and bent, the broken end of a bone jutting out raw and bloody. He brought up his pistol and aimed at the hyena. The gun shook violently as he held it and squeezed the trigger. The bullet went wide and missed, but it was enough to send the greasy beast running off into the night, leaving its meal behind.

Sirens cut through the night. Still far away, but coming closer. A thud and vibrations through my feet made me look behind me. I turned to see Charlotte pinned to the ground by the Were-shark only a few feet away. She was battered and looked broken. The giant shark-man lifted her up, pounding her to the asphalt again. Spider legs swung limply, broken and crushed. That giant maw yawned open, teeth bristling as he picked her up, moving her limp body up for a bite. A white skein slid wetly over his black eye.

Everything was in slow motion; the world encased in a thick syrup of time. I picked up half of the rifle the Were-lion had destroyed. I tried to run but stumbled instead, falling against the Were-shark's back. The skin on my arm tore, shredded by the sandpaper sharkskin. That close, I could see the silver-gray pattern of that rough skin. His big, triangular head swung toward me, teeth flashing death, the white skein over his black eye making him blind during his moment of attack.

I shoved the broken rifle into those jaws, ramming and wedging it as deep as I could.

The Were-shark jerked back, trying to shake its head and dislodge the thing holding its mouth open. I threw my body across that wide, triangular snout, using my weight to hold it in place. The skin ripped open on my side. Pain burst like a forest fire. It was distant, but there. I pushed it away. I'd have to deal with it later. My left hand fumbled out a handful of bullets that went to Bessie. They rattled in my palm, clacking together. They were heavy bullets weighing a few ounces apiece.

Big bullets.

Silver bullets.

I took that handful of silver bullets and jammed them as far down that big throat as I could.

Slick, wet muscle closed over my arm, the throat trying to pull me in farther. I let go of the bullets and jerked my arm back. It slid out with a moist sucking sound, coming free with a pop. The shark-man began to convulse and stagger around, smoke curling out of its mouth as the silver began to eat away his stomach.

I fell back, crashing to the asphalt. Exhausted. My brain rolled around in my skull. I just wanted to close my eyes and sleep. Every inch of me was weighted with lead. I was too heavy to move. The bitter taste of aspirin filled my mouth, and my throat was so dry the sides of it stuck together.

The sirens were louder. Closer. We had to go. There were too many bodies on the ground to stay and explain.

With a groan that hurt to make, I rolled over and pushed myself up to my knees. My vision tunneled down to a quarter-sized hole in a cloud of bruise purple. I took a deep breath that pulled in as much pain as it did air and sat up with my eyes closed.

My head spun, the centrifugal force of it trying to throw me back down. My mind screamed at me that I was not safe. After a second, I was able to drive my eyes open. A gorilla stood in front of me, its hand held out.

George was covered in blood, fur drying into a stiff, plastic-like shell. Cuts and gashes checkered most of him. His monkey hand was larger than mine as he pulled me to my feet. My stomach cartwheeled in protest to the movement.

I told my stomach to shut the hell up, I didn't have time for it.

Behind him stood the two Were-lions we had come to rescue. Marcus was still in his suit. That tailored, high-dollar suit with the faint chalk stripe. The silk tie was gone, but other than that he looked fresh and dapper, ready for a hard day at the office. His mate, Shani the lioness, had changed into a set of silk pajamas that probably cost about what one of my guns would. She was clean, bright, and shiny in the night. She could have stepped out of a magazine advertisement. Both of them stood in a parking lot filled with destruction and carnage completely unmarked. Not a hair out of place.

I guess we had done our jobs well. Their asses were safe. The sirens were closer. Blearily, I looked George in the eye.

"We need to get the hell out of here."

15

The sirens were close enough that the sound had separated. Instead of one loud chorus of siren, I could hear individual sirens caterwauling into the night, heralding the arrival of the police. It sounded like a lot of cops would be here any minute.

My forehead pressed against the open trunk lid of the Comet. The metal was warm, my forehead hot. My head weighed fifty pounds. It hung from my neck, stretching my vertebrae with its mass. Pain radiated out along my shoulders to crawl up my neck and across my scalp. Red and black pulsed from the edge of my vision keeping time with the wail of the sirens. I was looking at a problem. Inside the trunk lay a dead man in a pool of blood. He was naked and a huge rack of antlers curled out from his head.

The antlers were the problem.

"They won't fit like this."

Blearily, I looked over at the gorilla standing beside me. Blood caked his fur. A hundred tiny cuts and slashes crisscrossed his skin; deep ones yawned open like watermelon-colored mouths. He had his monkey arms crossed and his monkey hand cupping a monkey chin.

Monkey lips turned down in a frown. I would have laughed at the absurdity of it, but I know laughing would have made my head explode.

"You have to fold him up. You can't lay him out like that."

Big brown eyes cut over at me sharply. "I'm trying to be respectful."

We didn't have time for this. The sirens were getting louder. There were too many bodies on the ground for us to stand around playing nice. We had to go.

"You got three choices here, George." I stood up, still holding on to the trunk. "Fold him, break the horns, or drag him out and leave him here. Pick one, 'cause we are out of time."

He sighed. The air pulled long through his wide nose and then rushed out in a blast of hot air. His hands looked like catcher's mitts as they hooked the Lord of the Forest under his arms and lifted. The Were-deer was loose in his skin, death making him flop around, robbing him of all resistance. George pulled him up into a sitting position, then folded him in half like a towel and stepped back.

The antlers still stuck up too far.

My hands closed on the tines, hard antler cool and slick in my palms. Leaning in, my weight pushed them down. As they sank there were several loud, wet pops. I couldn't tell what was dislocating and I didn't care. When they were low enough, I shut the lid. The points of the antlers scraped the inside of the trunk lid with a loud, cutting screech that made my right eyelid twitch and flutter. I turned to George.

"Follow me close. If we get tagged by the cops, don't panic, just stay behind me."

His brow had a deep crease down the center. "Are you all right to drive?"

My head was a throb of pain that made my vision

shrink and expand with each pulse. My stomach was sour, threatening to spill at any moment. I turned, walking toward the driver's side, my hand on the roof to keep me upright. "Probably not, but nobody else is driving my car."

My fingers curled under the door handle. Tugging up radiated a dull ache from my knuckles to my elbow. The door swung out, the weight of it nearly pulling me off balance.

In the backseat, Ragnar lay against the side of the car. His leg was propped up. There was a burgundy smear under the place where his calf muscle used to be. His shirt made a filthy tourniquet just under the knee. Komodo dragon teeth marks showed white through the rusty blood covering his exposed shinbone. The pelt of hair on his chest was silver, blending in with the gray fur that covered Charlotte's body.

She lay against him looking dead. Her unblinking red eyes had clouded opaque. Long spider legs lay like wet ropes. They were supposed to be stiff and segmented, but the great white Were had crushed them. Every time they touched something, she would let out a moan and convulse. She shook while Ragnar tried to hold her.

I fell into the driver's seat. My feet were lead as I lifted them and pulled them inside. The slam of the car door reverberated up, bouncing through my bones, shaking my skull, rattling my brain. I fumbled with the key, trying to fit it in the ignition. Time stretched, moments felt like hours as I pecked at the ignition with the key.

A hand closed on mine, steadying it. The key slipped into the slot.

I looked over. Boothe was in the passenger seat. He had pulled his T-shirt halfway off and was using it to sling his right arm. Narrow shapes jutted up through the thin black cotton. It looked like a sack of broken sticks. *Multiple compound fractures.* His skin was pale and waxy. Fat droplets of oily sweat stood out on his face and chest. Slowly, he leaned back, careful of his arm.

A twist of my wrist and the Comet roared to life. Blues guitar cried out from the speakers. Pain shot across the space behind my eyeballs, white and hot. I grabbed the MP3 player, tore it off the console, and threw it on the floor. Pushing myself back into the seat, I dropped the Comet into Drive. The welded chain links of the steering wheel were slick in my sweaty palms. My foot dropped heavily onto the accelerator. The car lurched forward, yanking my stomach into my throat. I leaned and pulled to the left, spinning the wheel and turning the car to the exit.

Charlotte moaned in pain, the sound long and plaintive.

We pulled out of the lot lights and the world went dark, staticky black crossing the windshield. I pulled on the headlights. Without stopping, I whipped left out of the motel's lot, cutting the Comet across the road. The car straightened, rocking back and forth. I looked up into the rearview mirror. George's little Mazda chirped out behind us.

In the distance, just topping a hill about a half-mile down the strip of straight road, flashing blue lights split the night like spastic lightning. There were a dozen cop cars, if not more. I rammed my foot down on the gas pedal, the effort causing the pain shooting up my back and neck to blossom into fire and ache just behind my right ear.

The Comet rocketed forward, motor roaring into the night air. I had to put distance between us and them. Enough distance that they wouldn't think we just left the scene of the crime. Enough distance that they wouldn't follow us. We pulled into the curve of the road that would take us out of sight, blue lights getting smaller and smaller behind us. In the rearview I watched the first cop car jerk into the motel parking lot.

Tension I didn't know I had washed out of my shoulders. A wave of dizziness followed right behind it.

The road shimmered and the dashboard lights slid into a lazy revolution of color-filled light trails. I tightened my grip on the wheel, concentrating on pulling it together. Breathing slowly. In through my nose. Out through my mouth. Feeling the weight of the air in my lungs. Centering me. Exhale. Air leaving me more together.

I had my vision cleared to just crackling lines on the edges when the first car passed in the opposite lane.

Headlights blazed across the windshield, frying my optic nerves and blasting my vision to a white field of blindness. Pain slashed from my eyes to the back of my skull, like someone had hit me with a machete across the bridge of my nose. The Comet slewed to the side while I blinked back into seeing. I bounced in my seat as the hot rod chewed through the grass beside the road. Pain jolted up my spine with each bounce.

Boothe slammed into the door with his broken arm. Within seconds he began to dry-heave violently; his body roiled as his stomach tried to toss out what was not there. The sound of his throat trying to pull his stomach out slapped through the car. I jerked the wheel to the left, pulling us back onto the road. The car lifted then settled back on the asphalt with a *wub-wub* sound.

Charlotte moaned louder.

"How is she?" My voice was hoarse, rubbing the sides of my throat like gravel as I shouted over the rumble of the engine.

"Not good." Ragnar's voice was strange, a high-pitched wolf growl cutting through his words. "We better get her somewhere quick or I don't think she will make it."

Fumbling around, I managed to pull out my phone. I flipped it open and held it. I fished around in my mind for the way to dial the numbers. It took a second to latch on to the information. My fingers pushed the buttons to dial the club. It answered on the first ring.

"Polecats, this is Kathleen, how can I help you?"

I held the phone in front of my face. The thought of pressing it to my ear made my head throb, so I yelled at it. "Kat, we're on the way to Larson's. Multiple severe injuries. Less than twenty till we get there." Snapping the phone closed, I let it drop to the seat. Kat would call Larson and give him the heads-up. We wouldn't walk in and catch him unprepared.

Shutting one eye seemed to stabilize my vision a little. Things stopped swaying to and fro. Instead, my eyes only jittered when I looked at a new object. The signal ahead turned red. The light blared out in a halo around the fixture.

"Deacon . . ."

The halo around the red light was cut with blades of light that matched the ones around the taillights . . .

"Deacon . . ."

. . . of the cars stopped at the intersection.

"DEACON!"

My foot slammed on the brakes. Wheels locking. Car sliding. Tires screaming. The Comet skewed sideways as we skittered and shuddered to a stop. Boothe was braced against the dash with his good arm. Black acrid smoke boiled up around us where the tires had lost a layer on the asphalt. The nose of the Comet was so close to the car in front of us I couldn't see the headlights shine.

A scream ripped from the backseat. It rose, high and brittle, until it broke, cutting off with a wet, choking sound.

Turning around, I saw something that made my heart drop.

Charlotte was in the grips of a grand mal seizure.

She and Ragnar had slid halfway off the seat. The old

wolf held her, trying to keep her still, but she bucked and jerked in his arms. Her head flailed back and forth, every muscle she had pulled taut in relief under her short gray fur. A pink tongue lolled out of her mouth as greenish foam flecked her lips.

I had to get her to Larson. My power flared up and I could feel her fading. Dying. I turned back to drive.

"What the hell's your problem, man?"

Looking up, I saw a fat man at my window. His face was purple, sweat running from brow to jowl. T-shirt with some scribbled logo on it tented around him, dark blue shorts hanging off his fat ass. His hand held a short aluminum T-ball bat that extended out, pointing in my direction.

I don't have time for this.

My voice was a hoarse snarl. "Get back in your car and drive away."

The bat thunked hollowly on the roof of the Comet. The noise made me grind my teeth. "Oh no, pal. I ain't going anywhere until you get out of that car. You 'bout hit my ride, man, and I ain't cool with dat."

My hand went under my right arm and came out with one of the Colt .45's.

The fat man went white and dropped his bat. His hands were up and waving. "Whoa, whoa, whoa . . . No harm done. Take it easy."

I kept the gun pointing at him. "Throw down your cell phone."

He reached into his baggy shorts and pulled out a black square. He dropped it on the asphalt with a sour look on his face. Those damn smartphones cost an arm and a leg.

I motioned with the gun. "Get in your fucking car and get out of my way."

He jogged over and climbed into his car. It was a

tricked-out, rice-grinding, four-cylinder piece of shit. A
spoiler spread over the trunk like a gull wing, and a fiber-
glass skirt skimmed just an inch above the street.

Douchebag.

His car stalled once as he shifted it into gear and tried
to pull away. I stomped the gas, making the Comet's
engine roar. The little car started again with a whine,
moving off the road in a quick little jerk.

Putting the gun in my lap, I pulled off, the Comet sliding by the five-speed like a shark in oily water.

"We need to hurry if the spider's going to survive,"
Boothe said.

I glanced back. Charlotte had stopped convulsing, but
now she lay boneless across the old Werewolf. Turning
forward, my hands tightened on the chain link. I closed
my weird eye and pushed the accelerator to the floorboard.

"We'll get there. Just hold on."

16

My gun was heavy in my hand. Hell, my hand was heavy. I was feeding bullets into Bessie, one eye closed so I could focus. If I opened both eyes, the world went all liquid and shimmery. Someone was talking, voice low and quiet. Looking up, I found it was George.

He stood in the laboratory now, still a gorilla, holding Lucy in his big, furry arms. She was naked except for Marcus's suit jacket; big patches of the chalk-striped fabric looked black where her blood had soaked through. Her head lolled on his shoulder. Dark smudges filled the area under her eyes, stark against her chalk-white skin. George had his lips close to her ear. He whispered for her to hold on, it would be her turn soon.

Larson rolled around the exam table that held Charlotte, working frantically, hooking her up to IVs and machines. Kat was by his side, handing him things as he called them out. She was here when we arrived, waiting out front with a gurney as we slewed into the parking lot like a bat out of hell.

Larson had given me a handful of pills, mostly painkillers and caffeine, and I could feel them working. Exhaustion still sat heavy inside me; my bones were made of lead, but the pull of sleep had receded into a small tug. The pain in my head had dulled to a low, buzzing ache that didn't spike with movement. Or lights. Or sound.

Or breathing.

Speaking of breathing, my side was a giant scab of dried blood that stuck shirt to skin, pulling every time I moved, radiating hot pain across my side. It felt like sandpaper rubbing a sunburn. The bite by Cash, the dead Were-dog from earlier tonight, still throbbed on my forearm. I needed to wash it and apply ointment before it got infected.

Switching the eye I had open shifted my view of the room slightly. The corner of my vision caught Marcus and Shani on the other side of the room. They stood against the wall. Staying out of the way. Staying away from the wounded.

Wild, feral beauty radiated from both of them. They looked like models waiting for a photographer to wander by and capture their image of concern like some kind of absurd photo-op. Everyone else who had been at that motel tonight was injured and filthy.

Or dead.

They stood, perfectly coifed and tailored. Clean and whole. Anger tipped over in my chest like a cup of acid, pouring and running to settle deep in my gut. Climbing blood pressure drove the ache in my head to a throbbing pain.

Larson rolled up to me as I stared across the room, dragging my attention away.

"Charlotte's stable." He ran a hand through red hair, thin fingers cutting parts that fell back along his temple. "I don't know for how long, though. She has multiple fractures, her spider appendages have been crushed, and I am sure there is internal hemorrhaging."

"If we can wake her up and get her to change, will it help?"

"Probably, but I don't know if we will be able to get her conscious." His hand touched my arm. "I just wanted you to know that I've done all I can for her." Those hollow blue eyes stared at me, looking for something.

Understanding crashed into me. He wanted me to understand why he was moving on to another patient. He didn't want me to think he hadn't done enough for my friend Charlotte. He knew that of all the people in the room, the only one that truly mattered to me was Charlotte. She was my friend. She was mine to protect. Everyone else could be damned if it meant she would live.

It wasn't personal. They were new. I didn't know them. I didn't wish them harm, but they were not my friends. Something else dawned on me, rising up and spilling into me as understanding.

Larson was scared of me still. He didn't know what I would do if I thought he let Charlotte die.

Neither did I.

But he hadn't. Because he was afraid of me, and his own affection for Charlotte, I knew he had done all he could. It was out of his hands now.

My voice rang hollow in my own ears. "It's okay. Go help somebody else, they need it too."

With a nod, he rolled away and went to George and Lucy. I watched as he led the Were-gorilla to an empty counter and pointed for him to lay Lucy on it. Kat came over with a tray full of bandages and medicine.

Something cold touched my arm.

I jumped up. My feet tangled together. I stumbled, almost crashing into Boothe. He sat on the floor, twisted arm padded in towels to protect it. Cursing loudly, he threw up his good hand to try and ward me away. I pulled myself upright. I swung around, Bessie hanging at the end of my hand.

Tiff stood there, Sophia crouching behind her legs. The girl was still wearing her cowgirl outfit from earlier. The Were-dog trembled, spine bowed, tail curled underneath her. It had been her nose that touched my arm. My arm dropped, too heavy to hold up. I put Bessie back in her holster.

It took three tries.

Tiff stepped toward me when I was done, arms wide. Compassion rode her pretty features. Hard. "Sorry, baby. I should have warned her about sneaking up on you."

Tiny hands slipped softly across my shoulders as she moved against my chest. I pulled her close. Her warm girl presence felt good in my arms. My face touched the side of her neck softly. There, close to her skin was the warm scent of honeysuckle and Tiff. A small sound of contentment murmured from her near my ear. Voice soft, she spoke in my embrace. "At least you had clothes on this time." I felt her smile against my shoulder.

Soon after Tiff had rejoined my life she had surprised me in my sleep. I had put a gun to her head before I was awake. Then I tried to apologize, not realizing I was naked the whole time.

Awkward.

She never let me forget it either, bringing it up whenever the mood needed a little lightening.

Leaning back, I smiled at her. "It's good to see you. It has been a long, long fucking night."

Wide blue eyes looked up at me, framed by a fringe of dark lashes. Her hand was cool against the side of my face. "It's good to see you, too, honey." Full lips pulled into a sad smile. "You look like hell."

The chuckle it brought felt good and hurt at the same time. Tiff had a way of making me feel wonderful with her big-hearted sweetness. It lifted my heart to laugh, but it also sent an inferno of pain across my ravaged side, driving the air from my lungs. Pulling away, I doubled over and knelt down, trying to recover. Tiff rubbed small circles on my back in comfort. The pain subsided and breath came back to me slowly. I stayed leaned over for a moment.

Sophia darted in and licked my cheek. She sat wagging her tail. I reached my hand out and rubbed her along the muzzle. Her face leaned into my hand, a soft rumble of pleasure in her chest as my fingers scratched behind her ear.

"It's okay, girl. You didn't mean to startle me. I am just a little jumpy." It was hard not to talk to Sophia like a pet. I knew she was a human, but I had only interacted with her as a dog. It didn't seem to bother her as she licked my hand in response. My hands roamed down her side, alternately smoothing and ruffling long russet fur.

I heard them walk up behind me, expensive heels clicking on the tile floor of the lab. Tiff's hand stopped moving on my shoulder and she took a small step to give me room. Sophia turned and darted behind her. A throat cleared behind me. The voice that spoke was smooth and melodic, a soothing purr in full effect throughout the words.

"Deacon, I want to thank you for all you have done tonight."

Anger flared hot and seething in my chest. It flashed out from the well of rage I always carried with me, deep in the scar left from losing my family. Slowly, I stood. My head started throbbing. Hands clenched tight by my side to keep them off my weapons.

This was going to get ugly.

17

"And what *exactly* did I do to earn your thanks?" My voice was low. I had to force the words out through clenched teeth.

Marcus put both hands up in a deflecting manner. He didn't bow his head. He was too alpha, too dominant, too predator for that, but both empty hands were raised. I stared at the smooth caramel skin of his palms.

No calluses marred their surface. No blood dried in the creases of them. The cuffs of a rich linen shirt sat on his wrists. The cloth was a pale cream unstained with gore that contrasted nicely with his dark skin tone. Slick, shiny black onyx cufflinks held their edges together.

Opening my fist, I looked down at the contrast. My hand was almost black with grime—a mix of dirt, gunpowder residue, and dried blood. It obscured the tattoo across the back of my hand, dulling the colors, making my daughter's name unreadable. The knuckle of my thumb was split deep, not bleeding but glaring reddish pink as it opened up. When it healed, it would add to the web of scar tissue that spread across all my knuckles, building them thick and tough. There was a callus on the inside of my index finger, a rough patch built from thousands of bullets fired in the last five years.

Marcus spoke, that voice drawing my attention wearily back to him. I had to admit it was a good voice, very soothing and melodious. A voice for sermonizing and motivational speaking. "You put yourself at risk to protect me and my mate." He took a step toward me and reached out to take my hand and shake it.

I glared at that hand—smooth, clean, and manicured—and left it to hang in the air between us. My eyes snapped back up to his face. His skin was smooth and unlined. The same features as his brother, Leonidas, but softer, more delicate, less feral. He looked at me with dark amber eyes.

"What about the rest of the people who bled tonight to keep you two safe?" I swept the room with a gesture, taking in everyone who was injured. "Everybody else gave their pound of flesh and pint of blood for you tonight. So why the hell are you thanking me?"

Cat eyes blinked. "They are lycanthropes, you are human. You didn't have to get involved, you chose to." His hand thrust forward again. "I appreciate it."

I couldn't believe what I was hearing. Understanding crept up on me. Because he was a predator he expected the others to give themselves to his safety. And they had, willingly, but he took it for granted. I thought I couldn't get angrier.

I was wrong.

"Why didn't you join us? I can see not taking on your brother and his gang by yourself, but once we got there, you weren't outnumbered anymore. Why didn't you fight with us?"

Finally, Marcus pulled his hand back. It smoothed along his shirt, looking for something to do. "I am a pacifist. I do not believe in violence to solve problems."

His head tilted back and he looked down at me over his wide, noble nose. He actually had the gall to sound superior about it.

"Let me test my understanding here." Slowly, I stood. "Your problem tonight was that your brother was coming to kill you and your mate." My knuckles cracked and popped as I clenched and unclenched my fist. "Your problem was solved because we showed up and fought to pull you out of there. Violence saved your ass tonight. Being a pacifist would have gotten you dead without the sacrifice of the people in this room."

The lioness stepped up beside him. Her back arched, stretching her to the fullness of her height. She didn't speak, mouth pulled tight into a harsh line. A single crease pulled her smooth brow together as she glared at me.

Marcus flicked smooth fingers at me dismissively. "I don't expect a man like you to understand."

A giant throb of pain closed the eye I was having trouble focusing. My one open eye blazed at Marcus through a haze of red. The muscles along my shoulders swelled tight, fury coursing through my veins. The sound of teeth grinding together was loud in my ears.

"What the *fuck* do you mean 'a man like me'?"

"I know about you, Deacon Chalk." Marcus drew himself up, lion flashing in his eyes. "Your reputation is known far and wide among my kind. You are a man whose life is drenched in blood. Always fighting, always killing." He leaned in closer, the bones in his face sliding under the skin. Golden fur sprouted along high cheekbones and brow. When he spoke, his breath had a thick, meaty scent. "You have no idea what it means to live a life of peace." He leaned back. "You bring every bit of violence on yourself. It is what you want."

His words slapped me across the face. He was wrong. Not about the fighting and the killing, that he had gotten right, but he was dead wrong about the peace part. I knew peace . . . before my family was taken. My life had been full of fucking peace. I didn't *choose* this life, it was forced on me. All I wanted was out of this life, to go on and be with my family.

I couldn't do the job myself. That was a mortal sin and sure separation from them forever. I couldn't wait around for old age, living with the pain of them being gone for years and years. And with knowledge comes responsibility. Now that I knew monsters and evil existed, I couldn't sit by and let my fellow man suffer. Now this smug bastard had the *audacity* to sit in judgment of me?

Rage crashed through me, tightening my fists. I drew back without thinking, the desire to smash Marcus's face moving my arm.

A small hand touched me, firm but gentle. It was a shock through my system, cold water on the fire of my anger. Jerking my head around, I saw Tiff standing there. The look on her face was hard to read. Big blue eyes were brimming with sympathy, and full red lips were pulled into a line of determination. She gave a small nod and a glance down, black and pink hair shimmering around her face.

Her hand was on the Colt in its holster at her waist.

Tiff was ready to follow my lead with the two lions. Whatever I chose to do she was down with. Rock or roll, it didn't matter to her.

Looking at her, I realized I did know a measure of peace. Her. She had become a delicate oasis of calm in the storm of my life. No, she would never take the place of my family, but here and now she was a place of healing for me. Anger leeched away, ebbing, dissipating.

Not leaving. No, never leaving me. Just dropping to a simmer. Tamping down to the normal level I lived with every day. It left me tired in its wake, the adrenaline dump washing away my energy. I didn't turn around, speaking to Marcus over my shoulder.

"Get out of my town."

I could feel the change in the air behind me. Between the lion and me there was a cushion of static that bristled.

Marcus's voice was thick with offense. "What? What do you mean by that?"

"I mean get the fuck out of my town. Leave. Vamoose. Amscray. Hit the bricks, pal." Now I turned to face him. Tiff's hand slid around me, her fingers maintaining our connection. "Take you and your ass and get out of the South. I want you on the road by dawn."

The lioness stepped forward. "You can't throw us out of town."

I felt my lip curl on my face. "The hell I can't. You will leave voluntarily or I will tie you both up and stuff you in the cargo hold of a Greyhound bus." My finger stabbed toward her. "Do not test me on this."

Boothe sat up on the floor, still cradling his arm, still pale and wax-skinned. Pain threaded through his voice. "Deacon, if you send them away, then you'll be sending the Brotherhood to another town with them. Maybe a town without anyone to make a stand against them."

Dammit.

Damn *it*.

DAMMIT.

Boothe was right. I didn't like the fact that he was right, but that didn't change anything. Now that I was involved, this was my fight. It was my responsibility to put an end to Leonidas and his band of assholes.

None of this made me any less sick of the sight of Marcus and his mate. They were the reason I was standing in a roomful of injured people. It was squarely their fault. My hand waved in the air.

"I don't care. I will deal with Leonidas and his thugs.

I'll track them down if need be." My finger pointed at Marcus and Shani. "I still want you two gone where none of my people will be put in danger by your presence."

Shani seethed with fury. It was written on those aristocratic features, pulling them into an ugly, venomous mask. Claws unsheathed from her fingers with tiny pops, like someone cracked their knuckles. Sleek muscle swelled under caramel skin, changing her shape, giving mass to her feminine form. A deep purr rumbled in her chest, working its way into a roar. Her lycanthropy burned hot within her, pulsing along my skin like an open flame. It pushed on my power, making the room swirl just a little.

This was escalating too quickly.

I put my hand on Bessie. "Marcus, get control of your bitch or she is going to get you both hurt."

Marcus's face had slipped back into human, all traces of lion swallowed up. One manicured hand reached out in a blur, closing on the back of Shani's neck. His voice dropped two octaves, vibrating with a power I hadn't felt from him before.

"Stop. It." The command came out chopped. Muscles in his hand flexed against her throat as power rolled off him. I felt the raw edges of it even though it was directed at his mate. It rode through the air like the crack of a lion tamer's whip.

Shani tensed, her core fighting Marcus's influence, eyes wide and wild. Then her expression changed. It looked like a switch flipped inside her. She sank to her knees, face lax and loose. Marcus looked at her for a moment, watching her carefully. He let go, moving his hand back to his side. Two steps forward put his body in front of her. It was a dominant move, disregarding her, assuming she would obey regardless of his attention.

He was close to me, shoulders thrown back, chest

wide. He looked me in the one eye I had open, still playing the dominance game. I let him feel how little I cared. He blinked, eyes sliding away from mine. His voice still carried the edge of power when he spoke.

"We will go. But I refuse to leave without all that is mine." Honey amber eyes cut down to the Were-dog still huddling behind the cowgirl. "*Come* to me, Sophia."

The Were-dog crouched, lowering her belly to the ground. Her mismatched eyes closed. A whine, high pitched and thin, cut through the air. Tiff knelt down, her hand pulling skirt between thighs modestly. Sophia tucked her head under Tiff's arm still whining. The girl looked up at me, eyes questioning.

"Deacon?"

The power coming off Marcus doubled in strength, pressing hard against my skin. It stretched into a rope between him and Sophia. My nose wrinkled involuntarily as the rank musk of cat filled my nostrils. The Were-lion pointed his hand at Sophia and that dominant power jumped, sparking and crackling like static electricity.

"Sophia, come to me. *Now.*"

Shani's eyes bored into Sophia, upper lip pulled into a snarl. She didn't move from where Marcus had put her, but she vibrated with the desire to. Her upper body leaned forward, straining against the command she had been given.

Sophia pulled away from Tiff. Turning, she took a small step toward Marcus. Her belly skimmed the ground, her whine louder and sharper. Marcus smiled wide.

My fist smashed into his throat.

The connection between the Weres snapped in two as he fell to the ground. He floundered on his side, trying to yank air into his lungs. Shani roared, vibrating the air.

She came to her feet, claws out. Boothe and Tiff both had guns out and pointed at her.

I was grateful for the backup, because I couldn't have drawn my gun if I had wanted to.

I took a step back, hand finding a wall. Black spots clustered at the corners of my vision. My stomach soured, pushing bile up my throat. I swallowed convulsively, trying to keep from throwing up. Fever raged across my skin like an inferno. Punching Marcus had sent pain searing along the nerves in my head. My brain throbbed inside my skull, each throb another nail driven into bone.

Fucking head injury.

Breathe in, breathe out. Try to keep it together.

I leaned on the wall, helpless for a few moments. Slowly, the room stopped swimming around and the blackness pulled back until it crowded only the edges of my vision. My head was still pounding, but I could stand up now.

I almost felt human again when a beep cut across the room, high and shrill, sending another spike of pain through my eyeball into my skull.

There was a crash as Charlotte jerked and convulsed on the table in the grip of another grand mal seizure. Long spider legs flailed out, knocking equipment over. Foamy blood spurted from her mouth, spattering around her chest and face. Larson wheeled over like a madman, ducking spider legs and grabbing medical equipment.

"She's crashing!"

18

Larson was out of his chair, on the table, and laying across Charlotte. His legs hung limp off the edge, and ginger hair swirled across his eyes, sticking to blood running from a cut on his brow. One spider leg had clipped him in her convulsions, splitting the skin open over his eye. Defibrillator paddles hummed in each of his hands. Charlotte jerked and convulsed under him.

Kat stood by holding a syringe as long as my hand, finger-length needle gleaming wicked sharp. Her brow creased in concentration. Larson nodded in her direction. She didn't hesitate, driving the syringe through Charlotte's gray fur and breastbone. Once it was home, her hand flashed, pushing the plunger down. Clear liquid gurgled into the Were-spider's chest cavity. Syringe empty, it was yanked out cleanly and Kat stepped back, out of the way.

"Clear!"

The paddles came down against Charlotte's chest. The hum became a buzz, crescendoing into a loud, cracking *ZAP!* The smell of burnt hair filled my nose. Charlotte twisted up, torso raising off the table. Larson lifted up, riding the wave of her body. He jerked the paddles off her, breaking contact. Her shoulders slammed back down as the electricity stopped. She lay limp and boneless, like she had been spilled.

The heart monitor beeped.

Once.

Twice.

The long, uninterrupted beep was a small scream of anguish. That thin green line on the monitor cut with finality.

Larson started yelling orders to Kat in short, precise sentences; words clipped like gunshots. His hands pushed down on Charlotte's chest, performing CPR. The heart monitor continued its one-note wail.

I stood at the end of the table. Charlotte's lycanthropy washed over me. I could *feel* her slipping away. My power searched for her spider, dashing out, running to and fro inside her. I found it curled up on itself.

Shrinking.

Collapsing.

Dying.

Charlotte was my friend. She had stood shoulder to shoulder with me and mine to face off against that evil hell-bitch Appollonia. We were bound by bloodshed. Throughout the last several months she had taken in the spiders abandoned by Appollonia's reign of terror and made them into a community. A family. After she had lost her babies to Ronnie, we had shared food and drink and laughter. Many, many nights over the last few months had been spent in the company of her and Tiff. I loved Charlotte as a dear, dear friend, one that could be called on when needed.

She was my friend.

She was *mine*.

And I would be damned if I was just going to let her go.

Reaching out, I touched her leg. Short gray fur prickled my palm. I pushed my power out, unfurling it toward her spider, coaxing it, calling to heal my friend. I felt it stir, valiantly flexing legs and trying to move. The room spun and my head swooned with it, feeling like it was going to be thrown off the top of my neck. I shut my eyes so I could concentrate on Charlotte instead of the sick sensation of vertigo. The theater of my mind opened up and Charlotte's spider lay before me, strength spent. It twitched a death twitch, jerking once, then again. I felt it fading into darkness, carrying my friend away with it.

Desperate, I cast my ability out into the world, searching for strength to give her. For life to bring her back. I spilled out over the room. Searching. Seeking. Hunting.

George's gorilla fell into my power with a wash of jungle; all moist heat and the dank green smell of vegetable. His ape reeked of musk and blood as it was drawn up into my power. Pain filled him from hundreds of cuts and bruises. Both his weariness and his deep well of strength that came from love settled in my bones.

Love for the woman he held in his arms. His beast rode in the wake as my power washed over her. Her shapeshifting was different. I could feel Masego like watching him through an open door. The shaman's curse threaded through them, a bittersweet web tracing veins under both their skins. Lucy the human's was a delicate lace of humanity. It contrasted sharply with Masego's heavy net of strength, thick and solid as the earth. Both of them shared the deep wounds they had suffered tonight. They hurt and their strength was enough to hold on, but not to share.

I couldn't take from the three of them, so I pushed on. They hung on, still connected to me like currents in a stream.

In my mind's eye an ancient wall stood in my way,

trying to block my power. It was like a small rock in a river; I rushed around it, surrounding it completely. My nostrils filled with crisp, thin air and the smell of peat moss. Cold salt spray from the ocean splashed against my face and the world rocked up and down. Ragnar was old, ancient in fact. He came from an era where steel ruled. His wolf was from a time before there was even an America.

Pain crept into my joints, a deep ache that was constant; so constant that the throb from his ruined leg felt dull and distant. He had strength, but it was old and waning. I pushed away, still searching. His beast trotted along as I cast further.

Boothe's rabbit was deep in its burrow, pulling the comfort of the earth over itself to hide from the blinding, searing pain that arced along his mangled arm. The smell of dirt was strong and I felt pressed close, hugged by the security of the earth.

Strength ran from my knees like water, threatening to drop me where I stood as his injury was added into the sensations I was feeling. Grinding pain dropped inside me like a sack of bricks.

The urge to take my hand off Charlotte was blinding. If I just moved my hand a half inch, I could break the connection. I could stop hurting, stop aching, stop dying.

Charlotte's spider folded like origami. Crumpling smaller and smaller, twitches weaker as life fled from it.

The prickly gray fur under my hand receded, becoming smooth human skin.

No!

Desperation flared in my chest. Reaching down inside, I forced my power out further, pushing against it, stretching it. My head began to throb. Sweat ran in rivers under my shirt. My power felt like pushing through water, resistance dragging as I forced it to keep looking.

Each injured lycanthrope hung in the chain, creating more weight, more drag. My leg and arm were bolts of pain. My skin felt like every inch had been gone over with sandpaper. My bones felt like crushed glass. Every muscle pulled like overstretched rubber bands. Their pain became melded with my pain, knitting into a tapestry of agony. Acid filled my stomach, blasting into my throat.

Then I fell upon the lions.

I broke over them like tide pools by the ocean, rushing into them, sweeping through them. Cat musk filled my nose, and short, coarse fur rubbed inside my skin like cotton candy. Both of them roared in unison at the invasion, but I shoved on, clawing for the hot vitality that bubbled within the two of them.

I found it, two separate balls of power and vitality. The strength of the Serengeti, of the savannah. The strength of the hunt and the kill. The strength of rending claw and gnashing teeth. I latched on to it with all I had, jerking it from them and shoving it down the line. Their beasts dug in claws, fighting, but I would not be stopped. I would not be denied. Not when my friend lay dying because of them.

My power swelled around them, pulling strength and pushing it back. As I dragged it down the channel toward Charlotte, bits broke off with each lycanthrope it passed, washing them with vitality and healing. It was only the space of a thought, but it felt like minutes when I got the lion's life force to Charlotte. What had started as a blazing torch had dwindled to a bright candle. I poured it like oil over her spider, saying a prayer as I did. *Please God, save my friend.*

Nothing happened.

Larson still pushed on her chest, but he was slowing down, giving up. The monitor still sang a shrill dirge. Charlotte lay limp. I held my breath.

Beep.

Charlotte's spider twitched.

Beep.

It jerked and rolled over trying to right itself. Legs scrabbling to find footing.

Beep . . . Beep . . . Beep . . .

The spider fell flat, moving no more. Charlotte lay limp on the table.

My spine bowed, yanked out of shape as I reached deep and dug under my power. I threw it back out into the room. Searching, seeking, looking. It dove into Sophia and I pulled some of her strength, sending it down the line. I tasted the scent of the city in moonlight on my tongue mixing with the acid and bile that filled the back of my throat. Her beast did not fight me; instead, it ran to help, putting as much of itself as it could into the channel I called it through. It rippled down the way, spreading to the other Weres as it passed by, leaving just a little for Charlotte. Carefully, I pushed for more and found the three babies she held inside her.

Brushing them was like touching a match to a trail of napalm.

White-gold energy smashed out, stretching the channel to a roaring river. Rushing along, sweeping all the lycanthropes up in its wake. I felt Boothe's arm grind together as broken bone found its way whole. The pain from it flared along my spine and then ceased with a snap as his rabbit made him whole with the strength of Sophia's unborn children.

The wave crashed over Ragnar and I experienced the abrading sensation of muscle and skin regrowing and knitting together in moments. Cells rushed together in agonizing creation, the pain blinding until it was finished. Even the ache in his joints was soothed. I felt his wolf rise to burst through his skin and I knew it had been many years of denial because transformation had been too painful to withstand.

The power rolled around George and Lucy, smoothing cuts in stinging strips of healing. It wove in and out of the two of them. I also felt it lap out to Masego where he lay recovering inside Lucy. The power tripped along the life-lines connecting the three of them, binding tighter, tying knots of energy, forming a three-strand cord that would not be easily broken.

None of this diminished the wave of power. Instead, it grew with each lycanthrope it healed. It roared, it rushed, it raged. Just outside of Charlotte, it gathered into a large, quivering pool. I felt it pause and turn to me like a living thing. It searched me, sliding around my power, seeking a way inside.

Somehow I knew that if it could only find a way inside me, I would be healed just like the others. I stood for a second, head pounding, stomach geysering acid into my throat, and muscles feeling like they had all been pulled apart and stapled back together. Ache lived deep in my bones, haunting me with pain. My body was a lead weight. If I did not have the table in front of me to lean on, I wouldn't have been able to stand at all.

The power could not find a way in. That isn't the way my ability works. It's all outside. I can't take someone's supernatural inside myself; I can only feel it and manip-ulate it.

With the last dregs of my strength, I pushed the energy toward my friend. That white gold wave studied me for another second, then turned. It crested, rolling up and crashing over Charlotte like an ocean wave.

Her spider jumped as if it had been hit with a live wire. It skittered up, rushing toward her skin. Charlotte's body yanked, throwing Larson to the ground. The heart monitor began to scream. The leg under my hand grew hard, shifting and growing longer.

I opened my eyes. Black filled the edges of my vision, leaving me dim slits to look out of. Through them I watched Charlotte's body stretch and shrink, swell and elongate, until on the table stood a 200-pound brown recluse spider.

It crouched in deadly composure, completely still, eight eyes unblinking, ten-inch fangs open to strike. I didn't move because I didn't have the strength. Besides, fuck moving, this was my friend—I didn't care if her spider form was even creepier than her spider-lady form. The spider gave a shake and shifted again, arachnid washing away and leaving Charlotte in its place. She was whole and healed and unself-consciously nude like only a beautiful woman can be. Her smile was bright as she looked at me and spoke.

"Thank you, my friend."

I opened my mouth to say no problem.

And promptly passed the fuck out.

19

Warmth.

Not the fever heat my skin was before I blacked out, but a comforting heat that made me relax. I came awake sharply. No sense of time passed, no dreams, no memory of anything after blacking out. It was later, though. I knew because I was in my room at Polecats, under the covers of my bed, a woman pressed to my back.

I could feel her breathing, slow and even against me. The line of our bodies was unbroken. Her chest to my back, one arm laying across my hip light and tender. It felt very familiar and I knew who it was.

There had been many late nights and early mornings of talking with Tiff that ended in closed eyes and close embraces. Sleeping together without *sleeping together*. The comfortable companionship of two people who are attracted to each other on many levels, not just the physical one.

My relationship with Tiff was not something I had been expecting. I wasn't looking for it when I found it. After losing my family, I've been celibate. There were lots of reasons for this. The pain of their loss was just too much to consider moving on, and the danger I am in almost constantly kept me from forming close connections with anyone. Because my life is absolutely insane, with monsters and blood and violence, Tiff and I did not have a "normal" relationship. She was in my life, we were close, and there was care and chemistry between us. But we had not been more intimate than hugs and holding hands.

Hell, we had only kissed once, last year when I was sending her away from danger the first time. She had laid one on me and told me I'd *better* find a way to survive and come back to her.

I did. And since then we had been slowly growing closer to each other.

Gently, I slipped out from under her arm, sliding slowly across the mattress. With a small whimper of protest she curled into the covers left behind, snuggling down, not waking. I watched her in the dim light of the room, sweetly sleeping.

I stood up slowly, taking my time to see what kind of shape I was in. My head hurt, but it was a low-level ache in my skull instead of blinding pain behind my eyes. The room did not spin or tilt. That was a good sign. Taking the few steps to the restroom was easy. I closed the door and my eyes before turning on the light.

Keeping my eyes closed, I felt my way to the sink. Slowly I cracked them open and looked at my reflection in the mirror. I had been cleaned up, washed of dirt and grime, but I didn't have any extra stubble on my face or head, just the goatee I kept.

So I hadn't been out longer than a day. If I had, there would be stubble. You just can't shave someone who is unconscious.

There was a bruise going green that slashed along the left side of my skull, arching over my ear and disappearing around the back of my head. Several small cuts were scabbed up along my throat; I had no idea where they had come from, but they weren't deep. I could feel bruises on my arms and chest, but none of them showed under my ink.

Lifting my arm, I looked down at my side where I had laid across the Were-shark. It had also been cleaned and covered with a thin layer of ointment. Rubbed raw from the sandpaper skin of the great white, it was pink and angry looking; the tattoos there were faint under milky new skin. It didn't look like any of the injury had gotten to the subdermal level of skin where it would harm my tattoos. They would come back after it healed more and the skin turned back translucent.

Lifting my arm had pulled something on the other side of my back. It pinched, tight bites of pain in a line. I turned and looked. A gash started at the bottom of my ribcage, curved behind me, and ran up toward my shoulder blade. The edges of it were puckered together along a row of stainless-steel staples. They studded the wound like decoration every quarter inch or so. They pulled as I stretched, feeling like a long row of tiny teeth in my back. I had no idea what had caused that wound either. It was deep enough for staples. I could see the wound had sealed, the line of it angry pink instead of raw red. It would turn into one of my more gnarly scars.

Opening the medicine cabinet gave me two things I desperately wanted: ibuprofen and my toothbrush. I used both liberally and then stripped off the shorts someone had put me in and turned on the shower. I had been cleaned up, but there is only so much that can be done without a shower. The hot water would feel delicious on my bruises.

Making adjustments until there was a thick billow of steam, I stepped in. Water beat down on me, driving heat all the way to my bones. For a moment I stood under the shower, forehead pressed to the wall, and just let it roll over my neck and shoulders.

As I relaxed my mind wandered, moving around the events of the last day like a predator stalking prey. Charlotte was healed, and I was pretty sure the rest of the people injured in that room were too. Everyone except me. I never have been able to use any of the supernatural stuff I do to heal myself. Used to be I could only sense supernatural things, now I can manipulate it, but I can't steal it or take it for my own use. I do heal faster than humans, but that's a holdover from my encounter with that Angel of the Lord when I first started out. I am glad of it. It's why my bruises were already fading and I had new skin over my cuts. It was also why I was able to move around without feeling like I was on the verge of death.

I was glad my friend was alive.

The power that healed her had come from Sophia's babies. It wasn't from her or me. I have used my ability to feel out a lot of lycanthropes, but the explosion of healing from her unborn children was something new. An anomaly.

And powerful.

Hot water washed over my head and neck, loosening muscles as my mind worked the edges of recent events.

Everyone wanted Sophia. The asshole Were-lion and his worse asshole Were-lion brother were both trying to get her. I could only assume it had something to do with her pregnancy. It's been my experience when it comes to supernatural shit that if something looks like a coincidence, then it never is. So if the two brothers wanted her, then it was not by chance. It just seemed one wanted to kill her and one wanted to keep her.

They could both kiss my ass. I had signed on to keep her safe when Tiff and I rescued her the first time. She was now on the list of people I would stand in front of when scary shit came calling. If they wanted her, they would have to go through me.

I wondered where Marcus and his mate, Shani, were now. I didn't like them and didn't trust them. Hopefully they were in the wind like I told them to get. I doubted it. Trouble like them tends to stick around until the bitter end.

Marcus's brother, Leonidas, was on a fast train to getting his ass dead. Him and all his crew, that is, whoever was left among them. I try not to kill lycanthropes. Most of their lives they are human. But when they choose to go rogue, they have to be put down. They are way too dangerous to be out of control or evil.

A Were is a package of scary fast and inhumanly strong tied together with a string of almost impossible to kill without silver. You *can* do enough damage to a lycanthrope to put it out for the count, but it takes more than most can dish out. A hand grenade would do the trick, or a flamethrower, but then you have to smell burnt hair for hours.

Leonidas had crossed the line, and so had every member of his crew. Boothe had said they were all stone-cold killers. I believed him after going up against them. They were pretty high on my shit list. Number one with a silver bullet.

I washed up using the bar of Irish Spring in the shower, scrubbing and rubbing away dirt that had been missed by whoever cleaned me up after I had passed out. I was not surprised to be safe, back at Polecats. My people were there when I passed out. They had obviously taken care of the situation. Tiff, Kat, Larson, and Charlotte would have kept Marcus and Shani from doing anything stupid. No matter how pissed they were at me for using their lycanthropy to help heal the others. I don't know what it felt like on their end, but their anger had blasted through the connection clear enough.

I shut off the hot water even though I didn't want to and stepped out of the shower. After drying off with my towel, I hung it on the shower rod and slipped back into the clean shorts I had worn into the bathroom. I shut off the light, giving my eyes a moment to adjust before stepping out. I needed to get dressed and find out what the aftermath to last night would be.

I couldn't wait.

20

Tiff was awake and sitting up in the middle of the bed. Her hair was tousled, flicking out in kicks around her face. She was scrubbed free of makeup, leaving her features starkly clean. Big blue eyes closed, her cute nose scrunched up as she stretched and yawned. Both lithe arms lifted over her head, pulling up the edge of her tight, thin T-shirt to reveal the smooth, curved planes of her stomach. The low light of the bedside lamp glittered across the stone of her bellybutton piercing.

I sat on the bed in front of her and watched. Many, many times I found myself captivated by casual things Tiff would do. Whenever she was around, I was very *aware* of her. So whenever she did something like this, I couldn't take my eyes off her. She finished her stretch and leaned over, crossed legs still under the covers. Elbows on her knees, she tucked a tiny chin into her palms. Long fingers framed her face as she smiled.

"How're you feeling, champ?"

I smiled back. "Not bad. Better than before I passed out. How long was I down?"

"About eight hours. Larson said you pushed yourself too hard with the trauma to your head. Your body shut down for repairs." Her voice hitched at the end. A look passed over her face, wrinkling her forehead. She turned away.

"What's wrong?"

Shaking her head, she wiped at her eyes. "I was just worried about you."

I smiled at her. Reaching out, my fingers lightly touched her knee through the covers. "It's all right, little girl. I'm fine." My arm curled, flexing bicep muscle. "See?"

"Don't," she said sharply. "Don't laugh this off. I'm being serious." Her eyes flashed over at me, tears broke off and trickled down her cheeks.

My hands went up, palms out. "Hey, hey, I was just kidding." Gently, I wiped a tear off her cheek. "I really am okay." The droplet hung on my callused finger, shimmering between us in the low light. "You have seen me hurt before and I survived."

She blew a lock of hair out of her eyes. "Not like this. You looked terrible before you dropped. Weak and disoriented. I have never seen you like that. I've seen you hurt, but not weak. And I have *never* seen you fall like that."

Scooting forward, I pulled her over to my lap. She slid around, settling into my arms. Her head was soft against my shoulder. I held her, making low shushing noises while she cried quietly. Stress she had been holding since yesterday ran away like water. As she subsided, I rubbed her leg through the covers.

I felt like a dick when I leaned back so she would look up at me. I didn't want to say what I had to say. Sometimes things have to be put on the record. You can't ignore them because they won't go away. They have to be put into the universe to make them real. And sometimes leaving things open makes them hurt even more when they happen. I tried to be as gentle as I could, keeping my voice soft as I spoke hard words.

"If you stick around, little girl, there will come a day that you will see me in worse shape than that." She tried to put her head down against my chest again, turning away from what I was saying. My hand went under her chin, softly but firmly keeping her looking at me. She had to understand this. I would do her no favors trying to keep it from her.

"One day, you may have to watch me die. This is not a life that will end in sunset years and peaceful passing in the night as an old man."

She pushed my hand away. "I know that. Just like I know that you don't *want* to die an old man. You *want* to go on. You want to cross that line when you can." Pulling back, she crossed her arms over her chest. Her voice was quiet, an injured bird hiding in a bush. If we had not been so close to each other, I probably would not have heard her. "I know there is nothing here you want to live for."

A sigh left me. Dammit this was hard. Here before me was a wonderful woman who deserved a life full of love. And I did love Tiff, but my heart was a wound that never healed. It was always raw and open. Sore to the touch and bleeding if not ignored. The part I had to give was damaged, twisted because it was tied to the laceration on my soul. It would not stop hurting. And it was packaged in the life I had now, a life of violence and bloodshed.

I looked at her and realized that one of the things that made her so special was that she was pure. Everyone else in my life had been traumatized by evil in their past. Everyone. All the girls who worked the club, Kat, Father Mulcahy, Larson, Charlotte. Me. All of us had been dragged into this against our will.

Not Tiff. She had chosen to be here. Yes, I had taken her from a club owned by a vampire, but she didn't know what he was at the time. He hadn't had time to taint her with his evil.

She was a clean soul.

It made me ashamed to have involved her in my life as much as I had.

Blue eyes flashed at me. Her brow creased, full lips hardening into a line of anger. Tiff moved. Straddling me and pushing me back against the wall. One small fist thumped down on my chest, hard enough to get my attention. Hard enough to hurt. She loomed over me, finger pointing in my face.

"Oh, no, you *don't*." Her voice pushed through clenched teeth. Tears pooled in the rims of her eyes, glittering and shimmering, waiting for the one small thing that would send them tumbling down her cheeks. "Don't you *dare* get that look on your face. You are *not* sending me away for my own good. I am a grown woman and I want to be here. I'm. Not. Going. *Anywhere*." She leaned in, face close to mine. The tears had spilled and her voice was a fierce whisper. "The only reason I got so scared is that I love you, Deacon Chalk. I love you more than I have ever loved anyone or anything in my whole damned life."

Then she kissed me.

21

Her mouth was soft. The kiss was hard and fierce. Lips delicate and tender parted against mine. Her hands came up to my face as our tongues danced. I returned her kiss roughly, arms sliding around her. One hand went to the back of her neck, pulling her into me, holding her there even though she wasn't trying to get away.

The air was charged, energy dancing back and forth between us. My skin felt swollen with need. The kiss broke and she sat back. Both of us were breathless. My mouth ached with the absence of her. I could still taste her warm and sensuous on my lips. She turned her face away, sliding her bangs over to cover her eyes. Hiding.

"I'm sorry. I didn't mean for that to happen. I'm not trying to push you where you don't want to go." She leaned away, moving. "I'll leave."

Those two words stabbed me in the heart.

The inside of my chest collapsed, hollowed out by the thought of her hurt. The thought of her leaving. My fingers tightened on the back of her neck, holding her still, turning her face to me.

My voice was thick with the feelings storming inside me. Love. Heartbreak. Desire. They all rolled through me. She stared into my eyes through a veil of black and pink hair as I spoke.

"Stay. I couldn't stand it if you left now. I want you with me."

"But your—"

My finger touched her lips, stopping her words. "I am a grown man, darling. Let me worry about all that." I lifted her chin. "I love you, Tiffany. I'm fucked up and I have more issues than *Time* magazine, but I do love you and I want you in my life."

She shook hair out of her eyes. "Really?"

"Truly."

Her smile was a brilliant, beautiful thing. Sweet and happy, but mixed with a dark edge of desire. White teeth pressed into her bottom lip, drawing my eyes into looking as they made tiny, half-moon impressions. Her eyes were heavy lidded as we moved toward each other. Tentatively, so softly, our lips touched. A thrill tightened the back of my neck as we kissed. Tongues seeking, searching. A spark of desire shot through me, cutting through my chest. Hunger for her boiled up through me and I couldn't get enough.

Not enough of her kiss. Not enough of her. She matched me, hunger for hunger, small sounds escaping from deep within her.

The kiss broke, my lips afire with the taste of her. The taste of her burning on my tongue. Her forehead rested on mine. Our lips just far enough apart to catch our breath. My head swam with her warm honeysuckle scent.

The cover had slipped and I was suddenly aware of how little clothing was between us. I wore only shorts. Tiff was in a thin T-shirt and a matching pair of panties.

Need pressed against me hot and heavy. My veins ran hot with it, rushing and coursing under my skin. My mind swam with animal lust. I had to have her; if I

didn't, my heart would stop beating. Desire hung from
me to her, stretching and pulling. The air between us was
charged, heavy with anticipation, crackling with desire.

With a wicked grin, Tiff slid off my lap, moving back
on her knees. Shapely muscles flexed in her thighs, drawing my eyes to the hollows of her hipbones. She was
wearing a thin pair of panties, blue with orange flowers
meant to be cute, but now just enticing and teasing. Her
fingers grabbed the hem of her shirt and pulled it slowly
up. The fabric slid up her body, caressing smooth skin,
unveiling the edges of her curves. Like a work of art
being slowly, teasingly revealed by its creator.

I held my breath as the shirt slipped like water over
the swell of her breasts. It seemed to take an eternity to
slide those few inches, hesitating just before popping
free and being pulled over her head. She sat back, watching me through bangs that fell soft across her eyes.

A growl cut through the air and I realized it was me.
Everything stripped away and boiled down to bare desire.
We crashed together, clothes being pulled away by eager
hands, desperate to remove any barrier between us. We
rolled on the bed. My hands landed on each side of her
head as I rose over her. Nothing between us but heavy
desire and our swollen need for each other. She looked
up at me, hair fanned around her face, blue eyes sharp
and searching.

I was naked. All pretense stripped away. Every secret
laid bare. Every scrap of pain exposed for her to see, for
her to soothe. I was overwhelmed by what was in her
eyes. Desire, yes, but tempered with something deeper,
something richer. The texture of our feelings slipped between us, caressing our skin. Her hands moved up, sliding along the muscles of my arms, nails grazing the skin
across my shoulders. The connection between us

sparked, flaring into an inferno. We surged. She arched up to meet me as I fell and we spun away together.

A storm of passion unleashed between us. Driven by need, urged by desire, we rode the storm untamed. The world fell away until it was just the two of us chasing the lightning. Pleasure washed my mind empty. I couldn't think, I could only *feel*. Skin fevered and sensitive everywhere we touched. The pleasure rode us, driving hard, too much need for hesitation. The maelstrom carried us to the top of the mountain and threw us off the edge. Tiff broke beneath me as I broke above her and we crashed together, spiraling to the depths as passion washed away in a climax of ecstasy.

I fell away, landing beside her. Still touching, still connected as I tried to catch the breath she had taken away. My hand searched, fingers finding hers, twining together. She rose up and lay across my chest, skin slick and warm. Her arm draped as she looked down at my eyes, warm girl weight delicious against me. Her eyes were heavy-lidded, hair tousled, face soft in the low light of the bedside lamp. I leaned up and kissed her softly. Her lips were swollen, full and tender. Our hearts beat in time as she lay across me.

"Wow," her voice was throaty with satisfaction. She snuggled against me, stretching one smooth, sleek leg over mine. "Thank you."

No, thank *you*.

22

I woke up with the same warm weight against my back, the room dark once again. I stayed where I was so I would not disturb her. I felt good. Really good. Better than I had felt in a long time. Well rested. Sated.

Tiff and I had made love.

Yes, we did. It had been amazing. Passionate and caring. Everything lovemaking should be. She was insistent, and yet caring. Patient.

It had been a while for both of us and we worked to make it worth the wait. I felt a satisfaction deep in my bones. It had not been my plan, though. I didn't regret it. God no, not one moment of it, but things were different now.

I had been celibate since my wife's death five years ago. Consumed with killing monsters and saving people, there had been no time for romance. No inclination either. I loved my wife, still love my wife with everything in me. Even being separated by time and death had not lessened that. I miss her and my children every day. Every. Single. Day. I push their memories into safe boundaries just so I can function. The loss of them burns deep in my soul.

Tiff had come along and found one small piece of my scarred-up heart and made it her own. I did love Tiff. I knew that. She would never take the place of my wife, and truthfully would never want to. That made her the only one I could let in deep enough to go *there* with. She was very special. More special than she realized.

Part of me felt like I should have guilt over being with Tiff, like I betrayed the memory of my wife. Thinking about it, I realized that my feelings for Tiff didn't diminish my love for my wife. Not even a little. Realizing this made a small knot inside me loosen. It was okay. I could love two people, maybe not equally, but love nonetheless.

I rolled over carefully, slowly putting my arm around the person pressed to my back. With a sigh, she slid back, pressing bare skin against my chest. Sleepily, I took a deep breath into a thick mane of long hair.

Wait.

I jolted out of sleep, sitting up sharply. The girl next to me gave a little yelp as she scrambled away, pulling the covers with her. The person I had been holding didn't fit just right and she had hair well past her shoulders. She didn't feel right. She didn't smell right.

I realized it wasn't Tiff about the same time the light was switched on with a click.

"Well, this is interesting." Tiff's voice came from across the room.

I blinked in the harsh light. It took a few seconds for my eyes to adjust enough to see who was in bed with me. The girl I had been pressed against was huddled under the covers. Her skin was pale, translucent, almost glowing even in the low light. A thick tangle of russet hair cascaded around a finely boned face. She blinked at me with a mismatched gaze: one eye blue, one eye brown. Even with the covers pulled up to her neck it was obvious she was nude. It took a moment to realize I was too.

And she had taken all the covers with her when she pulled away.

Putting the pillow over my lap, I tried to make sense of what was happening. Tiff was dressed and standing in the door of the room holding two cups of coffee. The naked girl huddled as far away as she could but still be on the bed. Looking over at her, I had a guess who she was.

"Sophia?"

She nodded, her chin trembling.

"What the hell is going on?"

Her mouth opened to answer, closed, opened again, then slapped shut as her bottom lip curved down. Tears trembled in her eyes, shimmering on the edge of spilling. A long, quivering breath pulled into her nose, color bloomed on her cheeks, and the tears spilled over in streams.

Tiff strode around the bed, moving quickly and with purpose. Putting down the coffee, her arms scooped Sophia up and pulled her close. She shushed and caressed, making low, soft sounds of comfort as she rubbed the other girl's back.

Looking around, I found the shorts I'd had on earlier and slipped back into them. To do so meant flashing the room, but Tiff had already seen the show and Sophia had her head buried in Tiff's shoulder. I got up, moved to the closet, pulled an Orion Outfitters T-shirt off a hanger, and slipped it over my head. The shirt had a silhouetted demon skull in a crosshair with the words "ORION OUT-FITTERS: BUMP BACK."

It felt better to be somewhat dressed. I would really feel better if I had my guns, but somehow I didn't think they would help this situation. Pulling down a short-sleeved dress shirt, I handed it to Tiff, motioning toward the crying lycanthrope in her arms. I turned my back to them while Sophia slipped it on.

"Okay, you can turn around now."

My shirt fit Sophia like a dress that was too big. It swallowed her, making her look like a child. Her mismatched eyes were red rimmed, her skin ice water pale, except her cheeks, which were scalded with blush. She was pretty. The hang of tangled locks and fine-boned features drew her face long and lean, the delicate ethnic cast of Eastern Europe stamped there. She could have been Ukrainian or Russian, definitely something from that part of the globe.

Tiff sat next to her, hands around one of the cups of coffee. An amused look was on her face as she took a sip. Skintight jeans stretched up her legs as she sat with them crossed on the bed, leaning against the headboard. Her shirt was the same thin tee from earlier and she was in her socked feet, but the Colt hung from her hip in the gun belt. The sight of it made me itch for my guns again, but I pushed it aside. There were weapons stashed around my room, handy to reach, but only if you knew where they were.

Leaning against the doorframe of the closet, I spoke, "Okay, who wants to explain what just happened?"

Sophia looked at Tiff. "I'm sorry. I didn't mean to—"

Tiff cut her off with a pat on the knee. "It's okay." She turned to look at me. "I left you sleeping to get coffee and let Sophia in as I left. She was still in her other form, so I didn't think anything of her curling up on the bed." She patted the other girl's leg again. "I was thinking of you as a dog, honey; sorry if that was rude."

"No, no. I *am* a dog when I'm shifted. Not *just* a dog, but still a dog if that makes any sense." Her eyes turned to me. "That is why I came in. It was instinct. I wanted to curl on the bed for comfort." Her chin dropped in embarrassment. "I guess I got too comfortable." A small chuckle escaped her. "I didn't plan on changing."

Okay. It was good that Sophia felt safe enough to

relax into a change and Tiff was handling her being naked in the bed with me well. Not that I really saw anything. It was all an accident. I was sleeping, she was sleeping, she shifted. No big deal. Which brought my mind to more important matters.

"How are the babies since you shifted?" I asked.

Sophia's hand went to her own stomach. It was a gentle, rounding curve in the center of her. Until she framed it with her hands you wouldn't have noticed it. Her eyes closed, brow creased in concentration. Seconds ticked by until a smile broke over her face. "They're fine. It doesn't feel like my shift affected them."

"Good. Let's try to keep you from shifting again."

Sofia nodded.

Tiff stood up. "Now that you are human, let's go find you something to wear. Surely with all the girls around here we can find something appropriate."

My stomach growled. I hadn't eaten in almost twenty-four hours. "All right, then, I am going to get dressed. We'll eat and then you can both fill me in on what I have missed."

23

My boots made a nice sound as I stepped out onto the tile floor of the foyer outside the club's kitchen. They're harness boots—black and square-toed with a strap and ring across the instep. They're a style of engineer boot with a cowboy heel and oil-resistant rubber soles. They are a badass pair of boots. Look up badass in the dictionary and you will find a picture of these boots beside the entry. I've owned them for years.

They were a gift from my wife, on a birthday before the kids had come along. She had bought them for me and surprised me with them when I got home from work. I put them on and she liked them. She liked them so much I spent the rest of that birthday wearing nothing but the boots.

Enough of that.

That memory was a dark road with a bad end. Pushing it aside, I kept moving.

I had changed to an old pair of jeans, white-blue from untold washings and threadbare over the knees. The Orion Outfitters shirt remained, tucked in now to stay out of the way of my shoulder holsters. Both Colt .45's rode under my arms, where they were supposed to be, rows of extra clips stacked below them. Bessie hung heavy on my hip. The leather cords cut into my thigh where they were tied to hold the holster down. The big gun had pitting and corrosion from Were-snake venom splashing on her the night before. Spots of rust scattered on her stainless-steel frame, but she was still serviceable.

In my hand, I carried a katana.

The Japanese sword was past antique. It was downright damn ancient. It had been taking lives for almost fifteen centuries. The scabbard was ebony and wrapped with a crimson and saffron cord that was knotted and woven so the sword could be worn at the waist or slung over a shoulder. The handle was plain yellow wood wrapped in black cord. Inside the blade rode, tarnished and dull, spotted black from gallons of blood drank along its edge. It was a cursed and bloodthirsty blade. Every time I held it I had to fight its call to kill more than necessary.

I didn't know all of the sword's history. Kat had looked it up and found out that it used to belong to a Japanese emperor's executioner before being stolen by a group of Tibetan Demon-monks. I kind of zoned out as she told the story. It was one long of evil that ended in the hands of an asshole named the Kensai. He was a rogue Yakuza assassin with delusions of murderous grandeur. He was the one who had stolen Charlotte's egg sac a few months back with dreams of bonding with her offspring and using them as tools to assassinate people who cannot be gotten to.

I had put an end to that plan.

Everything ended with him dead and eaten by Charlotte's young, who then bonded with Ronnie from the club. I wound up with the Kensai's matched pair of Colt .45's and the katana, which now was home to an Oni, a Japanese demon I set free from being trapped in a tattoo on the Kensai's back.

I am not a master swordsman by any stretch of the imagination, but I can hold my own. Especially when my opponents only have claws and fangs. The sweeping curve of a katana makes it one of the most deadly weapons in the world. I wouldn't take it over a gun, but I would take it over bare knuckling a few rounds with a lycanthrope.

This cursed katana was a bloodthirsty blade. When used, the Oni inside it tries to seduce you over to the dark side. Whispering in your mind, promising you your darkest desires if you will just use it to spill more blood. It pulled to you, making it hard to stop killing, especially if you were prone to killing to start with.

Not that I would know anything about that. No, not me.

It also heightened your speed, your strength, and reaction time. It wouldn't put me even with Leonidas, but it would tighten the gap. After the level of injury taken the last time we tangled, I wanted every edge I could get. One day I would destroy the damned thing, but until that day I would use it to my advantage.

The smell of pizza filled the kitchen as Kat and Tiff opened flat cardboard boxes and set them on the long table. Larson rolled over with a stack of plates and napkins. My stomach clenched into a knot of hunger. I hadn't eaten anything in too many hours. My mouth started to water as I walked in.

Tiff came over to me. She reached up, arms around my neck as I pulled her close. She smelled good, warm honeysuckle scent making my head swim. I lifted her up in a hug, squeezed her firmly, then set her back on her feet. We pulled apart, her hand lingering on my arm, my hand still lightly touching her back.

She smiled up at me. "Detective Longyard is waiting for you out front."

"He probably wants to know what happened last night."

"I'm sure."

My stomach growled again. The smell of pizza filled my nose. "Did you offer him lunch?"

"I did and he said he had somewhere to be." Playfully, she pushed me toward the door to the main part of the club. "Go take care of business. The pizza will wait for you."

I walked out to find Detective John Longyard slouching against the bar, cigarette in one hand, a lighter in the other. He brought the cigarette up, flaring the lighter to life with a flick of his thumb. Inhaling sharply to get the cancer stick started, he then blew out a thick cloud of smoke.

With a squint he looked at me. "Nice sword."

I pulled up a bar stool next to him, laid the sword on the bar top, and slid over an ashtray. "Thanks. They're very fashionable this year; all the cool kids will be carrying them this fall."

Detective John Longyard. Good cop, good at his job, good man. He had been the investigating detective on the case of my family. He was smart enough to step back and let me do my work now, knowing it saved the lives of police officers to do so. He helped smooth over things when I had been too violent or left too much evidence behind during a hunt. I knew exactly why he was on my doorstep today.

We left bodies on the ground last night.

A *lot* of bodies.

He waved the cigarette in my direction, indicating the sword. "I'll pick one up for my kid then." One long drag and he stubbed the cancer stick out in the ashtray. "You got any hooch in this joint?"

I got up and walked behind the bar. "What'll you have, sailor?"

"Something dark. Neat, and plenty of it."

I pulled down a bottle of Southern Comfort and held it up. He nodded. Two shot glasses went on the bar. I poured them full, pushed one toward him and picked up the other one. We tossed back the whiskey at the same time. It hit the back of my throat and tumbled down to splash into my empty stomach. The low ebb fire of the liqueur set up residence. I turned my shot glass over and slammed it on the bar.

It had been a while since I drank whiskey straight. Déjà vu swept through me. I had tried to drown my pain through a lake of Southern Comfort when my family was taken. I had talked to Longyard while drinking back then, so this had the eerie feel of the familiar. Bad déjà vu.

I pushed the bottle over to him. He picked it up and poured another shot. As he tossed it back, I studied him. Every time I had ever seen Detective Longyard he had been wearing an expensive suit. Morning, noon, or night, he never dressed casual. For a split second I wondered if his pajamas were three-piece. The one he had on today was a rich cocoa brown matched with a blue shirt and a saffron-colored silk tie. It was rumpled, wrinkled at the elbows and knees like he had been wearing it too long. His light brown hair was still in place but had a slightly greasy shine in the low light of the club. Dark shadows filled the hollows under his eyes.

Normally, Longyard is always the same. Different suit, but the same level of styling, like he was going to a million-dollar executive deal rather than a crime scene. Today, he looked worn and raw, as if his nerves were too close to the surface of his skin and everything in the world was rubbing him the wrong way.

He set the shot glass down. His fingers smoothed down the mustache he kept trimmed above his upper lip. He poured a third shot but left it sitting on the bar. The brown amber liquid quivered in the glass.

I moved back to the bar stool. "Been a long day?"

"Long night. I'm still working from yesterday." He pulled out another cigarette. He tapped it on the pack, settling the tobacco into the tube of paper. He studied it, watching his own fingers intently. Without looking up, he spoke. "Do you have any idea what kind of mess you left at that motel?"

"Actually, I was pretty out of it when we ditched. So, no, I don't have any idea. How bad was it?"

He pulled out his phone. His thumb slid across it as he scrolled through information. He read off mechanically. "One motel unit destroyed. Eleven bodies. Approximately two hundred and four bullet casings of various calibers. More blood types than there are blood types." His phone slipped back into his pocket. He looked up at me. *"Eleven bodies."* His finger stabbed the bar next to the shot glass. "All of them nude as the day they were born."

Eleven was a lot. One of the good things about being an occult bounty hunter is that when I handle most monsters I can shuffle them completely off this plane of reality. This keeps too many people from tuning in to the fact that monsters are real. Vampires turn to dust, mummies crumble to dirt, ghosts go into the light, demons go to hell . . . you get the picture. Lycanthropes don't do that. Kill one of them and all of a sudden you have a dead human on your hands.

A dead naked human.

This can be awkward at the best of times.

I looked at Longyard with a cold eye. He generally took what I did in stride, smoothing things over, keeping the attention away. Was this the time that his help ran out? Had he been pushed too far? If I was on my own with the police, things could get real hard real quick.

I stood up. "Are you about to give me bad news, Detective? If so, just get to it; don't dance around."

He looked at me, meeting my eyes. I liked John, but I kept my face empty. I could feel emotion bleeding away, my subconscious preparing me. He broke the stare and picked up the shot glass. Southern Comfort spilled over the edge onto his fingers as he tossed back his third shot.

Grimace on his face, he turned the glass upside down and slammed it on the bar. "I like you, Deacon, and I appreciate what you do, but sometimes I forget just how dangerous you really are." He looked at me, something sitting dark in his eyes. "Was it necessary to kill all those people?"

I reached down and gave him as much truth as I could. "Werewolves. The dead were almost all Werewolves. They had joined the bad guys and tried to kill us. So, yes, it was necessary to kill all those Werewolves last night."

He stared at me, searching my eyes. I don't know what he found, but it seemed to satisfy him. He nodded to himself and stood, picking up his pack of cigarettes. "The official story is a drug-dealing, sex-trafficking ring had a deal gone wrong." He turned to go. My hand fell on his arm.

"Thank you, John."

He turned. His eyes cut over to the sword on the bar. "Is your case ongoing? Or do I have another long night in store for me?"

My hand fell away. I shrugged. "It's not over."

"Then thank me when it *is* over." He turned and walked out of the club without a backward glance.

24

Pulling a chair around, I sat across from Sophia. She had run a brush through her hair, pulling it smooth into big, loose locks, making it shine. My shirt still draped around her narrow shoulders, but underneath she had added a pair of black yoga pants from one of the girls. She sat quietly, but returned my smile when I gave it.

Tiff put a glass of sweet tea in front of me, leaning over my shoulder to do it, her warm girl weight gentle on my back. Her lips pressed quickly against my face, the barest kiss and then gone. Fingernails trailed up my arm as she kept moving. The honeysuckle scent of her cut through the air around me, causing my heart to speed up.

I caught Kat shooting me the same look I had given her about Larson with the same raised eyebrow. My chin went up in a small nod to her. She grinned, her eyes slowly sliding over to Larson.

I snagged a wide slice of veggie pizza and dragged it onto my plate, leaving a trail of cheese and toppings behind. I love veggie pizza. Put as many vegetables on there as you can. Anything but hot peppers and I am in like Flynn. The joint we order from does it right. The veggie pizza has thick-cut, fresh vegetables tossed on a sea of cheese over a homemade marinara sauce and dashed with seasonings.

The owner, Mario, takes good care of us. Making our pizzas with extra toppings, never charging us. Why does he hook us up? One, because he has a soft spot for the ladies, and two, a few years ago Father Mulcahy and I exorcised a minor demon out of his pizza oven. It had come in with a bad batch of parts from Indochina. Some Holy Water and a rite of Exorcism, and he was back to making the best pizza in the Metro-Atlanta area.

Kat looked at me while everybody sat down around the table. "So what is the story from last night?"

"Sex-trafficking ring and drug deal gone bad."

"Hasn't that one been used before?"

"I don't think so."

"Must be hard to sell a drug deal gone bad when there are no drugs around."

I laughed. "I've been to that ghetto ass motel. Trust me, there were drugs on the premises somewhere." I didn't share the peculiar way Longyard had acted. I would keep an eye on him. If things went south with the relationship we had, me killing monsters, him covering it up, then I would deal with it. There was no need to worry anyone else with it right now.

Everybody settled in with food, beginning to eat in a companionable silence. Just the five of us gathered around the table.

"Where is the good Father? He loves Mario's."

Larson wiped his mouth. "He's with Boothe keeping an eye on Marcus and Shani and making preparations."

"Preparations for what?" My pizza was hot, cooling on my plate as I spoke.

"They are getting ready for this Brotherhood group. Boothe and Father Mulcahy have a plan of some sort." Kat picked up her slice, pepperoni grease dripping onto her plate. Kat is a meatitarian. She will not tolerate a vegetable on her pizza. For her, the pizza world consists of only pepperoni, cheese, and more pepperoni. "Some kind of trap for them that is set up for tonight. I called and told them you were back among the living and they want you to join them."

"Why didn't they wait for me?"

"They couldn't. Leonidas and the other predators have been terrorizing Weres all over town. Nobody has died, but it's only a matter of time unless they are stopped." Larson's eyes blazed bright inside dark circles. "I've been treating a lot of shape-shifters in the last twelve hours. They're escalating. What started as simple cuts and bruises has grown into some serious injuries. I had to shut the clinic. Between the aftermath of yesterday and the injuries last night, we ran out of supplies."

"I ordered a rush shipment. We will be restocked tomorrow." Kat's hand went out and grabbed Larson's. He raised it to his lips, kissing it softly as they shared a lover's smile for each other.

"What's being done to protect these people Leonidas is hurting?" Somebody had better be doing something or there was going to be hell to pay. This had been pushed to the tipping point by Charlotte and the other lycanthropes' insistence that I get involved. They had given me their word that they were my backup. I had pushed myself over the line to heal them. They had damn sure better be trying to protect people. If not, I had a pocket full of ass-whoopin's to hand out when I saw them again.

For a spilt second guilt came knocking because I had been with Tiff while people were being hurt.

I looked over at the girl in question, who gave me a sweet smile, and told guilt to kiss my ass. My old friend anger, though? That I held on to, pulling it deep in my chest. It settled next to my heart, warm and cozy in the spot it had held for years now.

"Word has been put out for all the area shape-shifters to go to Boothe's neighborhood, the Warren, to be safe. They have been showing up all morning from all over the area."

"Word? How is this 'word' getting to them?"

Kat rolled her eyes. "Since Larson has been providing medical services to the Were community, we have put together a network of contacts. E-mail, social media, phone numbers, text chains . . . name a way to contact someone and we have it."

I should have known Kat would have set up something like that. She had a similar system in place for the few other people around the world who do what I do. Before Kat came along, I had a bunch of scraps of paper with random numbers on them. That was how I kept the contacts for other monster hunters that I had gathered. Kat quickly took those and made a database. Now I could call others in my line of work from my cell phone.

She lives to organize things like that, putting her Internet wizardry to work. When it comes to Web-based things, Kat is a genius.

"What about the predators? Are they with Leonidas or us?"

"We don't have very many predators here to start with," Larson said around a mouthful. "The ones that are in the area have gone to ground and are keeping to themselves until this is over." He looked at me pointedly. "They're scared of you."

If they chose to be with Leonidas, then they should be.

I turned to Sophia. She had eaten four slices of pizza while we were talking, with her fifth being brought to her mouth. Lycanthropes eat fast and they eat a lot because their metabolism runs ninety to nothing. Which is why you never see a fat Were. Sophia was eating for four, so I would not be surprised to see her polish off an entire pizza, despite being the smallest person in the room.

"Is this normal behavior for Leonidas and his gang? Or are they taking retribution for the other night?"

The Were-dog swallowed her mouthful, wiping daintily at tiny bow-shaped lips. "He does scare people into going back to the old ways. I don't know any details, those were kept from me, but this is the first time he has been in a city at the same time as Marcus. Normally he arrives just after we leave and undoes all Marcus works to accomplish."

"So, what's the story with you and Marcus?"

"There's no story. Not really." Her cheeks flamed crimson, voice falling away. "Not anymore."

I felt my face grow hard as I looked at her. "We are way past that line of shit." She flinched like I had yelled at her, even though my voice had remained steady. Ah hell, I wasn't trying to scare her. I softened my tone to try and take out some of the sting she had in her mismatched eyes. "I need to know the real deal before I go any further, Sophia. You can trust us here."

Pulling in a breath, she held it captive for a long moment, then slowly, shakily, she let it escape between her lips. "I was his assistant. My job was to go out and make first contact with prey groups before Marcus showed up. I was sent ahead because my other half is a non-threatening predator. I would also arrange our transportation, housing, and upkeep." Her words tumbled out in a rush. She quickly replaced them with another bite of pizza, moving her eyes away and hoping that was all I wanted to know.

Not that lucky.

I probed again. "Okay, but I know there is more to the story than that." Tiff elbowed me under the table. I ignored it. Sophia dropped her head, hiding behind a cascade of dark auburn hair. "Does he know that you're knocked up?"

She nodded slowly up and down just once, hair still a veil.

"Is the father Cash, that Were-dog I killed yesterday when they showed up to take you? Is that why he wants you back?"

Softly, so softly I almost didn't hear it, she spoke words that crashed like thunder and tilted the whole situation sideways.

"No, it wasn't Cash. It's Marcus."

Larson dropped pizza in his lap.

Without even looking down, he leaned over toward her. "Are you sure? Absolutely sure?"

Fire flashed in mismatched eyes as she looked up. "Yes, I am sure. I have only been with one person my entire life and that's Marcus."

I watched Larson carefully as he reacted to this information. His brow furrowed and he removed his glasses, cleaning them with his shirt. Putting them back on, one hand ran through ginger hair, pushing it back and letting it fall. He pulled the glasses back off and began cleaning them again.

Finally, Tiff spoke, "Why is that such a big deal?"

Larson shoved his glasses back on over wild eyes. "It's a big deal because it is impossible to crossbreed species of lycanthropes. Completely and utterly impossible."

"Obviously it's possible," I said.

Larson turned to me. "You of all people should know that just because something happens doesn't make it less impossible." I nodded that he was right. "The implications of this coupled with what happened last night when you healed Charlotte and all the other Weres . . ." Voice trailing off, his big blue eyes were far away as he looked up. "This is huge. Enormous. The implications . . ." And just like that we lost Larson as he began thinking, his brain in mad scientist mode calculating possibilities, probabilities, and repercussions. He hadn't been quite right since last year.

Tiff's eyes were narrowed as she studied the Were-dog. I could *feel* the wheels turning in her mind. Her voice was very gentle, softly trying not to spook or scare. "Sophia, did Marcus ever use that creepy voice to get you to sleep with him?"

Shame flooded Sophia's face like a switch was thrown, blossoming across her cheeks in crimson, big eyes shimmering as they filled, brimming with saltwater, threatening to spill. "No . . . not like the other night." Tears broke from her eyes and ran wildly down her cheekbones to hang and drip along the delicate jaw. "Sometimes."

She took a deep breath, drawing it in and pushing it back out. "He is so handsome and confident. When I met him I was scared to talk to him and I knew he would never notice someone like me, someone so plain and scared of everything. But then he did notice me. And he wanted me to help him."

A small, wistful smile played through her tears. "He made me feel so special. If someone like Marcus, who had people listening to him, hanging on his every word, if someone like him could see me, then maybe I wasn't so ugly. He said I wasn't ugly." Her mismatched eyes sparkled. "He was the only man to ever tell me I am beautiful."

She took a deep, trembling breath and went on, words coming in a rush, spilling out, cleaning the wound. "I knew he was mated and I felt terrible about that part of it. I was raised in a Southern Baptist home and you just don't do that. Mated isn't married, but it's the same thing. I justified it by telling myself that Shani doesn't want him, she just wants the position of being his wife. Which is true, but it didn't make what I was doing any less wrong, only easier to justify. Cash would help us to be together because Marcus was *so* lonely. He wanted *me*. He said I made him happy and that I was beautiful and wonderful."

A small pale hand wiped away saltwater. "He didn't have to use any voice tricks on me. Not at first, but once I found out I was pregnant, I didn't want to keep being his mistress. They might have been conceived in sin, but I wasn't going to raise my babies that way. The next time he came to me, I told him no." She choked a little, holding back a sob. Swallowing, she moved on. "He made me submit then, using the voice. But he was used to me just doing it without question, so I don't blame him." A sob broke, giving lie to her words. Her voice was small, brittle. "I don't blame him at all."

Kat put her arm around Sophia. With her past, she is acutely, painfully sensitive to victims of rape. Unfortunately, it is a sympathy born of experience. I had rescued her from the hands of sexually sadistic vampires who had used and debased her in ways that would have killed a lesser woman. She survived, even to the point of being able to have a romantic relationship with Larson, but because of her past she was attuned to any form of sexual trauma in others.

Sophia folded into the circle of protection, Kat looking at me over her head. Kat's lips were making low, soft sounds of comfort, but her eyes were flint-hard pieces of hate for Marcus. Tiff moved to kneel behind Sophia and add to the circle. The three women huddled, drawing strength from each other. Larson and I were left out by virtue of our gender, so we sat quietly, reverent in the presence of something we could never fully understand.

After long moments, the three of them slowly broke apart with lingering touches of comfort. Three pairs of eyes red-rimmed and wet. Larson and I watched the birth of a sisterhood before our very eyes. It was something sacred, something holy. Forged in the crucible of shared experience, it wouldn't break easily. Women already come equipped with a core of steel-fiber strength, depths of resolve a man cannot comprehend. It's not the dynamic strength men have, all power and show. It's a strength of endurance, fortitude. It is the strength that allows women to conceive life and to carry that life until the day it can stand on its own. These three women were now one, a three-strand cord not easily broken.

After everyone was back in their places I put my hand out toward Sophia, resting it on the table between us. "You don't have to worry about that anymore. You have my protection as long as you want it and longer. I will keep you as safe as I can. But I can guarantee that Marcus will never touch you again."

Tentatively, her pale hand moved toward mine. It hovered over my hand, not touching, just wavering in the air an inch or two above. The contrast was stark. Her hand was translucent, thin blue veins tracing below the surface, the fingers dainty along their length.

Mine was stained with a dark patina from years of violence, not unlike the katana blade I carried. Swirls and whorls outlined as if ink-stained. Scars and calluses standing, a topographical map of violence. Carefully, her palm descended onto mine, finally touching, landing lightly as a bird. Her fingers closed over mine, and with a nod she was part of the family.

It was that simple. A small decision on her part and just like *that,* we would all die for her.

Or kill for her.

"I have only two questions."

She nodded, giving me permission to ask.

"How long did Leonidas have you when Tiff and I came along?"

She left her hand in mine as her brow furrowed in concentration. "I was in and out of consciousness, so it's hard to tell, but not long. They tried to snatch me on the way to a group of predators to set up a meeting for Marcus. I got away and ran. I had to change to my dog and try to lose them that way. They chased me for miles and miles, and every time I thought I was safe, another one of them would be on me and I would run again. Until they herded me to that lot where Leonidas collared me and beat me." Mismatched eyes bore into mine as her memory flared.

They were done with tears. Now only deep banked fires of anger burned inside. "He called me the worst names as he beat me. Whore. Slut. . . . Worse than that. All the while he kept trying to hit me in the stomach." Kat rubbed her shoulders in comfort. Sophia still stared at me, straight in my eyes. "Thank you for saving me and my babies."

I shook my head at her. "Don't mention it. How did Marcus handle it when you told him about being knocked up?"

"With the fighting about not being his mistress and how busy we were on the road, I couldn't tell him."

"But you said he knows."

"I convinced Cash to claim it was his." Finally, she pulled her hand from mine. "I thought about just leaving but couldn't. So I told Shani I was pregnant by Cash. She thought all the times I was with Marcus were spent with Cash, so it fit." Her fingers fidgeted with a pizza crust. "She is the one who told Marcus."

"How did he act after she told him?"

"The same. But he hasn't had time to react. I told Shani the night before I was attacked."

Marcus, you dirty, filthy bastard.

25

The Comet rumbled, growling down the neighborhood street. The big motor slowly rocked us back and forth, back and forth, back and forth as we crept by the small ranch home. It sat just off the road in what used to be a good neighborhood. The lawn was about three weeks past needing to be cut. The neighboring houses were close but separated by large run-down yards and overgrown holly bushes. Trees overhung the roof, windows dark and empty.

"I don't think they are home."

I kept looking past Tiff, who was sitting beside me. "Is this the right address?"

Kat answered from the backseat. "Cooper residence, 843 Banty Lane. This is them."

We were on the way to meet Father Mulcahy, Boothe, and the others when we got the call that no one could get in touch with the Coopers. They had not shown up at the Warren and were not responding to the network. Since we were on the way, I offered to go over, check on them, and bring them in. Now I sat outside their perfectly normal, perfectly ordinary, perfectly *dull* suburban house, with dread clenching my guts in both hands.

"How many people in the family?"

Larson spoke up. "Four. Mother, Carol. Father, Ben. Son, Rudy. Two years old. Daughter, Mary. Eight."

"What kind of lycanthrope are they?"

"They call themselves gamefowl."

Game fowl. It took me a second to realize the term meant they were Were-chickens. I kept looking at the house, my eyes searching for something out of place or some sign they were out of town. No mail piled up. Two vehicles in the driveway; a Toyota that had seen many a mile under its wheels and a minivan with a caved-in fender. Empty trash cans were at the head of the driveway. If they were gone, it was recently. Earlier today, last night at the earliest.

Sophia leaned up, putting her chin over the back of the seat. "Does this feel wrong to anybody else?"

It was hard to look at her since she was so close. I kept studying the house. "Is that just a feeling? Or some lycanthropic-heightened-senses kind of feeling?"

She looked at me sideways out of her brown eye. "Just a feeling, but I can't tell why. Maybe we are all just on edge and it is giving us the heebie-jeebies."

I looked back at the house. It sat still and silent, growing darker in the fading sunlight of early evening. Heebie-jeebies was right.

"Take the wheel," I said to Tiff, opening the door and sliding out. She moved over to the driver's side, foot touching the brake as mine left it. Just like we had practiced. She settled in as I quietly shut the door. I had taught her to drive the Comet without adjusting the seat so that she could take the wheel at a moment's notice. Or give it up if I came in a hurry.

I squatted down so that my face was even with hers.

My eyes stayed on the house through the other window as I talked to her.

"Keep the car in gear. If I am not out in fifteen minutes, then drive away and call Father Mulcahy. He will know what to do."

"I could come in and get you." She said it plainly, like it didn't really matter.

I looked at her. Hard. "You will do exactly what I tell you, little girl. That's the deal. Your job is to get everybody in this car to safety if anything goes wrong." She looked away from my stare. My fingers touched her chin, turning her face back to mine. "Don't make me lose focus in there worrying that you aren't going to do your job."

Her pretty mouth drew to a hard line. "I'm on it. You can trust me."

"If I don't come out in fifteen minutes, what are you going to do?"

"Drive away and call Father Mulcahy."

"If someone, anyone, comes toward the car, what are you going to do?"

"Drive away and call your cell phone."

"What are you going to do if you hear a lot of noise from that house?"

"Count to thirty and drive away whether you are out or not."

All the right answers. I smiled. "Good girl. Your training is paying off."

"I have a good teacher." Leaning forward, she gave me a quick kiss, just a brush of her lips against mine. "Be careful in there, it really doesn't feel right."

"I will. Hand me the shotgun."

Her hand reached down to the passenger floorboard, unclipping the shotgun she had used earlier and passing it over to me. It was a Benelli .12 gauge pump action shotgun, matte black with a tactical green laser attached under the barrel. Some people think a laser is not necessary on a shotgun. Bullshit. Shotguns don't spray the entire room with lead, or silver shot in this case, no matter what television shows you. You still have to aim, not as precisely as a pistol, but you *can* miss with a shotgun. I checked the slide to make sure it was loaded and stood up, holding the gun along my leg. Without a second glance I walked around the car and stepped into the driveway.

My back was to the hedge that separated this house from the neighbors. It was a tall, wild holly bush grown thick and tangled with prickly leaves. I moved quickly, all my senses open. I rolled my power out, casting it around me, looking for anything.

Nothing supernatural that I could feel.

My boots clomped on the broken concrete of the driveway. I stepped carefully to be as quiet as possible. Each stride that brought me closer to the house brought me deeper in the bubble of silence that enveloped the house. The air grew heavier with every footfall, pressing down on my shoulders, oppression riding in my shadow.

Stepping carefully over a girl's bicycle, I passed between the minivan and the hedge. Heat radiated off the vehicle, washing across my face. I swung around the front, breathing as evenly as possible, and moved into the shadow of the carport. The temperature dropped with the sun gone from my skin. I stood for a second, allowing my eyes to adjust to the shift in light.

The carport had the normal collection of junk for a family to have—toys, boxes, and a rickety old wooden ladder that leaned haphazardly against the back wall. The screen door cried softly in protest when I opened it. Pulling the shotgun up to the ready, my hand moved carefully out to turn the doorknob. It was cold under my palm. With a turn and a push, the door swung silently inward.

I stood for a moment, senses screaming, waiting for a reaction to the door opening. Nothing happened. No movement, no noise. Pushing the door wide, I stepped over the threshold and into the kitchen.

The kitchen was as immaculate as the yard was un-kempt. Everything was in its place, tucked away and tidy. The linoleum floor gleamed even in the dim light. Water dripped slowly from the faucet, falling into the stainless-steel basin.

Drip.

Drip.

Each drop split the silence of the spotless room.

Drip.

Drip.

I stepped over to the sink to turn the handle and shut off the maddening noise. Inside the sink was a baby's pacifier.

It sat there, innocent and dreadful in its cuteness. Tiny cartoon animals frolicked on its surface. A damp baby blue ribbon hung from the ring, trailing toward the drain.

My blood ran cold.

Turning away, I stepped from the sink, moving into the dining room on the other side. Drawn blinds cut the light in the room making it hard to see. I walked care-fully through, my back to the wall. Carpet muffled my footsteps. A light buzzing sounded distant in my ears. Stopping for a second, I tried to figure out if it was a real sound or left over from my head injury. After a second I couldn't decide, so I kept moving.

I rounded the corner of the doorway into the living room. Like the kitchen it was immaculately tidy, every-thing neat and orderly. Blue couch, loveseat, and re-cliner. All arranged around a flat-screen TV that watched the room like a dead eye. The buzzing was louder in this room—just slightly, but louder nonetheless. Curtains were pulled tight across a bay window, leaving only three squares of waning, early-evening sunlight at the top of the front door to cut the gloom.

There should be toys here. I'd had two kids, and there was always a toy of some kind lying in wait to trip you. There was none in this room. The carpet stretched empty around the furniture, bare and void. The room sat like a hollowed-out corpse; the weight of its barrenness pulled at me like gravity.

Tension hung on the back of my neck as I moved to the hallway leading to the rest of the small house. Four closed doors lined the hall: two on the left, one on the right, and one at the end. It was dark like a cave; the only light was a thin sliver coming from under the door at the end.

It spilled out onto a naked Barbie doll that lay on the carpet. My eyes locked on the smooth plastic limbs that stuck stiffly in the air. Flat, vapid eyes stared at me surrounded by a mass of synthetic yellow hair. I tore my eyes away and began to check the first door on the left.

The buzzing grew louder with each step down the short hallway.

Slowly, I pushed the first door open, my eyes wanting to look at the Barbie one more time. Ignoring the pull, I moved on. Leading with the shotgun, I stepped inside. It was a little girl's room. Butterflies soared across the wall behind the bed in a mural of colors robbed of their vitality by the dim light of the room. The bed was made with a simple ruffled comforter, spread smooth and tucked into the corners. The floor was bare of toys. Tiny shoes lined the wall between the closet and a small child's desk. I stepped back into the hall.

Barbie still lay where she was, ominous plastic eyes still open.

The room across the hall was a bathroom; small and simple in spotless white. It only took a second to clear it.

The urge to step over Barbie and throw the last door open clawed at me.

I pushed it down. It's stupid to leave an unchecked room behind you. Stupid gets you dead in my line of work. I opened the second door on the left, pushing it all the way to the wall. Stepping in, there was almost no space to move. A king-sized waterbed swelled into the room, dominating the center. A South Carolina football blanket blared out on the bed in red and black.

The bedspread was soaking wet.

Carefully, I touched it. My fingers came away wet but clean. Water. Slowly lifting the corner revealed a small puncture through the sheets and into the bladder of the bed. Water had puddled slowly from it to saturate the thick blanket.

It would have taken hours.

I dropped the blanket and moved back to the hallway.

The buzzing was loudest as I stood in front of the last door. Now that I was here, I did not want to open that door. My hand closed on the doorknob. It turned with a soft click. I held it closed, drawing in a deep breath. Trying to stop my heart from pounding in my ribcage while Barbie looked up accusingly from my feet.

With a push, the door swung slowly inward. Light flared along the opening. The buzzing grew with every fraction of an inch the door moved. My stomach clenched as the buzzing grew angry, furious in its wrath.

Flies.

Thousands of flies.

So many flies that my eyes could only see them for a moment. Black and green, crawling and buzzing and darting. Tiny gnat flies, big black houseflies, giant green horseflies. They swarmed out into the hallway, pelting me with their sticky little bodies like hard pebbles, legs skritching, wings tickling. Their angry buzz filled my ears.

I closed my eyes and held my breath as they flew past me, seeking food and freedom. Carrion appetites driving them forward. Once they were past I drew in a breath.

That's when the smell hit me.

The smell of meat gone rancid. Green and moist and gag inducing, cut with the rusty metal scent of dried blood. It crawled its way in, worming through my sinuses. My lip curled involuntarily; my nostrils tried to shut down.

I didn't want to open my eyes, knowing what I would see. My mind wondered if it would be as bad as my family after they were killed. Would it be worse?

I forced my lids apart.

The windows were open in this room, blinds pulled off, letting light stream in. Cartoon vegetables made the wallpaper in the room. Blood, dark and tacky, dried in abstract patterns across them, like some mad painter had come in and flung it on every wall. Thick bits and chunks of gore stuck in random decoration for the leftover flies to crawl across.

Two bodies lay in front of me. They were female, their clothes removed and replaced with a sheet of congealed blood and a blanket of flies. Their arms and legs were pulled apart, sprawling akimbo in death. Neither of them had peaceful expressions on their faces. No, they were both frozen in screams, eyes shut with rigor mortis, mouths drawn wide with the rictus of death. One was average height for a grown woman.

The other was much smaller.

A man without eyelids was propped up against the wall. Bloodstained rope twisted around his body, binding him in a kneeling position, holding him there. He was dead, his throat torn open. The wound yawned apart to reveal the ivory gleam of his spine. He had been forced to watch what had happened in this room before he was killed. Every horrible second, helpless to stop it. Helpless to do anything but watch.

When he tried to not do that, they had torn off his eyelids.

The crib sat across from me. I did not want to look inside of it. Dread hung from my neck like a stone, weighing me down. With a bracing breath, I stepped over stiff-dried carpet and looked.

Inside the crib, nestled in a soft blanket of blue wool, lay a pile of tiny bones. Teeth marks stood in stark relief against their ivory color. A few white feathers tucked in here and there like a flower arrangement. The skull lay on top, cracked open and picked clean. Big eye sockets stared up at me, tiny square baby teeth underneath in a baby's gap-toothed smile.

I flinched. I looked away. My eyes moving up to the wall in front of me. It took a second for me to realize that the pattern of blood there was not abstract. My mind pulled, trying to make sense of it. Slowly it came to me.

Written in blood above a crib full of gnawed baby bones were the words: *Finger lickin' good.* I turned away, chest tight, hot fire burning in my guts.

Someone was going to die for this.

26

The gates to the Warren were iron monstrosities. They loomed into the dusk, soaring twice as tall as I stood. No curlicues, no decoration at all except for a wrought-iron rabbit welded onto each of them. Instead, they were made of thick iron bars the size of my wrists and banded together with straps of iron about twelve inches wide. They looked formidable, designed to keep things out. They swung open with a whisper on well-oiled hinges as Boothe buzzed us through.

I rumbled the Comet slowly across their threshold, nodding to the two men standing beside them with hard, pink eyes. They nodded back just slightly in unison and turned as one back to watching behind us on the other side of the gates. All around were wide fields of uncut hay grass that led all the way up to the high stone walls surrounding the neighborhood. One thin ribbon of asphalt led up to the gates.

The Warren was outside the city, outside suburbia, damn near to the country. It was as isolated as it gets in this part of the state. Which is good for the "fireworks" we would probably have tonight. We should be able to do this without interference from the police.

Following Boothe's directive from earlier, we rolled through the neighborhood. It was full of similar houses, small cluster homes with tiny yards and tinier driveways. They all had a sameness to them. This was exactly the kind of neighborhood I hate. Cookie-cutter houses in a cookie-cutter neighborhood. Give me an honest yard and a house that doesn't look like my neighbors'. And for the record, you can take your Homeowners' Association, turn it sideways, and shove it up your ass. Thank you very much.

This particular neighborhood didn't look too bad, though. Yes, the houses all looked the same and the lawns were tiny, but it didn't have the emotionless feel you get when a neighborhood is new and the HOA is on a power trip. In every yard there was a toy or some evidence of a child's presence lying about. A yellow truck here, a red ball there, and the sidewalks were murals of pastel chalk done in early childhood abstracts.

This was a neighborhood of families. Children probably ran safe in the streets, playing without a care in the world. It looked like a paradise for kids there. We had already passed four playgrounds.

There were no children to be seen.

Not one. Just a few adults on every street walking around, talking on porches, doing yard work. Anything to mask the fact that they were on watch. On guard.

I could feel the tension in the air as we drove by. Every set of eyes watched us pass.

Reaching the back of the neighborhood, we found the community center, a big square brick of a building. The windows were small with large steel shutters. I noticed they were hinged and not just for decoration.

George and Boothe stood talking on the steps leading up to the door. The Were-gorilla's tree trunk legs hung out of basketball shorts. They were pale, slightly bowed, and covered in black wiry hair. His right knee was misshapen, a knot of scar tissue that made his leg twist in. It was the reason he leaned on his cane. Getting shot in the knee with a silver bullet will do that.

Boothe was dressed in black military BDU's. Two plastic semiautomatic pistols hung unobtrusively under his armpits, their matte-black finish blending with his clothes. I assumed they were both Springfield .40 calibers like he had earlier. Both of them stopped talking and looked over as I turned off the car.

My car door swung open just as silently as the gates had. I pushed the seat forward so Sophia and Kat could get out, then walked around the car to the trunk. A twist of my key popped it open. The hot air inside whooshed out with a slight charnel smell from where the Lord of the Forest had laid until Boothe had taken care of the body. The trunk had been washed out, but the smell lingered. Inside lay a collapsed wheelchair, the katana, a box with a biohazard symbol stenciled on it, and a bandolier of grenades.

The grenades may seem like overkill, but after the fight at the motel, all bets were off. I was going to blow some assholes up if need be. I slung the katana over my head, settling it between my shoulder blades, then picked up the bandolier in one hand and the wheelchair in the other.

Kat took the chair from me and unfolded it with a shake and a jerk of her arms. I watched Larson haul himself out of the car and into the seat, adjusting his legs and strapping in. The wheelchair was light. Made of titanium and carbon fiber, it was also tough as hell. Two thin, knobby tires designed for multiple terrains hugged the seat. I saw straps and pockets on the tubes it was composed of, custom-fitted for guns and knives, which Kat was filling as I watched, her hands moving quickly and surely. When she finished, he was loaded for lycanthrope, but if you weren't looking closely, you would miss the weaponry strapped to the chair.

I reached in and flipped open the box. Inside were three sets of dark blue coveralls. I picked them up and handed them to Tiff and Kat. The coveralls were light as feathers, the material slick under my fingers. They took them and started stepping in and zipping up. The coveralls were made of a material called Tyvek. It's actually woven paper and standard issue for making biohazard suits. Slick and almost waterproof, it was also lightweight so the wearer didn't collapse of heat exhaustion. I handed Larson a long-sleeved jacket and blanket made of the same material.

The biohazard suits were necessary because we were fighting lycanthropes. Everybody who was just human had to wear one. Lycanthropy is a communicable disease. In fighting, you get blood and body fluids on yourself. You can't help it, it's just what happens. The suits weren't a perfect solution, but you do what you can. Lycanthropy is hard to catch and it isn't the worst thing to catch depending on how the strain you get reacts with your DNA.

If you survive your first shift, that is.

Lycanthropes who are born don't have a problem. Their shift works into the process of puberty, so their bodies are adapting to changes and growth spurts anyway. Plus, they generally have the help of their family and the gestalt of the animal group they are a member of. People who catch the disease don't have that. If they are an adult and their body is done growing, then sometimes the change can be violent enough to tear them apart.

I am not speaking figuratively here. I mean Grand Guignol-style, blood-on-the-ceiling tear them apart. The shift is a violent and gory thing for a lot of lycanthropes until their bodies adapt to allow the change.

As a secondary precaution, Larson had dosed everyone with an infusion of monkshood and colloidal silver. It wasn't a cure for lycanthropy, but the two distillations can sometimes prevent the disease from taking hold in the blood. It could also kill you if dosed wrong. Larson was very careful in his administration of it.

I didn't need the shot or the suit. Since my Angelic blood transfusion, I am not susceptible to lycanthropy. It's one of the long list of things I can't catch since then.

Tiff used a small knife to cut a slit in her suit by her hip. Reaching in, she pulled out the handle to the Colt so she could reach it. She handed the knife over to Kat so she could do the same for her 9mm. She looked at me, held her hands out to her side, and did a slow pirouette.

"How do I look?"

I gave her the once-over. The thin blue suit wasn't tailored, but it had been designed with a close fit to prevent snagging and tearing. It followed her curves, hiding just enough to be enticing. Studying her, I felt that aching pull from earlier.

I smiled, pushing my southern accent to the thickness of sorghum syrup. "Darlin', like my dad used to say before he took leave of this shitty old world, you could make a gunny sack look like a ball gown."

Her blush danced around her own smile. She gave a curtsey, stood on her tiptoes, and kissed me on the cheek. "Why thank you, kind sir."

Kat rolled her eyes.

Reaching back inside the box, I dug out three pairs of safety glasses and three face masks made of the same material as the coveralls. I handed them all around. Lycanthropy is able to be passed through mucous membranes, so the eyes and mouth needed covering. They hung the masks around their necks, ready to be put on when the fighting started. The goggles hung down by their chest on a tether. I handed out black latex gloves to everyone, a couple of pairs each. They slipped them on. Larson struggled a little even though he probably wore them more than anyone else in the group since he was the doctor for the lycanthrope community.

Tiff reached inside the Comet and grabbed the shotgun. She checked the slide to make sure it was still locked and loaded. Satisfied, she slung it up to her shoulder. I picked up the last set of equipment for Father Mulcahy and closed the trunk.

George and Boothe ambled over to join us as we moved up beside the car. I leaned back against the hood, engine heat leeching through my jeans, warming the muscles of my thighs. The evening breeze blew mist from the fountain, adding a slight chill to it. Tiny droplets of water peppered my arms. The two lycanthropes closed the semicircle around me.

"Nice sword." Boothe tilted his head. "You know how to use that thing?"

"Enough to get the job done."

He nodded, accepting it. "How are you feeling? You dropped like a stone after that healing bit you pulled on us."

I waved his concern away. "I'm fine."

He looked at me over his aviator sunglasses, pink eyes piercing. "I appreciate the mojo, but if you need to hang back, we can handle this."

"I'm. Fine." My knuckles cracked as I squeezed my hands into fists. The noise hung in the air between us.

Boothe slid his glasses back up and nodded sharply. My hands loosened at my side. All right, we could get down to business now.

"So what did I miss? I hear there's a plan of some kind."

Boothe gestured at the people milling around in the playground and picnic area beside the building. They were all doing normal things. Family things like cooking on grills, talking, even swinging on the swing set. Two things were off with the scene. One was that there were still no children. Not one. The second was the tension they all had. Every person looked tight. Wary. Their movements were forced, almost mechanical. They moved with the caution of a battered wife. Holding themselves together, trying to be normal while tensed and waiting for the first hint of violence.

"We've gathered all the shape-shifters in the area here. Our plan is to have Marcus give a speech about peace and goodwill later on to the group. We sent out word among the Were community that everyone will be here for a 'peace rally.'" His fingers made air quotes around the words *peace rally.* "The hope is that Leonidas and his gang want to take out Marcus bad enough that they will bite the bait and come here to our home turf." His fingers moved to the handgun under his arm, fingertips lightly stroking the grip. "Then we can take them out once and for all."

"You do remember that we got our asses handed to us at the motel?"

"We were outnumbered by them and the wolves. Here they'll be the ones outnumbered." Pride glinted in pink eyes. "The rabbits can hold their own."

My eyes did another pass over the crowd. Now I could see about a third of them were all wearing the same black clothes Boothe had on. The same black clothes all the people we had passed on the way in had on. My eyes found pistols tucked into waistbands, hidden under shirttails in unobtrusive holsters. All of the people in black uniforms had a device hooked on their ear that I assumed was some sort of wireless communication equipment.

I cracked an eye toward Boothe. "Are your people as good as you are?" I had seen him shoot at the motel. He was good man to have at my back.

He smiled. "No, of course not. But they have been trained to work together and handle their firearms." His voice took on an edge. "These predator assholes think of rabbits as nothing but prey. That we are weak, lacking teeth to bite and claws to rend. Predators think of us as only able to run, something exciting to chase and take." He shook his head sadly. "I have seen my people suffer some bad shit at the hands of predators just like these jackasses. That's why when I got old enough I took up martial arts and firearm training. I came back home and taught my herd what I knew so they wouldn't be helpless anymore." Fierce pride cracked his mouth into a grin, teeth shining white. "The rabbits can hold their own."

I nodded. Okay, so this time might be different. Larson had said we didn't have many predators in the area left to join up with Leonidas and his bunch. The Werewolves had been the biggest group and the most violent. The wolves had formed their pack around a neo-Nazi skinhead alpha named Krueger, so when Leonidas had come along and dropped Krueger, they had fallen right in line with him. That is why the Werewolves had supported the Brotherhood at the motel.

Even though we'd had to cut and run after the last fight, I knew we had taken a toll. There would be no Werewolves to help this time. If the rabbits knew how to use their guns, then we should be okay. Maybe this harebrained plan would work.

Sorry, I couldn't resist.

Sophia spoke up softly, "Isn't using Marcus for bait dangerous to him?"

"Fuck Marcus." Boothe and I spoke at the same time. I didn't say it harshly, just firmly. He had a more stringent tone to his words, voice cutting out of his lips. We shared a moment of complete understanding. I didn't know why he didn't like Marcus and he didn't know why I didn't like Marcus, but we were on the same page about the subject. And that reminded me.

"Speaking of Marcus, where is he? I need to talk to him about something."

George's eyes were wide in their deep-set sockets. "Everything okay? You look a little mad."

I could feel that. The skin was tight across the back of my scalp and my teeth were just barely on edge. It had been a long day and night of bloodshed, passing out, and death. The only bright spot had been being with Tiff, but because of a bunch of shape-shifting assholes, I couldn't even sit back and enjoy that.

Now that I knew Marcus was aware of Sophia's pregnancy, I had a growing feeling that he was in this up to his eyeballs and not the innocent victim I was first led to believe. Was I a little mad?

Nope.

I was pissed. I had a full-bore hate on, and I was spoiling for a fight.

Boothe's head jerked toward the building. "He's in there holed up in the game room with that mate of his until showtime. But I don't think either one of them will be happy to see you."

"You think they are unhappy now, wait until after I am done." I turned to Kat and Larson. "Stay here with them and keep Sophia away from Marcus. Tiff's with me."

"No problem," Kat said.

I was already walking away, Tiff at my back, so I spoke over my shoulder to Sophia. "Leonidas is after you, trying to kill your babies. I think Marcus is the one who told him about it." She said something after me, but I was already at the doors of the building and I didn't hear what it was.

The doors were heavy, solid wood with thick brass overlays that were decorative but would serve the function of reinforcement. If the lock on the doors was any indication, the place could be shuttered down like a fortress.

Inside the door lay a giant shaggy wolf. His fur was silver, shot through with coarse hairs of black. He jumped to his feet as I stepped inside. A wide triangle of a head came above my waist and looked up at me. Black gums split in a wolf grin to reveal yellowed teeth. Age had dulled them, but they were still sharp enough to crack bone. Thick pink tongue lolled out as he panted, wolf breath moist and hot on my arm.

Ragnar.

"Still feeling pretty good I see, old man."

The wolf bobbed his head up and down, sat back on his haunches, and immediately began to scratch behind his ear with a back leg.

Tiff and I had stepped into a large, square room. All the furniture had been pushed to the edges, leaving a wide expanse of floor space. Every inch of it had a child on it. Easily 300 little people packed in the space. Some were sitting, some were laying, all of them faced forward and were enraptured by Charlotte. She stood on a low stage in front of them telling a story.

I had no idea what the story was about, but it didn't matter. She was wearing a bright yellow sundress that swirled and flared with her animated movements, captivating the eye as it played against her dark mocha complexion. She gave a little wave to us, never breaking stride with her story. Father Mulcahy got up from the stool he was on at the side of the stage and began making his way to us.

The priest was dressed in his Roman collar shirt, white tab gleaming under a salt-and-pepper stubbled chin. His pants were black military-issue BDU's. Combat boots on his feet didn't make enough noise to disrupt Charlotte's story for the kids, although some of them did turn around and watch him walk over. He hugged Tiff, pulling her tight, mussing her hair with affection. Next his hand fell on my shoulder. It was warm and hard with calluses. The firm touch was masculine and reassuring, like a father's would be. Me and the priest have a long history and a lot went unsaid in that hand on my arm.

He motioned to the left where a hallway branched off the back of the room. We both followed him there to a table. It was odd to see him without a Kool cigarette hanging from his lip. He didn't smoke in Mass or around children, but any other moment he is awake, Father Mulcahy has a Kool in his mouth. A Kool cigarette and a cup of black coffee.

He kept his voice low when he spoke. It was good to hear his light brogue again. "It's a fine thing to see you up hale and hearty, son."

My arm went around Tiff's shoulders. She leaned into it. "It's good to be back on my feet." I nodded toward Tiff. "This one was worried about me."

"Hey!" Her hand slapped my chest lightly. "I have never seen you that hurt before."

Father Mulcahy's face grew somber and still. He had seen me hurt far worse than that over the years. He'd been my medic in the field more than once. Patching me up and praying me back to healing with hands covered in my blood. "It has been a quiet six months." Hard, appraising eyes scanned me again. "I thank the Lord that your Angel blood fixes you up quickly."

Yep, die and get a blood transfusion from an Angel of the Lord that resurrects you and you get accelerated healing. It doesn't lessen the pain at all, and it isn't instantaneous by any means, but my head injury was completely gone after giving my body some hours to heal.

"What the hell is that?" I pointed.

On the table lay what looked like a rifle, kind of. It had a giant scope, a rifle barrel in shiny stainless steel, and a handled trigger mount, but after that the resemblance to a rifle ended. Where the stock would be was a bulbous tank of metal that was about the same size as a two-liter bottle. Off it was a gauge of some kind and a series of tiny metal mesh hoses that ran to various points on the rifle. Jutting from the side was a curved clip made of clear Plexiglas that held a row of wicked-looking darts almost the length of my hand.

I've got really big hands.

Father Mulcahy picked it up, cradling it in his arm. "This, my son, is the Airsnipe Armageddon T-38. I ordered it last year when we were dealing with that troll problem downtown, but it didn't get here in time."

We had been hired by a building owner in Atlanta who had a pack of trolls squatting in one of his empty warehouses. He wanted to put it up for sale, but it's a hard sell when all your potential buyers who come to look over the property wind up with their bones broken by what are essentially eight-foot-tall garden gnomes with bad hygiene and an attitude problem.

It took a bit of work, including some "negotiating" with a sledgehammer, but we got them relocated to the Okefenokee swamp in south Georgia. Now they live happy working for Wildlife Management, listening to country music, and brewing the best moonshine I have ever tasted.

Father Mulcahy's gruff voice brought me back. "It was designed originally to down elephants from long distances for tagging. This one is Orion Outfitters' modified version. It should work fine for our current critter control problem."

Father Mulcahy is a real Catholic priest. Genuine, one hundred percent man of the cloth with all that goes along with that. He held his priesthood dear. It was a part of him that couldn't be set aside. He was a Catholic priest down to his DNA.

But somewhere in his past, before he put on those black robes and Roman collar, he had led a different life. Somewhere on the way he had learned how to knife fight like a convict. He had also learned the skills of a sniper. I have seen the man shoot a penny glued to a tree from 500 yards.

I don't know the details of where he learned that skill, but it wasn't hunting. There was blood on his hands. Righteous blood spilled in service to his country, but blood nonetheless. I didn't know any details, but I did know it is one of the reasons he became a priest to begin with.

He has helped me take out countless monsters, and I knew with no uncertainty that he would shoot to kill if it would save someone's life, especially one of the children who filled the room we were in. But if he could drop a lycanthrope without killing it, he would. They were human and he would do everything he could not to take their life.

Myself? I wasn't willing to work quite that hard.

Not after all that had happened with Leonidas and his crew. Not with what they did to Sophia. Not after the motel last night. Not after the Coopers' house and the things that had been done to them. No way in hell.

I guess that's why I would make a really shitty priest. "Where's Marcus?"

The priest jerked a thumb over his shoulder, pointing down the hallway. "Last door on the left."

I handed the bandolier of grenades to Tiff. "Stay here and keep people out of the back room. I need to have a talk with Marcus. Alone."

She nodded. Standing on her tiptoes, she kissed me on the mouth. It was a warm kiss made sweeter by how quick it was. The priest looked at us, scar tissue masquerading as an eyebrow cocked up in askance. I ignored it. He could ask Tiff while I was gone if he really wanted to know. If I knew the Padre, I wouldn't get halfway down the short hallway before the first question was out of his mouth.

Turning away, I began to settle back into the task at hand. As I walked down the hall, my hands moved quickly around my body, checking my weapons. The fingers of both hands touched the .45's, one under each arm. My right hand moved down and across my body to my waist. My palm brushed Bessie's handle, pushing slightly forward to ease my ability to drag her from the holster slung low on my hip. I reached up to settle the katana between my shoulder blades.

Each step down the hallway carried me closer to the Were-lions and closer to my center. My being settled around the molten core of anger I carried in my chest. Inside, I huddled around the heat of it like a homeless man in winter. Rage sparked through me, roiling and building like thunderclouds.

Both Marcus and Leonidas wanted Sophia and her babies. Again, when it comes to supernatural shit, there are never any coincidences. The only way Leonidas could even know that Sophia was pregnant with Marcus's babies would be if Marcus told him. I had no idea what kind of game they were running, but I damn sure was going to find out. Too much blood had been shed by people I loved to let it go.

The last door on the left was painted dark green and was made of steel. I stood outside of it for a moment, gathering myself. I could hear voices in a heated conversation but could not tell who was talking or what they were saying. The thrum of lycanthropic anger throbbed through the door itself. It pulsed and crackled along the surface, popping the air in front of me, spitting at me like bacon grease. Marcus was on the other side, mad as hell.

Fine by me. I could walk that road with him.

My hand closed on the knob, tensing to turn.

I was in an ugly mood and betting this was going to get real nasty, real quick.

I looked forward to it.

27

Marcus and Shani stopped talking as I strode into the room slamming the door behind me. They had been arguing, energy spiking off them, snarls still pasted across both their model faces. Marcus swung his finger at me as I walked across the room at them. His throat was knotted in anger, spittle flying from his mouth as he growled at me.

"Get away from us, Deacon. I don't want to see you after the shit you pulled last night."

I didn't answer, just kept walking across the room until his finger hit the center of my chest. My left hand clamped down, squeezing and twisting. The wet, brittle snap of broken bone shot out of my grip and Marcus's knees gave out, buckling him toward the floor. Right fist knotted in anger, I drew back, ready to smash him in the mouth.

Hot lycanthropy washed over me from the right and a flash of golden fur in a blue dress caught my eye. Shani launched herself at me, claws out ready to rip and rend. Letting go of Marcus's hand, I twisted, dodging the razor tips of her fingers. They slashed the air under my chin, missing my throat by mere centimeters. My arms closed around her waist as she went by.

Muscles in my back pulled against her momentum,

the staples on my left side pinching as they pulled tight. I swung her up to my chest. She kicked and flailed the air. With a heave, I lifted, spun her body around, and slammed her back down. The pool table she had jumped from cracked as I tried to drive her through it with my weight. The breath shoved from her lungs washed over me with a rank, carrion scent that watered my eyes.

"Stay down!" I yelled at her. She lay in a heap, heaving breath in and out. She wasn't truly injured. It takes more than that to hurt a lycanthrope. But if you can't breathe, you can't fight. I left her there while I spun to find where Marcus had gone.

My face was met with a hard punch. The taste of blood exploded into my mouth, hot and metallic. It would have broken my jaw if I hadn't been turning away already.

My feet went out and I fell to the floor. Sharp pain blossomed as my shoulder took my weight, slamming into the cold tile. Rolling with it, I scrambled back up to my feet. The room pulsed, waving in and out just once in my vision. I shook my head to clear it.

Marcus charged across the room, arms wide to grab me in a bear hug. Leaning back, I braced on a video game. I threw my foot up as he closed in. He smacked into my foot, hard leather boot heel driving in just below his collarbone. The jolt of it slid me and the game back almost a foot.

His dress shoes slipped, skidding out from under him. He fell flat on the ground. The hollow thunk of a ripe cantaloupe sounded as his skull bounced off the floor. My hands knotted around the expensive cloth of his suit. My head was full of what he had done to Sophia. Using his influence as a predator to get her to sleep with him, knocking her up, setting her up to be caught by Leonidas and beaten. I hauled him to his feet.

BAM! My fist smashed into his eye socket. Skin split under the blow. Thin red blood welled up, spilling out immediately.

"Tell me . . ."

BAM! My fist drove his nose crooked, one nostril flattening closed, the other shooting blood and snot out of it.

". . . what's going on . . ."

SMACK! His bottom lip broke apart, swelling instantly, pushing blood out of it to run and pool in the cleft of his chin.

". . . with you and your brother."

His hands came up weakly, waving away any more violence from my fist. His eye had swollen shut, turning purple as I watched. Nose too broken to breathe out of, blood bubbled into foam under the one open nostril he had. He panted through lips swollen to the point of throbbing, each pulse trickling more blood from the split. His voice drug out of him, oatmeal thick, chunky from the broken nose. "Stop. Just. Stop. Hitting me."

He hung limp in my grip, knees buckled, head lolling back. "He hates me. He hates that I am a pacifist. He hates that I try to change the way things are." It was a struggle for him to swallow. "He just hates me. Always has. Since we were litter cubs."

I shook him, ivory teeth rattling in his head. Pulling him up to me, I snarled in his face. "What kind of game is going on with you two?" I shook him again. "Why did you tell him about Sophia's pregnancy and send him to kill her babies?"

His one unswollen eye flashed wide, white around the light caramel iris. "Sophia's pregnant?"

"You didn't know?"

He shook his head. Blood had run into his tiny dreads, soaking into them like a sponge.

My skin went cold. I dropped him to the floor with a

thud. Whipping my head up, I scanned the room wildly, one of the .45's in my hand tracking, seeking a target, the laser sight dancing over an empty room. The door was slowly drifting closed again.

Shani was gone.

That bitch. That damned bitch had set me up. Set Sophia up anyway; me and mine just got caught in the crossfire. Stepping over Marcus, I stalked toward the door.

When I caught her I was going to make a rug out of her traitorous ass.

28

"Did Shani go by here?" Father Mulcahy looked at the gun in my hand and nodded. "Is she still in the building?"

"No, she went right out."

Shit. There was no way to catch her in a chase, not by myself. I'm built for power, not speed. Holding my free hand out, Tiff put the bandolier of grenades in it. "Go find Boothe. Tell him to put word out to every one of his people that Shani is to be stopped, even if she has to be shot. She's dangerous, so they don't need to take chances; but if she gets out of the Warren, then she will spoil the trap." She nodded. "And tell him to get in here ASAP so we can plan our next move."

Tiff nodded, spun on her heel, and moved quickly out the door. I watched her stride across the room. One leg in front of the other, with a nice up-and-down rhythm that was distracting to say the least. The old Werewolf got up and followed her out, slipping through the door as it shut.

"You seem a bit distracted."

I turned to see Charlotte stepping up to join us. A man and a woman had taken her place onstage with puppets over their arms. I shrugged. "It happens."

The door swung open again. Boothe came in speaking low into a walkie-talkie, head cocked to the side. He let go of the button as he came to a stop in front of us. The rubber soles of his boots gave a little squeak as he drew up short. "What the hell is going on? I just gave orders to shoot to kill if Shani resisted being taken in and I am not sure why."

Charlotte cleared her throat, lifting her chin to indicate the room behind me. I turned to find dozens of wide eyes staring up at us. The two adults were trying to get the kids' attention, but they were having no luck at all. "Maybe we should take this conversation somewhere else."

She was right. We were about to discuss killing someone. Even though all these kids were lycanthropes, and while some of them would know bloodshed on a level equal to a third world country when they grew up, they were still kids. The oldest one I could spot looked to be about twelve. If we could keep them from this, then it was our responsibility to do so.

"Follow me," I said, and began walking back down the hall to the last room on the left.

Marcus flinched as the door swung open. He was sitting on the pool table gingerly touching his broken nose. Blood was drying on his face, becoming darker. His fancy linen shirt, once a clean butter crème, was now tie-dyed with spatters and blotches of blood drying to a dark burgundy. His eye was still swollen shut, although not as much as before, and the purple bruise was fading into a sickly greenish color. His lycanthrope healing was hard at work.

"Where is Sophia? I need to talk to her." His voice was still chunky through the broken nose.

"No, Simba, you need to shut the hell up or I will kick your ass again." I walked past him and went to lean on a video game as everybody else came into the room. It was a fighting game of some kind, cartoon kung fu guys battling across the screen. "Everybody here will have questions for you. Answer them, but other than that, keep a button on your cock holster."

Anger swept the Were-lion's face like a grass fire, flashing hot and burning out quickly. I could feel the contempt on my face, staring at him until he dropped his eyes again.

The others all stood in a semicircle around us. Charlotte took a step toward Marcus and was stopped by Father Mulcahy's hand. The priest lit up another cigarette, drawing the flame into the end and smoke into his lungs. With a sharp exhale, a stream of gray-white shot from the corner of his lips. He spoke around the cancer stick.

"So what is going on, son?"

"Shani is a traitor. She's the one who called Leo and his gang in to kill Sophia's babies."

Charlotte held up her hand. "Wait. I thought Leonidas was trying to kill Marcus, and when did Sophia become pregnant?"

"Apparently Leo just wants to kick Marcus's ass, which having just done so, I can highly recommend." I looked over at Marcus, waiting for him to take offense, but he just sat there, still touching his nose gingerly. "The reason Leo and his merry men have come to town is because Shani called them and wants them to terminate Sophia's pregnancy."

"Why would she do that?"

"Marcus is the father." I waited for their reactions. Charlotte looked as shocked as I knew she would. As a lycanthrope, she knew that breeding between species was impossible. Boothe's face got harder as the muscles in his jaw clenched. The priest took another drag on his cigarette. I kept talking. "Sophia told Shani she was pregnant by Marcus's bodyguard Cash, but truth is it was Marcus who knocked her up."

Marcus looked up, his hand falling away from his face. Arrogance swept back into his battered features. "It can't be mine. I am not a dog."

"What you are is an asshole who takes advantage of young girls. Sophia has never been with anyone else, so that makes you the only suspect." I stepped up and uncrossed my arms. My voice was low when I spoke, coming up from that dangerous place inside me. "And I know about the end, where she tried to stop sleeping with you and you used your predator powers to 'persuade' her." I leaned in close, letting my size loom over him. "We will be visiting that situation again. There will be a reckoning for that. Mark my words."

He turned away, not looking at my eyes. Good. One wrong word from him and the desire I had to break his neck would explode. I stepped back, shaking out my hands from where they had been clenched tight. I caught Charlotte from the corner of my eye and looked at her. Her eyes were pinned on Marcus, face harder than flint. Marcus looked at her and reached out a hand.

"Charlotte, please . . ."

"Is it true, Marcus?"

"It's not like you think."

"Is. It. True?"

His hands went up toward her, supplicating. "Let me explain . . ."

Charlotte moved toward him. Between one footstep and the next her humanity washed away, leaving her spider-lady form. Long spider legs loomed over her, waving back and forth toward him. Eight unblinking, red eyes pinned Marcus in their gaze. Her voice took on the strange metallic sound as it passed through her Were-spider larynx. "Did you force that girl to sleep with you after she said no?"

Marcus backed up a step. His head dropped. "Yes."

Charlotte's right hand was a streak as it flashed across Marcus's face. His cheek slashed open. Each finger of her hand was a needle-thin claw. Marcus's blood dripped from each of them, falling to the floor. She turned away, dismissing him. Her humanity swept back in before she completed her turn. She stepped back to us, wiping her hand on her sundress.

Boothe nodded in appreciation. Father Mulcahy placed a comforting hand on her arm. I gave her a big thumbs-up and a wide grin.

"Back to the pressing matter at hand. What do we do if Shani is gone and warns Leonidas of our plan?" Boothe asked.

"Then he won't come and we posse up and go after them. Until we know they've been tipped off, we have to stay ready. Lure them in and take them down. If we have to go on the hunt, it all gets more difficult." My gaze met his. "Leonidas and his followers are psychotic and they have to be put down. If we have to, we will follow them to the ends of the earth."

Boothe's radio squawked and he hit a tiny button on the earpiece he had on. He listened for a second, head down, body turned slightly away. After a moment, he looked up. "I don't think that will be necessary."

The words were barely out of his mouth when an explosion rocked the building we were in.

29

People were pushing and shoving, trying to get inside the building and away from the explosion. They were also trying to get to the children, parents willing to push anyone aside to make sure their child was okay. Bodies crammed close, arms flailing, legs pushing. They pressed against us, a river of lycanthropes to swim against.

I shouldered my way through, knocking people aside as I strode forward. Boothe was a few feet away, his head and shoulders above the crowd. He talked on his radio as he moved people aside. Charlotte had shed her human form for the hybrid one. She was swinging through the doorway after crawling up the wall and over the top of the door frame. Father Mulcahy moved in my wake, using Shaolin skills to sidestep around the people who closed the gap behind me.

A thin young man stumbled in front of me, falling to his knees, threatening to be swept under the tide of people behind him. My hand clamped around his arm, it was like a stick in my hand, and hauled him to his feet. He gave me a grateful look before I shoved him on past me. A few more long strides and we broke through, stepping outside the doors and onto the stone patio out front.

To the left, a house was in flames, thick black smoke billowing out of the hole that had been blasted into the side of it.

To the right, the playground and picnic area had thinned out. All that were left were men and women dressed like Boothe in dark clothing. Every one of them had a weapon out and had taken cover behind different apparatuses. Some crouched behind grills, some behind playground equipment. All their guns were pointed in the same direction.

Leonidas stood on the roof of a house on the other side of the playground, holding the still-smoking tube of a rocket launcher. His voice was heavy, rolling out of his throat in a roar, vocal cords stuck between human and lion.

"You thought you could make a stand against the Brotherhood of Marrow and Bone? *This* is what happens when you try."

Smoke began to billow up from around the Warren as houses caught fire around the perimeter. Smog began to fill the air with a chemical smell like burnt diesel fuel. I knew that smell. It was the smell of napalm.

When the hell did it become fair for lycanthropes to use rocket launchers and napalm?

Boothe began yelling orders and the Were-rabbits began scrambling. I looked over and Boothe had *changed*. He was even taller, black shirt pulled tight against bulges of muscle. His skull was now oval, and his ears had moved up the side of his head, lengthening and morphing. Short silver hair covered his body, and his teeth had become two-inch-long enameled blades surrounded by whiskers. His legs now jointed in two different places and bulged, splitting his pants up the side seams. His eyes were large, round, and blood red as they rolled around, surveying the scene.

A seven-foot-tall Were-rabbit may sound like a joke, but it was a scary sight.

Other Were-rabbits were changing as they ran, muscles thickening, legs stretching. Their steps became strides and their strides turned into leaps as they ran like quicksilver to try and contain the fires. Soon the only ones left in the playground with me were Boothe, Charlotte, Father Mulcahy, Ragnar, and Marcus.

The priest, the rabbit, and I crouched behind the Comet. Charlotte was on the wall of the building, using the angle of the corner to cover herself. Ragnar lay at the base of the fountain, droplets of water glistening on coarse wolf fur. Marcus stayed in the doorway, out of sight of Leonidas.

Leonidas tossed the spent rocket launcher tube over his shoulder, letting it spin away into the night. He crouched on the peak of the roof. The moonlight and the firelight made him look like the feral beast he was. His dreads had grown out into a mane with his lion-man form and cast his face in shadows; only the glint of his yellow eyes and the gleam of his white teeth shone out. I stretched my arm across the roof of the Comet, black metal still warm under my skin, and pointed one of the Colts at him. The green laser cut across the distance and danced in the center of his silhouette.

He looked down, spotting the dot of death. A thickly muscled arm reached back, dipping below the roofline and out of sight. With effort he dragged someone up, pulling them around in front of himself like a shield. It was a woman, hands behind her back, probably zip-tied like her legs and ankles were. A gag cut across her mouth, keeping her quiet even as Leonidas held her up in one hand by her thick, blond ponytail.

Kat.

Fuck.

I kept the gun pointed but took my finger off the trigger. They were well over a hundred feet away. There was no way in hell I could make that shot around Kat. I looked over at Father Mulcahy. He was standing, tranquilizer rifle pointed at Leonidas. He was stone-still, cheek pressed against the stock, eye squinting into the scope. "I have no shot." Speaking didn't change his position one iota.

I yelled out across the playground. "What the hell are you doing? Let her go and I'll let you walk away." I was lying. Leonidas was dead, he just didn't have the sense to lie down, but it was worth a shot.

"If I let her go from up here she will break her pretty little neck." He stood up, dragging Kat with him. Her eyes were wide with pain, but she didn't struggle. "But if you insist." His arm flexed to toss her off the roof like he had the rocket launcher.

"Do it and you are dead right here!" I fired a shot into the roof at his feet, the bullet kicking up chunks of shingle in a spray of black bits. I put the green laser back on him. "She is the only thing keeping you alive right now."

The lion-man pulled her closer to himself. His free hand came around her body. Black talons began to lightly trace swirls and patterns across Kat's chest, caressing around her breast and trailing down her stomach.

"I would not throw away a fine morsel like this. Bring me the rhinoceros." The golden furred hand flexed, ripping open the jumpsuit she wore. Black talons sank slightly into Kat's skin, drawing her up in an attempt to escape the sudden sharp pain. "I am still holding a grudge from the last time we fought."

I glanced at Boothe, the earpiece and microphone still clung to his ear, even with the drastic shape change. I hoped Leonidas couldn't hear when I spoke to Boothe. "Get on the wire and tell George and Lucy to come up from behind us and to stay hidden until they get here. That feline sonuvabitch has something up his sleeve." He nodded and turned away to use the microphone.

I stood up and walked around the end of the car. The Colt hung loose in my hand, ready to fire, but pointing at the ground as I took slow steps toward the building Leonidas stood on.

"Are you sure you don't want to come down and finish what we started? I was kicking your ass pretty good last time."

Thick dreads shook as he threw back his head and laughed, the sound rolling across the playground. "Oh, I plan to finish with you, Deacon Chalk, but I have something special for your rhino friend." His face drew back into a snarl and he shook Kat. She grunted in pain around clenched teeth. "And you stop right there or we will see if your friend can sprout wings and fly."

I stopped. Everything in me screamed to open fire and blast him off that roof. I could feel it like the clothing against my skin, pressing against me, smothering me. So I stood and watched, waiting for a slip up on his part.

The seconds stretched into a minute.

The minute stretched into five.

Leonidas crouched, holding my friend hostage, waiting with the endless patience of a predator hunting. I stood listening to the far-off shouts of Boothe's people trying to stop the fires from consuming the close-knit houses. I breathed in the air that was tinged with oily smoke. My hand opened and closed on the grip of my gun. I shuffled and I fidgeted.

I am not a patient man.

Finally, George and Lucy stepped out from behind the building and began walking up toward the Comet. George was in his gorilla form, still wearing the rags of his white basketball shirt. It was smudged black with soot. Lucy was dressed in a pair of short shorts and a T-shirt with cartoon animals that made her look even younger than she was.

The Were-lion stood up again, dragging Kat back up by her thick hair. She tried to be tough, but a squeal of pain escaped from behind her gag.

"Glad you could make it," Leonidas called out. "Now the fun can really begin."

Then he threw Kat off the roof.

30

I wasn't going to make it.

There was no way I would be able to catch Kat before she hit the ground. Leonidas had thrown her up in an arc, her bound body twisting, rising and rising high in the air. High enough to break her when she hit the ground.

Probably to kill her when she hit the ground.

I pushed off, muscles churning, trying to reach her. My feet drove into the ground, moving me forward. I pushed, a scream tearing out of me. She fell, speed increasing as the ground rushed up toward her.

I wasn't going to make it.

A sharp blow hit me in the shoulder, twisting me around and taking my footing away. I stumbled, the ground hard on my knee, dust billowing up into my face making me blink as I swung my gun around toward whatever had struck me.

Boothe was a silver streak, rabbit legs churning, fur-covered arms outstretched. He leaped low to the ground, diving into Kat's falling form a split second before she struck the ground. His body wrapped around her, insulating her from the impact. He rolled to a stop, limbs flopping out onto the ground, and lay limp with Kat on his heaving chest. His arm came up holding something. His fingers moved and a wicked-looking blade sprung out. He used it to cut Kat's hands free.

Someone began to clap behind me.

I spun around on my knee, gun pointed, laser hot, searching for a target. I found a small, unassuming man standing there. He was dressed like the Brotherhood, all-black fatigues. Hair buzzed so close to his scalp I couldn't tell what color it was; small eyes sunk on either side of a blade-thin nose. He looked like nothing as he clapped sarcastically. The laser dot danced on his face, shimmying around. Beady eyes squinted when it would cross them. I had not seen him before, so I shoved my power out to feel what flavor of lycanthrope he was.

My stomach muscles cramped as I pushed power across the space between us, sweat forming between my shoulder blades and pooling uncomfortably above the press of the katana where it rode. My eyes slit as my power rolled up onto him, washing across him, seeking, looking, tasting. Reaching for some clue as to what I was about to have to deal with.

And came up empty.

Nothing, nada, zilch, zip. The man before me was not a lycanthrope. He was a big metaphysical empty spot reading completely human.

So why was he with Leonidas's crew, and why did he stand there with no weapons?

I kept my gun trained on him. "What are you? Human?"

He chuckled, slowly shaking his head. "No, I haven't been human for a long time. The lab coats saw to that."

"Whatever you are, this is your one shot at a walka-way. I have bigger beasts to catch tonight."

His chuckle became a guffaw—a belly laugh that

shook his entire body. He slapped his knee and wiped tears from his eyes. "Oh, man, you have no idea how wrong you are."

I had a bad feeling about this. I stood up, stepping into a shooter's pose, both hands on the Colt to steady my shot. The laser dot quit dancing and centered on his forehead. "What the fuck does that mean?"

The man didn't answer. His face turned serious, brow creased, lips pushed together in concentration. The skin on his neck began to mottle, spots of red blossoming angry and bright. Thick, oily drops of sweat squeezed out of his brow, breaking and running down cheeks to drip from his jawline. A tic began to pulse under his eye and a tremor ran through him.

His twitched once, then again, and then jerked and seized. Convulsions twisted him into a contorted pose. Ropes of muscle pulled into stark relief and began to pulsate and swell. A growl tore from his throat as his body began to change and grow. Faster than the eye could keep up with, his skin began to split and reknit as bones thickened and lengthened, muscle bunched and swelled and split to make new groups of muscle. Scale began to ripple from his skin, red and angry, interlocking into rows with audible clicks and clacks. His head became a dull square of bony ridge, deep-set eyes spreading around a massive reptilian snout. The bottom jaw unhinged, expanding and shifting into a new formation as teeth sprouted into six-inch daggers. A long red tail swept the dirt behind him as the creature rose to stand on legs the size of tree trunks. Two much smaller forelegs clawed empty space, ridiculous against a wide, red scaled chest. That big square head shook, thick spittle arcing into the air from those giant deadly teeth. A roar split the night, so loud that it made vibrations you could see like heat waves. My mind struggled to believe what I was seeing.

A blood-red Tyrannosaurus rex stood twenty feet away from me.

You have got to be fucking kidding me.

31

Thunder rolled out of my hands, the Colts spitting bullets as fast as I could tap the triggers. I didn't aim, I didn't have to, my target was damn near thirty feet tall and big as a house. Sixteen .45 caliber bullets shot out and struck the T. rex across light pink belly scales and its left thigh. The bullets bounced off, ricocheting away into the night. The dinosaur roared in annoyance, swinging his big square head toward me. Yellow, baleful eyes glared at me under a ridge of scaly bone.

Like magic, six or seven darts from Father Mulcahy's gun whipped over my head and struck the thick slab of neck under the jawline. One or two of the darts bounced off harmlessly, but most of them stuck, pumping their anesthetic liquid centers into the creature. He reared up, tiny forelegs flailing, trying in vain to reach the darts. That massive head swung wildly, red skin on the neck flexing and bunching, tossing the darts out. They bounced and rolled down its body to lay on the ground at its feet.

I shoved the Colts into their holsters under my arms. A shrug tossed the bandolier of grenades off my shoulder. It slid down my arm. My fingers clamped down on one of the grenades hanging from the bandolier in my left hand. A swift tug and it was free and heavy in my hand. I saw from the corner of my eye Boothe firing his gun at the dinosaur. It worked about as well as when I did it. Kat was running back to the Comet with the others.

The metal ring made my teeth hurt as they clenched on it. The metal tasted dusty, cheap steel causing my wisdom teeth to ache. A swift yank pulled it free from the grenade with a ping. The paddle under my fingers snapped against my grip as the spring inside was released. Reaching back, I tossed the grenade underhand; it spun toward the T. rex like a deadly, shrapnel-producing softball and bounced off the ground between the two black taloned feet.

Pushing off, I spun and began to run, my feet driving into the ground, trying to get enough distance between me and the blast radius. The sound of the explosion hit me at the same time as the concussive wave that shoved me along. I didn't lose my footing and I didn't feel the biting sting of shrapnel. Hopefully it wasn't just adrenaline masking away the pain. I hit the hood of the Comet in a jumping slide, my body slithering over the warm black paint job and dumping out on the other side. I felt a wet tear as a few of my staples pulled free.

Looking back over the playground, I saw that the T. rex was staggering. Blood ran from its abdomen and legs. It was black against the boiling red scales that covered the devil dinosaur. It stumbled back, crashing into the garage that Leonidas had stood on, caving the wall in, siding peeling back like a banana. The beast roared again, shaking the night. The hole in its belly reknit itself, the edges pulling closed and sealing like plastic melting together. Blood still covered its scales but no longer ran.

Boothe shouted at me, "Do we have a plan for this?"

"Oh yeah, of course, it's the 'Find a Way to Kill the

Fucking T. rex' plan." I pulled Bessie out of her holster while I looked around at our situation.

Boothe, Kat, and the priest were on my left keeping their heads down behind the car. Boothe was still in Were-rabbit form; Father Mulcahy had his back to the dinosaur on the playground, watching out behind us. George, Lucy, and Charlotte crouched to my right. George was still a go-rilla, and Charlotte still in her spider-lady form, red eyes watching me unblinking. Ragnar stood a few feet away, silver-shot fur standing down his spine, hackles raised. A low growl rumbled in his chest.

Marcus hugged the doorway of the recreation center looking shell-shocked. I hated him in that minute. All of this came pretty squarely down on his shoulders and there he stood. Worthless.

I tore my eyes away and looked out over the play-ground. The T. rex was getting to his feet. Slowly, yes, but still rallying to attack. It would take him seconds to get to us from where he was. Three or four T. rex strides and we would be dinosnacks. Nothing stood between us but a few charcoal grills and a few picnic tables. To the right was the playground. Tall, elaborate monkey bars and rope courses built for kids. Arm-thick cables strung between cut-down telephone poles and swing sets made of pipe set in concrete.

An idea began to form in my head.

An insane idea.

I turned to Boothe and Father Mulcahy. "You two go get the kids out of that building and take them to safety."

Boothe waved his hand, shooing away the idea. "They are already safe and in the Burrows."

"What the hell are the Burrows?"

"Our neighborhood is over a network of tunnels. Every building, every home connected by underground tunnels that access from the basements. They dump out into the forest as a getaway if needed."

"How the hell did you manage that?"

He looked at me, red eyes still managing to look condescending even though they weren't human. "We're rabbits. We dig. It's what we do."

Good to know. I looked at Kat. Her hair was a mess and her face still puffy from crying in pain. She was rubbing her wrists where the zip ties had cut ugly red marks into her skin. There was a bruise blooming along her jawline, going from her ear, under her cheekbone, and curling up just before it got to her lips. She looked okay as I got her attention. Roughed up, but okay. "Where are Tiff, Larson, and Sophia?"

"We got separated when the houses started burning and then I was snatched by Leonidas and that man." She pointed at the T. rex, which was shakily getting to its feet. The monstrous red lizard was still wobbly but getting steadier with every second. We were running out of time.

"Okay. Boothe, Father Mulcahy, and Ragnar, take Kat to the place where she got split up from the others and find them. Get them into the Burrows and out of here. Leonidas and the rest of his crew are still out there, so be careful and shoot first. I will keep George, Lucy, and Charlotte with me and we will join you underground when we get done here."

Boothe nodded his head at where Marcus still stood in the doorway. "What about him?"

I wasted a second to glance over at Marcus. He was now sitting and looking around the edge of the door. "Fuck the cowardly lion, he's on his own. Now go."

They turned and went, Kat flanked by the Were-rabbit and the priest, the ancient Werewolf trotting in the lead.

I breathed a small prayer that they would find the others without a problem. I turned to the ones left with me.

"Lucy, we need you to do your thing."

She nodded and stepped a few feet away. Her head dropped, eyes closed. She took several deep breaths, gathering her resolve, diaphragm swelling and contracting as thin hands lifted her shirt. Fingers scrabbled inside her belly button, nails digging, looking for a purchase. Her face twisted as she found one and began to pull, her hands moving slowly in opposite directions, stretching the skin apart at her navel like a special effect. A pointed black triangle slid wetly from inside her stomach, pushing its way free. The skin began to waver and roll as the horn became a massive head that belonged to Masego. His beady eyes stared at me from the middle of Lucy's thin body; she stood above and below him, her body trembling and her face stretched in pain. With a snort and shake of his head, Masego tore Lucy to shreds and stepped into our reality. He was as big as the Comet and just as black, gleaming wetly in the electric lighting and the fire glow from the burning houses.

"You with us?" I asked him. He nodded his head and shook all over, sending strips of jelly-wet flesh plopping to the ground at his feet. I tossed the bandolier of grenades to Charlotte. She deftly snatched them out of the air. "Can you web these up by their pins so they can all be pulled at one time? I need about an eight-foot tether."

She looked at them with her alien, unblinking stare. She turned back to me, head tilted to the side. "I can."

"How long do you need?"

"Just a few minutes, five at the most, and some privacy would be nice."

My mind flashed back to a conversation between me, Charlotte, and Tiff comparing Charlotte's half form to Spider-Man. There may have been some whiskey involved. Charlotte revealed that the reason she doesn't swing from webs is because her spinnerets are located where a spider's are. As she described it, in the backside of her lower abdomen.

She was gonna need some privacy.

"Okay, we'll keep devil dinosaur busy. Fix it up and then get it to me wherever I am." I turned to George and Masego as she hurried to the other side of the building. "Let's go keep him distracted. Be careful and watch what I am doing. I want him over by the play sets when Charlotte gets done."

"What do you want me to do to help?" George looked at me with brown gorilla eyes.

The T. rex was on his feet and looking our way. I stepped around the car and raised my gun. "You can be King Kong or Donkey Kong, I don't care which, just keep him busy and move him toward the play sets. If you think of a way to kill him, then even better." I began to run toward the dinosaur as he began to run toward me. The ground shook under my feet, rattled by the weight of my enemy.

Oh, this was going to completely suck.

32

Two roars ripped across the space between us. The T. rex's vibrated the air and stunk of carrion. Mine was torn from the pit of anger inside my chest and thrown at the devil dinosaur I charged. I ran headlong toward an enemy so superior it was insanity. A creature who could swallow me in two bites, razored daggers of teeth cutting me in half to be choked down that massive gullet. The dinosaur rushed toward me, head low to the ground, mouth open to crush down on me. I got close enough to count the scales on its snout when my finger squeezed the trigger on Bessie.

She bucked in my hand, spitting a massive, flesh-cleaving bullet in the face of my enemy. Dark blood spurted out where the bullet struck between those reptilian eyes. It cut a channel through the scaly red skin, furrowing back tissue from the bony ridge of the skull. The dinosaur's scream of pain was shrill as the head jerked upward and away. I fell into a slide along the ground, slipping low and under the head. Four more times I shot Bessie as I slid under the massive running body above me. Three of them hit, raining black blood that looked like crude oil down on me. Instantly, I was covered in sticky, stinking blood, dirt clinging to it, coating my skin and clothes.

The T. rex reared up from the pain, stopping short.

Oh shit!

I was under that bulk, trying to wipe crud made from dirt and dinosaur blood out of my eyes. I could feel it looming above me as I scrambled to get clear. My eyes cleared, still bleary but open, just in time to see a massive red tail swinging through the air at me. I tried to jump out of the way, but it caught me across the stomach and drove me into the ground. Air was pounded out of my lungs and I lay there, trying not to suffocate.

I gasped and fought to pull air into my lungs. After what felt like an eternity I somehow dragged in one short, sweet breath. Pain, sharp and clear, stabbed through my left side. A rib moved, popped out of place. The pain was excruciating.

I rolled over, the hurt stitching from my spine out to my chest. I tried to stretch, hoping it would settle back into place. It felt like I was being stabbed by a knife as wide as my hand.

A knife dipped in sulfuric acid.

Masego charged into the leg of the dinosaur, knocking it sideways. A grill bounced off the thick skull. George pulled another one from the ground, leaning back, getting ready to throw it too. Bessie was gone, thrown wide and missing when I was knocked down, and the .45's weren't enough to do any damage to the monster we were facing. I needed to get back to the fight.

I twisted away from the pain in my side, stretching, trying to fix the rib that was knocked out of whack. It pulled like a fist of pain pushing through my skin. The rib slid back in place like a punch, leaving me gasping for air. The pain dropped to a dull bruise of hurt. Sucking in air, I got to my feet. Reaching back, I drew the katana from over my shoulder.

The blade sang free, vibrating slightly in my grip. Its thirst for blood blossomed up my arm, running along nerves. A schism formed in my mind as the demon in the sword spilled into my brain. It surrounded my own fury with a membrane and began to drink, allowing me to coldly look at my enemy. My eyes traveled the form of the dinosaur, looking for weakness.

The T. rex had his back to me. I disregarded anything above its hips as being out of my reach, concentrating on everything else. I began to walk, blade swishing through the air, calculating my targets. I could carve a chunk of the tail off. Cleave it through and take a piece of my enemy. Immediately, I dismissed the idea, that wouldn't hurt my enemy. Not enough.

Masego made another charge at the dinosaur's legs, trying to cripple it. George was throwing things at its head to keep it distracted. A picnic table spun through the air in a lazy arc as the rhino closed in, thick, stubby legs driving and horn lowered to clip the low joint of the T. rex's hind leg.

As I watched, closing my distance, the dinosaur ducked the table, letting it bounce off the wide muscles of its back. A massive foot kicked out, driving into Masego and punting him across the picnic area. The four-ton rhino flipped end over end and crashed into the fountain. Stone shattered and water shot into the air around its bulk. He did not get up.

George screamed, his voice rending the night with anguish. Muscles bunched under silver fur as he picked up a charcoal grill. Holding it like a club, he charged the dinosaur.

The leg swung back toward me. I could see individual crimson scales as they overlapped each other. I could see the thick cord of tendon running from heel to knee. The katana rose above my head and I swung it down, my strength boosted by the influence of the sword's demon. The long, sweeping blade bit into the cable-thick tendon, pulling through, sinking inches deep as it slid down to the bone. Black blood gushed, soaking into the blackened blade as the dinosaur let out a roar and listed to the side. Its massive dino-drumstick folded under all that weight.

The blade in my hand rang out triumphantly as the blood and gore absorbed into its metal edge, sucked in like a vacuum. A humming frequency made the bones in my arm ache and drove me to my knees. A sick, delicious thrill ran up the nerves and into that membrane sack of fury in my mind. It swirled and swelled and burst, washing me with insanity and desire.

My mind snapped like a cheap rubber band.

I wanted to throw the sword as far from me as I could, flinging the dark thing out into the night.

I wanted to turn the blade on myself, letting it drink deep of my life's blood as I held it, power and pain and death dancing together until I faded, absorbed into the sword.

I wanted to take the blade and kill the whole world with it, finally letting it drink its fill.

The demon in the sword pulled at me, screaming at me. The ocean of rage that lived behind my breastbone swelled into a tidal wave that threatened to sweep me under. I fought against the tide, scrabbling to hold fast to anything good in me, looking for safety to keep from drowning in homicide.

The memory of my wife and children was sucked under, drowned deep in a whirlpool of rage. Their memories followed my love for the family of people who were in my life now. My love for Tiff was too new, not built high enough to rise over the swell of madness.

Desperately, I held fast to my faith, clinging to it like a shipwrecked sailor clings to the mast of a sinking ship. Waves battered me relentlessly, driving into me over and over and over again.

The tide of madness was pulling me under.

I drove the blade into the earth, grounding it. The ocean of homicide began to settle just a little. I grabbed hold of all the faith and love inside me and pushed back. The demon's voice fought, screaming at me at first, cursing me and damning me in a language I did not speak. My mind clamped down on all that was good and holy inside me and I shoved back.

We fought in the battlefield of my soul. The sword trying to kill my soul, to forge me into a wielder that would do its bidding. I raged back. I had enough murder in my heart, I didn't need the sword's influence. I dug in and held my ground.

We were locked in a stalemate. Stuck. Slowly, the tide began to turn as I shoved the demon back into its blade. As I began to come back to control, it started begging, offering me anything I wanted to just do its bidding. Finally, it shut down to the whisper of temptation I was used to dealing with.

I had not used the katana since killing its previous owner. I didn't know it would be such a struggle to keep my control.

Shakily, I got to my feet. I was covered in oily sweat, a slightly sour smell coming off my skin. Every muscle I had felt like it had been pulled too tight, strained almost to the breaking point. I pulled the sword from the ground. The voice surged up, trying to talk to me again.

I told it to shut the hell up. I had work to do.

The T. rex was back up on its feet, moving slower, but after George. The Were-gorilla had done what I asked him to and led the dinosaur to the playground. The dinosaur's colossal bulk couldn't maneuver among the close-packed play sets, but George could. He swung and scrambled around them like the monkey he was, taunting the devil dinosaur, always darting just out of reach. The T. rex was tangled in the rope course, trying to stomp its way free so it could crush George between its deadly jaws. That massive red skull swung to and fro in frustration, jaws clamping, dagger teeth grinding.

Charlotte dropped down beside me, so silent in her approach that she appeared like magic next to me. She held up the bandolier of grenades. Each pin had a thin strand of white silk attached to it, these fed into a thicker strand that coiled like a rope in her other hand. She looked at me with unblinking red eyes. "Are you going to do what I think you are going to do?"

Reaching back, I slid the katana into its sheath. As the blade disappeared, the voice became quieter, but more frantic. My hand came off the handle, breaking the connection. My palm itched. I wanted to scratch it. Instead, I took the bandolier and the web rope from her.

"Probably."

Her head cocked to the side as she studied me. "You know it's a stupid, crazy idea, right?"

"Absolutely insane." I grinned. "Now, go help George distract this big Godzilla-looking bastard."

She turned and darted off. Her spider legs came down and pushed her off the ground. Using them, she made the playground in three big leaps. She began to harass the dinosaur from the other side, being even faster and more nimble than the gorilla.

I watched as they drew the T. rex into a turn that put his back to me. Its thick red tail swished back and forth, wrecking playground equipment with every swing, tangling more metal around its legs and hemming it into one place.

Excellent.

The bandolier slid over my shoulder with the lasso of webbing hanging heavy against my side. It thumped into the spot where my rib had popped out of place, sending a harsh jab of pain. I ignored it. Tying the end into a slip-knot, I looped it over my wrist. I was tired as I forced myself into a run, building speed as I came up on that deadly swinging tail.

I circled to the right and jumped up on a mangled slide, climbing up its jumbled pieces. My hands scrabbled to find handholds on the twisted pipes and steps. Pulling myself to its highest point got me even with the T. rex's hip. I held tight to the structure I was on as that tail swung back and struck it. Vibrations jolted up through me, threatening to toss me off.

My feet slid to the left and out from under me, banging my hip on a piece of pipe that stuck out. Dull pain sunk into the joint and I could already feel where it would be bruised later. Pulling with my arms, I muscled my way back to the top.

The dinosaur's side stretched wide in front of me, angry red scales slick and tightly woven. In that moment of waiting my mind noted that Tyrannosaurus rexes were never red in the movies.

Maybe the movies got it wrong and they had all been the color of raw blood. Maybe it was just this one. *It doesn't matter.* I pushed the random thought from my head.

Boot leather tightened across my instep as I crouched. Thigh muscles pushed, shoving me into the air. There was a split second of weightlessness as I was uncon-nected to anything but the space between me and the di-nosaur. I had only one thought pass through my mind.

This really is a dumbass plan.

My body slammed into the scaled back of the di-nosaur. I began to slide down, fingers scratching for purchase. They dug in, bunching slick scaled skin in my grip. Pulling with my hands and pushing with my feet, I climbed up the T. rex's back. Realizing I was there, the beast began to buck, trying to dislodge me. It was tangled in mangled play sets, its movements hindered and constrained.

Hand over hand I got above the shoulders. My fingers tightened on the bony ridge of the back of the skull. Pulling myself upward, I wrapped my legs around its thick neck, hooking my feet together. That massive skull whipped back and forth, spittle flying from dagger teeth; thick, bumpy tongue whipping out of the wide-open jaws. My left hand clamped firm to the ridge on the back of the skull, and with my legs locked I wasn't going anywhere.

The end of the web lasso was still tight around my wrist. A shake of my arm sent the bandolier sliding down into my hand. I was only going to have one shot at this, so I held on, waiting for my moment. The dinosaur saw what I was doing and somewhere in his mind he understood. That big reptilian eye rolled back to look at me.

I could have given him one more chance. A chance to live. Turn human and surrender. But he had chosen this. He had signed up with Leonidas, and he had been party to any evil they had done. Nobody had forced him into being with them; he was too strong to be under anyone's control. This was the most powerful creature I had ever seen a lycanthrope turn into. He had chosen to do evil.

He had to die.

I whipped my arm out as that baleful eye stared at me. The weight of the grenades slung out and away from me, held tight in my hand. It tried to pull away from me and fly off in the night. My arm flexed, pulling the bandolier into the trajectory I wanted. My eyes watched it draw close. I felt the moment I needed and opened my hand.

The bandolier spun away from me in an arc, the tether of webbing flowing behind it like a streamer.

It circled around and arced down over the snout of the dinosaur. It hung there, slowly rotating around, snagged on bone ridges and teeth. My stomach tightened as it looked like it was going to fall away. The weight of it tilted it up, threatening to flail away. I didn't breath. Time folded in, slowing to a crawl. If it fell off, I would not get the chance to try it again. The dinosaur would throw me off, crush me beneath him, and eat my flesh. The world was the slow spin of the bandolier.

Finally, it canted to the side, slipping across red scales to settle around the ridge of the skull above my hand. The T. rex and I looked at each other.

"Via con carne, asshole."

I let go, tumbling backward off my perch, sliding down the dinosaur's long spine. The bumps of vertebrae bounced me, rattling my teeth. The web lasso snaked out above me. There was a sharp yank as I reached the end, stopping me for a split second before the pins in the grenades popped out, pulling like a busted zipper.

I hit the ground and scrambled to get under the slide set I had climbed.

I had just pulled my feet in when the explosion sent charred bits of dinosaur skull flying into the night.

33

George knelt beside the black rhino. His fur was slick and wet from the geyser of water shooting into the air around him. Two deep gashes cut across his shoulders, blood mixing with the water and running pink off his fur. He ignored it. His eyes were on the fallen form of the rhino. I couldn't tell if the water running down his face was tears or from the fountain.

Masego lay completely still. I couldn't see any breath. No movement at all.

Charlotte in her spider-lady form took a step forward and went to one knee beside him. She reached out a hand, tentatively toward his shoulder, when it touched him it was human. "Is he?"

The gorilla nodded.

"Does this mean she is?"

He nodded again.

"I am so sorry."

I slid fresh clips into the .45's I had emptied earlier on the dinosaur. Its carcass lay in the wreckage of the playground, still smoldering from the stump of its neck. It had not changed back to human. That was going to be a helluva mess for someone to clean up. A flick of my finger hit the slide release on each gun, jacking a bullet into the chambers. Charlotte looked up at the sound.

I tried to make my voice soft. "I am sorry about Masego and Lucy, but I have to go find the others. Leonidas and the rest are still out there."

She nodded and gave George one more comforting pat. She stood, and as she did her spider-lady form washed back over her. George didn't say anything. He leaned up and put his hands on the side of the noble beast that lay in front of him.

Thick gorilla fingers dug in, splitting the black hide. Pulling and yanking, he tore a hole. Pushing both hands in deep, he pulled back, shoulders bunching under wet fur. The gap widened. Inside there was nothing—no gore, no blood, no organs. Just empty blackness.

He began to pull away pieces of rhino, throwing them behind him. They were like black pieces of jack-o'-lantern rind left over from Halloween. The more pieces he pulled away, the more frantic he became, scooping away bigger and bigger pieces of Masego.

I caught a glimpse of a pale-white form lying thin and still inside the hollow before George shoved both of his arms inside, along with his head and shoulders. He pulled back and drew out Lucy's body. She lay limp and wet in his arms. His chest folded around her. Sobs wracked him, squeezing from deep within to choke out thin, strained, painful.

I know what that feels like. When sorrow swallows you and the world ceases to exist. Shards of pain coat the entire world, slicing and cutting you with every turn. Your heart goes black with grief, and nothing in the world can soothe that agony. I was in that same place five years ago. I knew better than anyone that George was lost to a harrowing grief that would not let him go anytime soon.

There was nothing I could do for him.

I turned away from his grieving, Charlotte only a step behind me.

Thick smoke clung in the air, billowing out of houses set afire. The cluster homes were so tightly packed that flames leaped from one to the next without hesitation, crawling over rooftops, devouring shingles and siding. The collar of my shirt rubbed across my nose, a make-shift mask against the oily, choking smog. My eyes still burned from it. Charlotte ran alongside me, unbothered by the smog.

Heat from the fires hammered the air on either side of the streets, browning the postage stamp yards. The wind blew in hellish gusts full of cinders and ash. Everywhere the rabbits had hydrants opened up and were trying to quell the raging inferno, desperate to stop the loss. At least the houses had been empty, everyone centralized for Boothe's plan.

My left hand fumbled out my cell and pushed the button to speed-dial Kat. The phone connected with a roar. I heard shouting and the pop and crack of gunfire. Kat's voice yelled out to be heard. "North side of the neighborhood on Oakleaf Court!" the connection broke like fine china in an earthquake. Taking my bearings, I spun on my heel to turn north.

Marcus was following us a few feet behind.

Ignoring him, I broke into a sprint, the fire falling behind us. My ears picked up the sound of gunfire in all the confusion and ran in that direction, slowing down as it got louder. The street sign on the corner was for Oak-leaf Court.

I stopped short. None of us was wearing any type of Kevlar. We couldn't run into live gunfire blindly. Well, we could, but that would be a dumbass move. Dumbass moves get you dead. I try to avoid dumbass moves.

I have wildly varying degrees of success at that.

The cluster homes were back-to-back beside us, tiny yards fenced in with wooden privacy fences. A thin strip of space opened between them, just wide enough for a normal person to walk between. I am not a normal-sized person, so I turned sideways, gun out, and ran in a side shuffle to keep the katana on my back from smacking into anything. The wooden fences skimmed by my face as I followed the sound of gunfire. There were openings every fifteen feet or so to a space between houses.

Five or six houses down, we came to the opening with the loudest sound of gunfire. I began to creep between two houses as quietly as possible. All light was blocked by the looming homes. I could face forward but not stretch my arms out to the side. The space pressed in, seeming to swallow us. I worked to control my breathing and still keep moving. My rib pulled with each breath, cracking pain along my spine. Running had not helped it. At the corner I stopped and peered around to look, the sound of gunfire very close. Charlotte hovered above me, using her spider legs braced on each house to suspend her in the air. She was looking where I was.

On the porch of the house stood three lycanthropes. Two of them were upright and strapped with flame-throwers. They looked similar, both half human, half reptile. One was the snake-man, fangs mismatched where one was growing back. The other was the Komodo dragon, his head elongated into a reptilian skull, skin covered with tiny teeth for scales. Both of them fired burst after burst of flame, spacing them so there was a constant barrage of napalm in the air.

I could see Kat, Larson, and Father Mulcahy pinned behind a car parked in the street. Paint that was once metallic blue bubbled and peeled off the Honda. Rubber gaskets caught fire, flaming on their own like candle tapers. The glass on the car had blackened and cracked. Puddles of burning napalm scorched the ground. Boothe lay on the ground behind them. I couldn't see Tiff or Ragnar. Kat was firing blind at the flamethrowers, every shot wide as she kept her head down from the gouts of burning chemical hellfire.

They were trapped. The car in front of them was a mound of fiery metal, but it was the only cover they had. If they tried to move away from it, they would be wide open. The flamethrowers would chargrill them in a second.

The third lycanthrope, a huge jackal, paced around behind the other two, greasy hair waving around from heat blowback. Short hind legs appeared comical under a wide, powerful chest. A heavy bottom jaw slung down to reveal a bone-cracking, yellow-toothed grin as he danced around.

We were behind them. I pointed my pistol, aiming carefully, slowing my breathing, making my shot count.

"What do you see?"

My eyes jerked to the left. Charlotte had already put her hand over Marcus's mouth, shutting him up. I looked back, hoping we still had the element of surprise.

Black eyes glittered in a black mask as the jackal looked around at me.

Dammit.

A high-pitched yip cut through the whooshing sound of the flamethrowers. A leap carried the Were-jackal over the porch rail. Claws tore up the grass as he charged at me, foam dripping from flesh-tearing jaws, closing the space in an eyeblink. I aimed both Colt .45's, squeezing off two shots.

Both bullets hit the tank of napalm strapped to the snake-man's back the exact moment that Charlotte took down the jackal.

Charlotte and the jackal tumbled end over end, greasy

fur and grass flying. The jackal came out on top, jaws snapping as Charlotte held it back with one slender arm. The Were-jackal was rabid, foam flecking along its snarl, dripping from vicious teeth. Its head whipped back and forth at the end of Charlotte's arm.

Her spider-lady face was expressionless. The nails on her other hand lengthened, becoming long, thin, razor-sharp needles. With a flash, she raked them across the snout and eye of the canine. Blood splashed out over her face and chest. The Were-jackal screamed and flung itself out of her grip.

I turned back to the porch.

Napalm squirted from the pressurized tank, coating the porch and the back of the Were-snake's black fatigues. Frantically, he tried to shake his way out of the tank's straps. I put another bullet in the tank and one in his leg. He screamed and crumpled like a used tissue, napalm tank thunking as it hit the wooden porch.

Gunfire erupted from behind the burnt Honda, bullets striking the Komodo in the chest and pitching him backward. His finger convulsed on the flamethrower's trigger, spewing a gout of liquid fire as he fell. The flames struck the spilled napalm. The combustion was instantaneous. The porch and the Were-snake burst into flames.

Turning to Charlotte, I found her standing, greenish blood running from deep bites on her arms and legs. She held the struggling jackal in front of her, spider legs clamped on its sides to keep it suspended in the air. The beast struggled, claws striking out in the air, jaws snapping. Slender fingers with too many joints shot out, shoving between crushing jaws. One hand closed on the snout, the other hooked into the bottom jaw.

With a shrug, she tore the jackal in two. A geyser of black gore and entrails splatted on the grass at her feet.

She casually dropped both pieces and stepped away, wiping her hands on her dress.

"Deacon, over here!"

I ran to where Kat was. She was pushing Larson away from the burning car in his wheelchair. It had been battered, one wheel bent out of shape so that the chair listed and swayed like a drunk man. Larson was slumped over, out cold, Uzi clutched in his hands still. Kat's jeans and skin were shredded from the knee down on one leg, blood bright red against her pale skin. Father Mulcahy was dragging Boothe's limp form into the street. Ragnar had a mouthful of belt, tugging to help. Blood slicked his fur against one shoulder and he kept favoring that leg. The priest had a gash across his forehead, blood pouring down his face.

The Were-rabbit he was dragging looked the worst of all. Half of his upper body was scorched, flesh raw pink and blackened crisp. Silver fur was singed away, curling brown and brittle at the edges. The burns splashed across his face, one ear a blackened stump. He moaned in pain with every movement, barely conscious.

My hand reached out for Larson's chair. Kat slapped it away. Her voice was tight with pain and stubbornness. "I've got this. Go help Father Mulcahy."

"Charlotte will get him." I took the chair from her. The warped wheel made pushing the chair a bitch. I had to pick it up to make it move. Kat limped along beside me as I pushed Larson across the street to where Charlotte was carefully moving the giant Were-rabbit and laying him on the grass. Marcus was following her, still looking lost.

"Where are Tiff and Sophia?"

The priest sat on the grass next to Boothe. "The two lions have Sophia. Tiffany chased them into that house. We got cut off by the ones with the flamethrowers."

I turned to look at the house. Flames were racing up the front of it, chasing each other. The front door was a black spot in a lake of fire. The two dead lycanthropes were crumpled, roasting in front of it. I checked the clips on my .45's, making sure they were full. I came up with one full clip for each gun and one full clip for a spare.

My fingers scrabbled at the buckle of the gun belt around my waist. With Bessie lost, it would just be extra weight. Boothe gave a choking cough that drew my attention back to the others. I turned and he raised his unburnt hand, weakly waving me near.

I knelt beside him, the smell of burnt hair coming off him made my nose twitch. His voice was raspy, thin, and mostly empty air. "They are going"—he swallowed, moving his tortured throat—"to use the Burrows. Downstairs . . ." The one good eye rolled back into his head, the other eye was a ruin in the burned half of his face. "Door is always . . . in basement. S-s-s-steel door."

I touched him, trying to thank him for what his effort had cost in pain. My power flared, a wash of hot agony seared across my skin and the smell of roasted rabbit filled the back of my throat, hanging on my palate like a clump of curdled cheese. Moving my hand back broke the connection. The agony stopped sharply, leaving the skin on my right side feeling raw. I swallowed against the taste still stuck in my mouth.

Father Mulcahy was wiping blood away from his face. "Can you heal him? Like you did before?"

Boothe was in bad shape. I didn't know how he was still conscious. Burns do damage like nothing else. I would rather be cut to the bone than suffer a bad burn. That one touch and I had felt the agony he was in. My skin still felt sunburned. The rib that was busted by the T. rex pounded from moving Larson, driving like a fist in my side with each deep breath. My hip was bone bruised and getting stiff, getting weak.

Without my power, Boothe could die.

If I used my power to save him, then Sophia, her unborn babies, and Tiff would die.

Time pressed down on my shoulders.

34

I tossed my car keys to Father Mulcahy. He caught them from the air. "Go. Get the Comet and get him medical attention."

"You could be killing him with that decision."

"If I choose him, I could be killing Tiff and Sophia." I stared into his eyes; they were stark in the mask of blood smeared across his face. "Go."

The priest stared at me. I stared back, deep inside the cold place that lets me kill.

Boothe began to choke, his body convulsing. A grand mal seizure twisted his burnt body, pulling it tight and bowing it off the ground beneath him. Father Mulcahy broke the stare to cut his eyes over at the dying Were-rabbit.

"My decision's made. This is on your hands now."

Father Mulcahy looked back at me. "Take the air rifle." He held it out to me.

We both had to get moving, so I didn't argue. The rifle was slung over my shoulder and the extra clip of palm-sized darts shoved into a pocket. I pulled one of my .45's out and handed it to Father Mulcahy. His mouth opened for a second and I gave him a look that closed it. The priest set off at a run back toward the community center and the car without a backward glance.

I turned to the group. "Charlotte, Ragnar, you're with me."

"Are you sure about this?" Charlotte was kneeling beside Boothe. The seizure had passed and he lay still on the grass. Her hand kept fluttering toward him and then away, unsure of whether to touch him or not as she looked up at me.

"Get up." My voice was flat, without emotion or inflection. Charlotte rose to her feet. "Father Mulcahy and Kat will take care of Boothe; our people still need rescuing. Nobody else can do it." I turned without waiting to see if she would follow.

My chest hit Marcus's as he stepped in front of me. The nerve under my right eye started to twitch.

"I am coming with you. I need to make up for what my mate and my brother have done." Big amber yellow eyes were brimming with sincerity, begging for permission. One moist hand lay limply on my gun arm. All my frustration with delays focused in on him like a laser. I drove my shoulder into him, pushing past, moving him aside.

"Follow if you want, but don't slow me down. The next time you get in my way, I *will* put a bullet in you." He fell in behind Charlotte as I moved toward the burning porch, my stride getting longer as I walked. Ragnar trotted beside me.

Dark orange flames ate at the porch, chewing the white painted wood and licking across vinyl siding to leave long streaks of soot and trails of heat bubbles behind. Napalm dripped from the overhead covering onto the wooden porch in scorching streamers. Heat slammed into me like a fist as I hit the bottom step. The air was thick, oxygen eaten away by the flame. My hip ached. I pushed on.

The door to the house was solid blackness wrapped in fire. I had one shot to get through that door. We were going to get burned, but if we stopped on that porch, we wouldn't make it off. The heat would sap our strength, driving us down so that the flame could finish us off.

The wood under my feet was spongy, threatening to crumble with each footfall. The two lycanthropes lay spread in the center of the porch. The napalm and heat had liquefied them, turning them into puddles of Were lava. I pushed off the balls of my feet, my thighs flexing to shove me into a jump. The second I committed my stomach dropped. I knew I was not going to make it across. My boot heel struck the edge of the puddle, splashing the mixture of napalm and liquefied lycanthrope up the back of my leg.

It felt like someone threw boiling acid across my calf.

The muscle clenched, locking in a knot, drawing up tight with hot agony. I stumbled forward, falling the rest of the distance. My shoulder crashed into the door. It sagged but held. Blackness swirled on the edge of my vision. Lungs burning from lack of oxygen, I drove forward, bashing against the door again. My rib pulled and stabbed. The door buckled under my weight and I fell into the house, slamming onto the hardwood floor.

My leg was on fire, smoldering holes were being eaten into my jeans, my boots, my skin. Frantically, I beat at the flames. Ragnar landed beside me, nails digging into the dark mahogany finish of the floor. His wolf coat was singed on one side down to the skin. He began to lick at one paw, then the other, swollen blisters on the pads breaking, running like egg yolks full of saltwater. Charlotte flew into the room with a leap that carried her past Ragnar. Smoke swirled off her as she crouched, heaving in air. One long angry slash of burn cut across her shoulder and chest. It looked like a drip of napalm she hadn't avoided. It looked like my leg.

Marcus fell inside, dreads singed, little swirls of smoke rising off them. His once butter crème shirt was dingy gray with soot, matching the charcoal gray slacks. He had shifted, clawed hands jutting out the ends of his sleeves. His face was a lion's, surrounded by a smoldering mane made of the same tiny dreads he wore as a man. His fur was a light honey color, short and tight against his skin. He was a smoother, lighter, tamer version of his brother.

He grabbed the door in taloned hands and pushed, shutting out the inferno on the porch. The backdraft through the house caught it closing, slamming it loudly.

"There goes the element of surprise for the second time, asshole." I looked at my leg before scrambling to my feet. It was ugly. The burn was an abstract pattern across my skin. Half-dollar–sized blisters already swelled over red, cracked skin with blackened bits scattered through. It hurt, not as bad as it looked, which was a bad sign. It meant there was damage below the nerve level, third-degree burn level. I would have that scar for the rest of my life.

The boot was ruined. It had protected my leg from the worst of the splash and had suffered for it. Black leather was eaten away and the heel was dissolved on the back half. They would get me through this, but then they were done. Regret cut through me. I had worn these boots for years. They had been a gift from my wife. The loss panged inside me, hurting worse than the burn on my leg.

I pushed it away and stood up.

A deep breath pulled clean cool air into my lungs. Inside the house it was quiet and peaceful. Orange light from the flames on the porch flickered across the hardwood from under the door. Exhaustion dropped on me like a wet towel. I just wanted to lay down, sink to the floor, and close my eyes. My bones ached. My joints were swollen and stiff. My skin felt like it had been scrubbed raw by a steel brush. I wanted to rest. I wanted to lay down. In that moment, for a split second, I wanted to quit.

I pictured Tiff and Sophia. They were somewhere below me. I could see them, terrified in the hands of my enemies. Hurt and afraid. Hoping someone would come to save them.

Hoping I would come to save them.

I started walking through the house, looking for the door to the basement.

The air rifle was gone, lost somewhere on the porch. I didn't remember it falling, but it was gone. The .45 filled my hand with a comforting weight as it slid from its holster. I held it out front as I moved through the house opening doors and searching. Each closet I opened pushed that sea of rage closer and closer to spilling over inside me.

My hand twisted the knob on a door in the kitchen. It opened on oiled hinges. Steps disappeared down into darkness. Cool air pushed up, the smell of earth clean in my nostrils. It was pitch-black down there. My fingers found the switch on the wall. It flicked up with a tiny click. Light sputtered to life somewhere out of sight in the basement below, spilling across the bottom of the stairs, which ended in front of a wall, the space to either side of them cluttered with boxes and used junk. I stood, listening, ears straining to hear anything.

Softly, low and near silent, I heard a moan.

A female moan.

Gun in hand, I started down the stairs, stepping carefully, being wary. The other three gathered around the doorway, watching me descend, waiting for the okay to follow. Each step took me farther down, each step deeper into the hole. Each step strained my calf, weakening it, threatening to dump me down the stairs. My neck was tight.

Taking another step, I lowered my foot slowly, the sole of my boot sinking, falling, to land on the wooden step. A creak cut through the silence, drawing the muscles in my lower back into a web of tension. My hand clenched tight to the grip on my gun, holding on as sweat slicked my palm.

The stairs were torn out from under me, wood splintering with a sharp snap. Stomach clenched, I hung in the air for one thought before crashing.

Oh shit.

35

Tiny shards of glass cut across my upper back. Something had broken inside the box I crashed into and the pieces were cutting me. I flailed about, trying to get up. Something tangled across my legs, pulling me. Tripping me.

Christmas lights. A strand of Christmas lights were wrapped around the shredded boot.

A shadow loomed over me, blocking the light. My power sparked. Cold, wet, and salty from a place that never saw sunlight, pressed in against my skin. Hunger filled me, gnawing away at my insides. The feel of rough skin scraping. It was the Were-shark.

He was mostly human but still monstrous as he hunched over in the shortened space of the basement. Light from the single yellow bulb gleamed off his unnaturally pale bald head. His eyes were glossy black, mouth stretched wide with too many teeth in too many rows. Arms the size of my thighs reached down to grab me.

My hand was empty. The Colt .45 had skittered out of my grip when I crashed and was laying on the concrete floor of the basement. It mocked me over by the hot water heater—shiny, deadly, and out of reach. My knees banged into the concrete floor as I scrambled for it. I ignored the pain, moving to get the gun before I was caught unarmed. I threw my hand out toward the pistol.

Reaching.

Stretching.

Just touching the grip, metal and ivory cool under the pads of my fingers. Something thin cut across my calf, shooting fire through the burns, pulling tight. Yanking me away.

The Colt lay unmoved by the water heater as I was dragged back across the floor.

Twisting, I saw the Were-shark had the Christmas lights in his hands and was using them to reel me back to him like a fish on a line. I dug the heel of my boot in, trying to stop myself. The wire of the lights cut in deeper, my boot heel slipped and I was sliding again.

Looking up into the doorway where the stairs used to be, I saw Charlotte. She was frozen, one hand over her mouth, body shaking. Fear rolled off her in palpable waves. I could see terror stamped on her every feature. She wasn't coming to help.

I reached up for the katana, bracing myself for its invasion of my mind.

A flash of silver fur struck the Were-shark in the back. Ragnar dug in, nails sinking into skin. With a snarl, canines sank into the Were-shark's throat, blood running scarlet from the old Werewolf's snout as he held on.

The Were-shark roared out in pain. He let go of the Christmas lights and I scrambled away. The monster reached behind him. One gigantic webbed hand closed on the thick ruff of fur on Ragnar's neck. Bending sharply and yanking, the Were-shark tore Ragnar off his back and swung him out in front. The ancient Werewolf hung like a pup, claws flailing the air, jaws snapping, bloody spittle slinging everywhere. The Were-shark's other hand swung back and crashed into Ragnar's skull. The Werewolf went limp, legs twitching as they hung loose. The great white's back loomed at me as he turned, drawing Ragnar up to that horrible maw. Blood began to gush, spattering the concrete between his feet. Wet, gnawing sounds filled the basement.

I stood up with the Colt in my hand.

My finger jerked against the trigger, stitching holes in that broad, inhuman back. Seven bullets struck like magic. Blood spurted out, thick like syrup. The Were-shark dropped Ragnar in a heap but did not fall. He turned toward me, slowly. My thumb hit the magazine release, dropping the spent clip to the floor. I had my last one in my hand. It slid home with a click. The Were-shark stood facing me. My thumb hit the slide release, clacking it forward and locking a bullet in the chamber. I pointed the pistol at him, laser cutting through the gray haze of cordite in the air and dancing on his chest.

"Where are the girls?"

His voice was a choke, wet and thick from that too-wide mouth with too many teeth. "Leonidas has the dog-bitch."

"Are they in the tunnels?"

He nodded.

"Where's the human girl?"

Those black eyes rolled to the right. There was a room, walls unfinished, door framed in but not hung. Inside that room were two things: a steel door in a blank wall and Tiff laying on the ground.

She was a sprawl of limbs. Black and pink hair swirled around her face. The coveralls were ripped into rags; her shirt was torn to shreds.

I couldn't tell if she was breathing.

Turning my eyes back to the Were-shark, I looked at him through a tunnel of blood-red hatred. My teeth hurt as they ground together.

"Is she alive?"

"She was before you showed up."

Desire to shoot him burned in me. My knuckles creaked around the grip of the Colt.

"Why are you still here and not with Leonidas?"

"I am the rear guard. I kill you and let him and his new mate get away. The girl was left for me as a reward." A pink stump of a tongue swirled around that lipless maw, leaving an obscene trail of saliva. "She looks yummy."

"You were planning on eating her?"

Massive shoulders shrugged dismissively. "I still am. After I'm done with her." He looked up at where Charlotte stood above, still frozen. "Maybe for dessert I will have some of your spider friend. Remember what I did to you last time, little spider?" Charlotte cringed away from his tooth-filled grin, moving out of my sight. "This time I will do so much more to you."

My finger squeezed the trigger.

The boom of the gunshot drowned out his scream of pain. Blood shot out of the hole I put in his chest, spilling into the air and down his shirt. He staggered back from the shot but still did not fall. Eight silver bullets in him and he still did not fall.

"That hurt, you bastard!" Blood slicked webbed fingers as he touched the wound. "You are going to pay for that and for what you did last time." The smell of brine filled my nostrils and that saltwater cold splashed over me as he began to change. His head pulled to a triangle and his neck spread out joining to his shoulders like clay being molded. A gray dorsal fin ripped his skin to jut from his back. His voice began to rasp as he screamed at me. "I had to have those damned bullets *cut* out of me!" His voice choked off as gills split on his neck and he lost his ability to talk.

He turned into the monster that had nearly killed Charlotte. A hulking beast that should never be seen on land. A nightmare of teeth and murder. A killing machine. He had taken eight silver bullets and was still coming to kill me. My power was wild and out of control as his lycanthropy washed over me. I was choking on the taste of saltwater as he charged me.

I dove to my left, crashing into a workbench, tools clattering down around me. I fired a shot, missing the Were-shark and hitting the water heater. A fine spray of hot water shot out, covering the floor in slick wetness. The Were-shark turned, black eye rolling to find me. The awful sucking sound of its breathing was loud in my ears as I scrambled to my feet, slipping on the growing puddle of hot water. An idea formed in my head.

Pointing down, I fired two shots into the Were-shark's crotch.

Blood burst onto the floor as he fell to his knees. Head back, his mouth gaped open in a silent scream. Monster or not, he was still enough man for that to hurt.

But it wouldn't kill him. He was too strong. His skin was too thick. I didn't have enough bullets to kill him, and I did not want to use the katana again so soon. I walked over, grabbed him by the fin, and shoved my hand into his gill slits. It was wet and sticky against my fingers, like thick jelly.

My power welled up inside me from the contact, moving down my arm and into his lycanthropy. I pushed in farther, driving my power into him. Saltwater choked me. My nostrils burned with it. Cold settled deep inside me. The shark in him was swimming near the surface, silent and hungry. I pulled it closer and pushed my power in deeper. It was close to the technique I had used to save Charlotte before, but I was looking only inside this one lycanthrope.

My mind translated my power into a visual and I found the cords that tied the beast to the man. I reached out for them, sorting them. His shark turned teeth on me, trying to throw me out. Metaphysically I yanked one of the cords and the shark folded in half, then swam away. I looked with determination, knowing it would be back in a thought.

The shark turned, swimming back toward me. Its mouth yawned open as it picked up speed with great sweeps of its tail. My power found the cord I was looking for and closed around it. The shark struck, slashing pain through my guts as I pulled and twisted the cord that tied the Were's lungs to his gills. With my power I could see his lungs shrink like tumors destroyed by radiation as gills took over their function. They yawned open wide to drag oxygen from water.

Water that didn't exist in the basement.

The connection was broken with a sharp pain that drove me across the room and crashed me into a dryer.

I shook my head, trying to clear it from using my power. Pain echoed deep inside my body; my guts filled with glass shards of it from the metaphysical shark strike as I stood. Bracing on the dryer, I got my feet under me.

The Were-shark writhed on the floor, thrashing around and clawing at his gills. One giant foot crashed into a table that had power tools on it, dumping them on his legs. A moist flapping sound came from the gill slits opening and closing desperately. Black eyes rolled, white skein clicking across them like a camera shutter.

I turned away. It would take him hours to die, suffocating slowly unless the house burned down on him. I didn't care. Carefully putting one foot in front of the other, I walked to where Tiff lay. Still, so still, no movement in her at all.

Dread grew with every footstep.

36

Oh dear God, please . . .

My knees were swollen as I knelt beside her. Puffy against the concrete, they felt like they were full of liquid, sloshing inside if I moved too much. Tiff lay like a broken doll, arms askew and legs akimbo. The soft cotton shirt was torn open, skin scraped raw in streaks of burn from the cloth being twisted and yanked.

Don't . . .

Her jeans were undone, pulled down over one hip, revealing the pink unicorn tattoo on her hipbone. She had gotten that tattoo on her eighteenth birthday. I had given it to her seven years ago, a lifetime ago when I was a tattoo artist. Before my family was gone and I was this. It had been one of those crazy coincidences of life that I don't believe in anymore, a connection we shared that I did believe in.

Her chest wasn't moving.

Don't do this . . .

Blood soaked black and pink hair, plastering it over her left eye. I reached out to brush it away, fingers staining crimson with her blood. The hair moved in a clump to reveal four razor crisp slashes across her eye. Deep.

To the bone of her eyebrow and cheek. Her lovely blue eye had been stolen. Ruined.

Her chest still wasn't moving.

Please . . .

A tiny breath washed across my hand as I touched her face.

My heart jerked. Chest tight, I touched her throat, fingers feeling for a pulse. Her skin was still warm. I pushed the hollow under her jaw. Searching. Seeking. Desperate.

Please, God . . .

I found it. Fluttering like a moth against my finger. Barely, but there still.

Thank you. Thank you.

I screamed out Charlotte's name.

She scurried in, dropping beside me. Tears ran from red eyes, all eight of them stacked along each side of her forehead. Her hands shook as she reached out for me. "Deacon, I am so sorry. I froze. I saw the shark. I was terrified . . ."

"Shut up."

Her mouth slapped shut.

As gently as I could, I picked up Tiff, holding her close to my chest. Against my skin I could feel her breathing, so shallow and light, like a tiny bird. I turned to Charlotte.

I stared the Were-spider in the eye. "I don't give a fuck about any of that." I passed Tiff over. "Take her." Charlotte cradled her gently. "Your only job now is to get her the fuck out of here. There has to be a response team here by now after all the shit that has blown up. Get her medical care and do it as fast as you can."

Charlotte stood up, shifting Tiff so she would be more stable. "I will—"

My hand shot up. "Shut up. Go." I focused on her main set of eyes. Blank space filled my head, emotions shutting down. The indifference that lets me kill people poured out in my voice. "Do *NOT* fail me this time."

Four spider legs picked her up and began crawling away. Marcus stepped into the door frame.

Blocking Charlotte's path.

My gun was out and in my hand, the laser dancing on his chest. My voice tore out of me in a roar. "Get the fuck out of her way!" He jumped, stumbling aside to clear the path. Charlotte moved like quicksilver through the doorway, carried aloft on her spider legs. They rose above her, pulling her up where the stairs used to be, making her disappear.

Ragnar limped into the room. He stopped next to me, swaying. His tail was broken, bent at a sharp, painful angle. The skin on his shoulder and neck ruff was a bloody mess of flesh and fur. One ear was torn off, leaving his ear canal open to the world, gory and eviscerated. The side of his wolf face was distorted, the bone caved in along his snout and eye. There were gaps where teeth were before. I was surprised to see him alive. He was one tough old bastard.

"They still have Sophia. You got a little more fight in you, old man?"

His snort came out with a whistle. Something in his face broken just enough to block the airway to his nostrils. He staggered over to the steel door, looking over his shoulder at me, his meaning was clear.

You coming?

I stood slowly, walking to join him. Marcus spoke from the doorway.

"Where are you going?"

I didn't look at him. I didn't give a damn about his reaction.

"To kill your fucking brother."

37

The tunnels were claustrophobic. Red clay pressed close, packed hard into low arches. I had to run hunched over, struggling to breathe. My rib shot pain under my arm, deep into my chest with each labored draw of my lungs. Ache radiated from my hip and knees, the strain of moving with my body bent over screaming at me. The skin across my calf pulled tight, ripping with every step. Hot fluid ran down my calf to fill my boot.

A string of lights ran down the side of the tunnel. They made pools of 100-watt incandescence that seared my eyes as I passed. Between the pools of light were gaps of pitch-black, made even blacker by the contrast of the lights. Every little bit we came to where another tunnel would cross ours and it would open up into a small area tall enough for me to straighten up. Marcus would spill into the opening with me, clawed hands on his knees as he drew in deep breaths.

Fire still burned deep inside me from the attack by the metaphysical shark. I knew what it would feel like to have a gut filled with glass shards. The old Werewolf would sniff the ground, tracking the scent we were following. He would take off down another tunnel and I would follow, hunched over, my head and shoulders brushing the tunnel ceiling, raining small rocks and dirt down my back.

We ran through those damned tunnels for what felt like miles.

I struggled to keep my gun in front of me. Each step it got heavier, weighing a hundred pounds. The smell of earth became cloying. Filling my mouth, it parched my throat. I started tripping on the uneven floor of the tunnel, dragging along the wall to stay up on my feet. I was moving on hate alone.

We came to another crossing. Ragnar trotted out, nose to the ground, scenting the path. I stepped out, straightening up, my back twinged.

With a flash of claws, Leonidas tore Ragnar's head off.

Blood arced out, spattering across my chest and face. The Werewolf's body stumbled for a step or two and then crumpled to the ground. Leonidas stood with his chest out, a wild grin splitting his face. Behind him, near a tunnel, Shani held a rope that was tied around Sophia's neck. Sophia's eyes were wide, staring at me. With a yank and a snarl, Shani dragged her off down the tunnel.

The laser from my gun tracked up to Leonidas's chest. I squeezed the trigger, popping off bullets. Like quicksilver the Were-lion twisted out of the way. Four bullets shot past him. One struck him in the arm, spinning him around and throwing him to the ground. He crouched, roaring in pain. Taking a step, I pointed the laser at his skull. My finger itched to finish the job.

Marcus grabbed my arm, jerking it off target. He stood close to me, so close that I noticed his dreads were full of dirt. Red clay smudged under yellow predator eyes. His voice was pleading and quiet, but his clawed hand was closed hard on my arm.

"He is my brother. Please let me try to reason with him."

My mind sparked, flashing with everything that had happened since Marcus and his brother crashed into my life. People were dead. Charlotte had almost died, so close to the brink that it had taken a miracle to save her. Tiff still could die; I didn't know how badly she was injured. The image of her ruined eye sparked in my mind lighting a forest fire of rage. Inside my head became a theater of pictures. Boothe's charred body, possibly too damaged for his lycanthropy to overcome. Larson unconscious. Kat dangling from Leonidas's hand. George sobbing over Lucy's body. Sophia was still a hostage. She could still die. So could her babies and Boothe. Blood had been shed by Leonidas and because of Marcus.

I remembered what Sophia had told us at the table just earlier that day.

I remembered what I had told him when he wanted to follow after his brother.

My calf throbbed in my boot, fire cutting deep in the muscle.

I twisted my forearm and jerked it against the weakest part of his grip. My arm came free. Raising the Colt, I fired my last two bullets into Marcus's face. Silver jacketed death exploded into his head from inches away. Gore blew back, spitting across my face and chest. The slide locked back on a clip as empty as his skull.

I slid the pistol back in its holster under my arm as the body slumped sideways and fell to the ground with a thud.

Wiping the blowback from my face with a grimy hand, I watched as Leonidas got to his feet. He stared at his brother's corpse. His arm was a mess of blasted muscle and tendon, the bone jutting out sharp and jagged.

My nerves were like his arm—open, frayed, and ragged. Even from across the dirt room I could feel his lycanthropy working to heal that mess. Blood had already stopped dripping from it. He looked up at me.

"That was some cold-blooded shit."

I didn't say anything.

"If I didn't have to kill you I would recruit you for my unit. You would make one hell of a shape-shifter." He took a step forward. "I bet the lab boys would use you to make another fucking Godzilla. They're already going to have a blast with my brother's crossbred bastards."

"No thanks, I'm immune and I would make a shitty soldier." We were both buying time, recuperating. Pulling our shit together in a race to see who would be first. I began to circle to my right. He matched me, moving to stay even. "What branch of military do you work for?"

"None of them. All of them. Contract work, going where the money is. Going wherever they let us do what we were made for."

I stopped moving. "What were you made for?"

"Killing."

With a roar, he sprang, claws out for blood.

38

My hand whipped up, closing on the handle of the katana. A lightning strike of homicidal rage cracked through me. The demon in the sword screamed through me, dark voice calling for blood. I was ready for it this time, riding the connection, letting it wash through me. Savage bloodthirst roiled down, crashing into the deep well of rage I always carry. It boiled over, filling me with murderous strength. I drew sword from scabbard, ringing steel slicing through the Were-lion's roar.

Time compressed. Stretching, distilling into a thick syrup as I watched Leonidas come at me. The cursed blade swept back in my hand, taking forever to reach its apex. A sharp pull and it begin to swing forward again, driven by the muscles in my arm. All the while Leonidas inched his way toward me, hanging in the air. Silence rang in my ears as I felt every contraction of my arm, every synapse firing in my spine to drive the edge of that blade toward my enemy.

Toward a feast of hot lycanthrope blood.

The sword bit into the Were-lion, slicing deep across his furred chest. Blood sizzled along the blade's edge, absorbing as quickly as it could be shed.

Time snapped back into place like the crack of a whip.

The lion-man moved past me in a plume of blood. My foot dug in, turning, leading with my hip, cutting back with the sword. He ducked, twisting under the blade as it sliced air with a flash. He came up close, snarling carrion breath in my face, claws tearing into my side. Burning pain flared as I shoved myself away.

Blood runneled down my ribcage in four slashes. My mind flashed to Tiff's eye, the four lines razored into her face. The sword called, thirsting for more blood, urging me to kill. My hand tingled around the handle, cramping to lock on with a death grip. I answered from a primitive place. A place of tooth and claw. Kill or be killed. A place of tearing flesh and blood for blood. I didn't fight the homicidal compulsion of the sword. I embraced it, bloodthirst washing away the pain of my injuries. Twisting, I turned to face my enemy.

Leonidas had torn off his shirt and was looking at the gash on his chest. It yawned open like an obscene grin, flesh pink under fur-covered skin. His right arm was still a mess but was less mangled. The bones pulled back in. Healing. He was growling to himself, a deep thrum that filled the room. Yellow eyes flashed up to me, his own murderous intentions banked deep inside.

Velvet lycanthropy washed over me. Scorching hot like the sun-blasted savannah, slamming into me so hard it drove me back a step. Piss rank musk filled my nose, choking me. Leonidas crackled as his skin swelled to hold more mass. Shifting, his body became heavier, thicker, as his beast tore out of him. He stepped out of the ruin of his clothes and shook off the last of his humanity.

Leonidas was a lion the size of a luxury sedan.

He stood titanic and enormous. Majestic. Lord of the jungle. His fur was dark liquid honey over a mountain of muscle. Four-inch talons flexed from paws the size of hubcaps. Teeth made for tearing carcasses apart gleamed in the glaring light of the naked bulbs around us. I watched his chest flex and expand, drawing in air. He unleashed a roar that tore my hearing away, so loud I felt it vibrating my bones instead of hearing it with my ears. That great mouth yawned open, full of death. Cold, predator eyes closed as it thundered out of him.

I struck, slashing the katana down across his lion face.

The edge bit into that heavy skull, skin splitting as I yanked on the handle to drag the blade down across his eye. It burst, adding a clear, gelatinous liquid to the gush of blood soaking his fur. The roar turned into a scream, high pitched and human sounding, but loud, so fucking loud it was like shoving icepicks into my eardrums. A giant paw flashed up, smashing into me and driving me into the rock-hard clay wall.

I bounced off the wall, sword still locked in my grip. It screamed in my mind for more blood, pushing me to get to my feet. I came up. Leonidas was shaking blood out of his ruined eye. A surge of dark thrill ran through me as I watched, thinking about what he had done to Tiff.

Serves you right, you son of a bitch.

Pushing off with my foot, I jumped, swinging the sword in a deadly arc. The black blade flashed in the incandescent light. Leonidas twisted away and leaped at me. His chest rammed into me, smashing me against the hard-packed clay floor. The air raced from my lungs and my rib shot pain across my body, drawing my left arm up in a rictus. The muscles locked and twisted in on themselves. I was being crushed by his weight. I couldn't draw a breath.

My vision began to squeeze down into a tunnel, the lights growing dim. The sword was still mine, but it was trapped uselessly against the floor with my arm. Those massive jaws snapped the air above my head, trying to reach me. One giant paw slammed the ground by my head as he lifted up so he could get at me with his teeth. Bloody clumps of mane slapped across my face as the pressure let up. I sucked air into my lungs, clearing my vision. Kicking and scrambling, I got out from under the lion.

I wish I had a fucking gun.

The cursed blade screamed at me to give it more blood. Leonidas was back on his feet, turning slowly, looking for me.

I was on his blind side.

Pulling from deep inside, fueling my movement with every ounce of rage I held and lacing it with the murder locked in the katana, I slashed the sword down. The edge cleaved across the back of his neck.

The demon's scream climbed into a keening that filled my mind. The blade poured strength into my arms as it drank deep. Bloodthirst exploded in a crescendo as the sword sheared through muscle and tendon to the spine. It bit into bone, locking there. The monstrous lion stumbled to its knees dragging the sword from my hand. That shaggy head lolled forward, kissing the red clay floor. His life drank down by the katana.

The connection to the sword was torn from me. The cursed power ripping out by the roots from somewhere deep inside and dragging up through me like a hook through the guts of a fish. My legs went out from under me and I crashed to my hands and knees, the world swirling in a lazy circle.

My lungs constricted as my busted rib twisted pain across the inside of my torso. The burn on my calf flared with hot agony in a vicious slap. All my injuries returned with a vengeance. My stomach dumped its contents on the clay floor in one great heave, sick splashing into the ever-widening puddle of blood around Leonidas's shrinking form. Acid burned along my throat. Exhaustion pressed on me, crushing my bones. I almost lay down in my own vomit.

I could lie there until someone found me or I moved on to be with my family.

I was empty.

Spent.

A cry for help echoed out of a tunnel. Sophia's cry for help.

Reaching down, I found the strength to slowly get to my feet.

39

I found them at the end in a room carved from the
earth. There were no more tunnels. It ended in a blunt
circle of hewn clay, lights strung around the edges. Sophia
was kneeling on the floor. Even with her hands tied
behind her back she managed to fold around her stomach and the babies inside. Shani paced in front of her,
chewing one lioness claw.

As I stumbled out of the tunnel entrance into the room,
she moved like quicksilver to jerk Sophia to her feet.
Using her bound hands as leverage, Shani bent Sophia
painfully back, making her stomach extend out front.

One clawed hand cupped across, resting just below
Sophia's belly button.

Shani's voice was a savage purr. "Do not take another
step or I will gut her."

Sophia spoke, her voice thin through teeth clenched
in pain. "Please. Don't. My babies . . ."

Shani snarled, teeth close to Sophia's throat, a vicious
sound like paper tearing to shreds. "Whore! You shut
your mouth. I know that's Marcus's bastard in there."

I could hear the echo of her lioness in her voice. Short

fur rubbed coarse inside my skin as my power picked up lycanthropic feedback.

"Is that what all of this has been about?" I asked. Her head jerked to look at me, lioness eyes cutting under her scowling brow. "Did you start all of this bloodshed, all of this death, because of your wounded fucking pride?" *No pun intended.*

"To hell with you, human. You don't understand our nature. You don't understand the ways of a predator. You do not know my pain." Her hand left Sophia's stomach, rising to point at me. "I was with Marcus for *years*, denying my nature for his dream of peace. All I ever wanted was what all lionesses want. Cubs. Marcus could never give me that. By the time he took up with this slut I was glad for it. I had grown sick of his touch. Sick of his weak ways." She coughed, a harsh cat sound from the back of her throat. Her face twisted in disgust as she spat on the ground.

"If he was sleeping with her, then he was leaving me alone. So I played along with the act that she was with Cash. I didn't care. Not until she came to me and told me she was pregnant." Her face tore into a mask of rage. "Not until she was having babies that should have been mine!"

The pieces fell into place. "So you called his brother and told him where he could catch up with Marcus and you sent them after Sophia too."

Her eyes shone, fever-bright. "Leonidas understood. He didn't fight his predator side, he *reveled* in it. Hot blood and torn flesh. He knew that what Marcus did went against the laws of nature. He understood the blasphemy of what Marcus did to me with this whore. He was glad to come here. Glad to take care of my problem."

Fury simmered deep inside me, adding volcanic heat to my voice. "A lot of my friends and loved ones have been hurt because of what you did, you stupid, petty bitch. People have died because of you and your wounded worthless pride. Some of my people still might." Tiff and Boothe flashed through my mind.

She rose up and pointed a clawed finger at me. "This is not my fault. If you hadn't gotten involved, this would have been simple. Marcus and his slut would be gone and I would have been free to be what I truly am, at the side of a mate who deserves me."

Fury boiled into wrath and washed through me. It pushed my pain aside, giving me a low hum of energy. I began to walk toward her, limping, but steady in a straight line. My voice was harsh. "Don't try to play that card, bitch. *You* chose a murderer to do your dirty work for you. *You* brought him to my town and turned him loose. He had to be put down and I was glad to do it."

Her hand flashed back over Sophia's stomach, talons digging into flesh. Blood began to trickle around where the points sank into skin. "Stop moving or I will tear this baby out of her!"

I stopped, still too far away to reach them. I was unarmed and injured. Blood still ran down my side from the fight with Leonidas, and my chest felt like my sternum was split in two, the edges grinding together from my busted rib. My hip was locked stiff, wrapped in chains of pain. The skin across my calf ripped with hot agony at each step. There was no way I could close the distance and save Sophia. Not against Were-lioness speed.

If Shani decided to rip her apart, I didn't even have the strength to avenge her.

Her lycanthropy snapped the air between us, popping and crackling with anger.

My frustration and rage roared back at her. The two energies wound together, slapping and cracking.

My guts ground the glass shards of hurt in them as I

pushed my power out, trying to latch on, straining to make a connection. It slipped through my metaphysical fingers. I reached out again, staring at Shani through dancing black spots in my vision. I grabbed one of the ragged edges of her lycanthropy, clutching it desperately, my power running down the line of it. Dry grass and dust filled my nostrils. The African sun beat down on me in my mind.

I was locked in.

Her lioness turned to swipe at me. I felt the claws tear across my shoulders, under the skin. With a vicious twist I forced my power to show me the cords that tied Shani's lioness to her humanity. There were hundreds of them dashing between the two lifelines of lycanthropy. Thin silken threads, three-strand cords the size of rope, and nets woven of both humanity and beast sparking with lycanthropic energy in blues and purples. One arm-thick cable tied both hearts together. I threw my power at that, clutching it and twisting it in my mind. All the cords and strands began to knot and gnarl together.

Shani screamed as I forced her body to change. It wasn't like the Were-shark, not one part for another, I made her lioness come out all at once.

And I did it as slowly as possible.

Shani jerked, body convulsing as it restructured. Sophia fell to her knees, crawling away. The Were-lioness stumbled back against the clay walls as her legs broke into new joints and her bones stretched. Feline eyes rolled white into her skull and foam spilled out as her jaw reformed.

My knees became water and I fell down. Ignoring my body, I kept shoving my power into her, still yanking metaphysical cords, still stretching her lycanthropy like taffy. The strain ground my bones together at the joints. Shani's neck stretched and her skull flattened as I pulled. Her organs tumbled, rearranging as my power forced her spine and ribcage to morph. The harsh yank to make her tail grow sent my head into a spin. Not a spin, a full-on exorcist twist.

She yowled, her agony cutting across the room. There were no more cords to knot, she was transformed. Draining the last of my strength, I used my power to cut the ties to her humanity in one sharp blow. Falling back, my power reeled into me with a snap that made my vision go black.

My head pounded as I crawled over to where the lioness lay quivering on the hard packed floor. Her breathing was labored and shallow. My fingers felt like water balloons, thick and full of liquid as I fumbled with the hard plastic case in my pocket. The spare clip for the air gun came apart in my hand, spilling out darts filled with liquid narcotic. I remembered what Father Mulcahy had told me.

It was designed originally to down elephants.

I pulled out three of them and slammed their wicked needles into Shani's shoulder. They shook in my grip as they dumped their narcotic load into the lioness. She gave one last, sharp convulsion and then lay still, her breathing fast but even.

I sat back on my heels, head spinning.

Take that, you bitch.

40

"She's all set up for you to see."

My hand fell on the man's arm. It was still thin under his gray coverall, but had wiry, redneck muscle to it. It was before opening and he wasn't wearing his cap. His hair swept up shorter on the top and slicked at the sides of his head. The back hung long, like a thick curtain of wavy brown hair.

Jimmy the zookeeper still had the biggest damn mullet I had ever seen.

"Thanks, Jimmy. I appreciate the trouble."

He waved the statement away. "No trouble at all. Anything for you. I still owe you."

"How's Cinnamon?"

His spindly goatee split into a wide, tobacco-stained grin. "She's real good, man. She's about ready to pop. The doctor says she might deliver early."

"Good. Tell her we love her and miss her down at the club. I am sure the girls will be throwing her one helluva baby shower."

I met Jimmy the zookeeper last year. The zoo had a Nosferatu that had set up a nest and was trying to grow a baby. He had helped me kill the damned thing and I had introduced him to Cinnamon, a sweet girl who worked at Polecats. They had hit it off and gotten married pretty quickly. It was nice to hear and I was happy for both of them.

We said our "see-you-laters" and I went back to work.

The hallway I walked down was wide and clean. One side was taken by a mural, the other with displays. There was no one else there, it was before opening and the crowds would not come until then.

My new boots sounded good on the tile floor. The leather boot heels landed with solid determination. Deep blood-red leather flashed at the end of my jeans with every step. They were a gift from Boothe and the rabbits. The dinosaur skin was thick but flexible and actually very comfortable.

I had asked what happened to the rest of the T. rex and been told that the rabbits had buried it where it lay. It was too big to move, so they just dug under it, sank it, and covered it over.

They're rabbits. They dig. It's what they do.

Boothe was back on his feet, his lycanthropy healing him slowly but surely. The skin on his right side was still shiny and pink, still thin like plastic wrap as it regenerated. Most of his hair had grown back, and even his eye was back. Mostly. He kept it hidden behind aviator sunglasses as it filled in. It had taken a few weeks, but he was starting to look almost normal.

He had brought the boots by the club on a particularly rowdy night when I was playing bouncer. He came in the door as I was hauling out two drunk frat boys who had gotten touchy-feely in the VIP room. He helped toss them out by their flipped collars, remaining calm and professional the whole time.

I offered him the job.

He took it and now ran the front door, checking IDs

and keeping the chaos of the club to a dull roar. Some of the girls had been very excited when he came to work. I mean, the only guys who worked there were me and Father Mulcahy. Boothe was fresh meat. They preened and flirted with him. That is until he came to work and introduced them to Josh, a Were-rabbit accountant whom he had been dating for three years and shared a house with at the Warren.

I rounded a corner, walking up to the viewing area. It had a giant Plexiglas window that was roped off. Benches lined the area in front of it where families could sit and watch. I stepped in front of the floor-to-ceiling window.

On the other side sat the Atlanta Zoo's newest addition: a dark furred African lioness.

Shani.

Feline eyes burned with hatred as she watched me. Her head was lowered, hackles raised like a wolf. I could feel the vibration through the glass as she purred with anger.

I closed my eyes and gave a small push, rolling my power out. It moved slowly toward the lioness. I probed in, making my power show me her lycanthropy. It was still a knot of silver cords, tangled up and wrapped tight.

Good.

The sound of rubber squeaking made me open my eyes and turn my head. My power rolled back up inside me like a tape measure.

Tiff rounded the corner, pushing a covered baby stroller.

My heart sped up seeing her. She had lost weight in the hospital, and once she got out she began a punishing cycle of training that had burnished her down and refined her. She was lean with muscle, still womanly, but all the little girl had been burned away.

The pink had been stripped out of her hair and the black had grown out, leaving her natural color, which was a deep chestnut brown. It hung over her left eye, making it hard to see the eye patch she wore. My heart hurt just a little to see her self-consciously keep it hidden. Her eye was gone, in its place were four dark red scars that slashed across the empty socket.

She stepped up beside me and I kissed her gently on the cheek. She gave me a little smile and a squeeze. Turning to the Plexiglas cage in front of us, she studied the lioness coldly. "She's not happy to see us," she said.

I turned to find Shani pacing in front of the window. Her head was down, lip curled in a snarl, hateful eyes glued to us even as she shifted direction from one side to the other.

"Just wait," I said.

Reaching up, I flipped open the covering to the stroller. Shani stopped, frozen midstep, eyes locked on what was inside that stroller.

Three sleeping babies.

One was a bouncing baby boy with a head full of hair that striped gently in russet red and dark honey tawn. He sprawled, arms and legs kicked out. His skin had his mother's pale European tone, and even this young you could see he had her ethnic European nose, but his face was his father's. Marcus's face.

On the other side of the stroller lay a cub. It was on its side, paws crossed in front of it. Its fur was thicker, shaggy and striped like his brother's hair, russet red and honey tawn, making a pattern along his back and sides. A tiny mane circled a face that had a canine snout in a feline face. Mother's nose, father's face.

Between them their brother slept. His hands tucked by his face, claws retracted. Short fur striped up his chubby arms and legs, covering his skin. His hair was long and thick around a face that pulled the best from both brothers.

If their eyes weren't closed, Shani would see that all of them had the same eyes: one blue, one brown, just like their mother.

Sophia's babies had Larson in a frenzy of research. They were growing incredibly fast. They were only a few months old and already looked almost a year. They were all walking and eating solid food.

There was always a human, a cub, and a half-Were.

And they switched. Shifted. No one ever saw them do it, not even Sophia, but they would. One would change, then another would become what he had been. They had three distinct personalities, so you could tell when they were in a different form, but no one ever saw them actually shift.

Larson wanted me to use my power to feel them out. I refused. They were healthy. Strange, supernatural, and weird, but healthy and happy nonetheless. I wasn't going to fuck with them.

Shani began to scream, a high-pitched caterwaul that shrieked through the glass. Her claws slashed at the thick barrier, trying to tear through. Trying to get at the babies.

The Plexiglas held, vibrating like a tuning fork and sending waves of percussion through the air that bounced off my skin, but it held nonetheless.

Tiff nudged me with her elbow, underimpressed, and pulled the stroller back. "Let's go before she wakes the kids. Besides, I want to see the Monkey House."

I gave her a grin. "You got it, babe." We turned from the frenzied lioness, walking away without looking back.

"I wonder if the cotton candy stand is set up yet?"

FROM THE AUTHOR

Dear Loyals and True Believers,

Wow, book two. Thank you. Thank you so much for all the wonderful support you have given me. I hope you liked this installment in the adventures of everybody's favorite occult bounty-hunter, Deacon Chalk.

Wait until you see what is coming up next!

More mayhem!

More monsters!

More Deacon!

It's going to be a blast!

Now, I want to take a second and tell you just how important you are to me. Every book you bought, every review you posted, every time you came out to an event where I was, every time you sent me an e-mail or a letter or a comment, it was important to me. It all means so much in ways you will never know. I write these books for you my friend and I love it, truly love it, when you tell me you enjoyed them.

It means I am holding up my end of the bargain.

And that's what a man does.

So keep reading my friend I will make sure it's worth your time!

Take care until next time,

James R. Tuck